CENTAURI

REACH FOR THE STARS - BOOK 2

JOHN WEGENER

Centauri

John Wegener

To those of us who know.

1

ARRANGEMENTS

Ethan looked across at Jade as she sipped her wine. He knew he was being corny, but he couldn't help but think she resembled a goddess as the sunlight silhouetted her hair, giving her an almost angelic aura. Who said scientists couldn't be poetic?

They had met over five years ago, but it had taken him those five years to muster the courage to ask her out on a date. More correctly, she had needed that time to persuade him to ask her out. He smiled as those awkward moments raced through his memory.

"What are you thinking?"

"I'm thinking I'm one of the luckiest men in the world."

"One?" Jade queried, raising a quizzical eyebrow in mock seriousness.

"OK. *The* luckiest."

"That's better." Jade sat back in her chair, looking smug. "By the way," she added, "I'm the luckiest woman, too." She turned her head and glanced across at him.

Ethan's heart skipped a beat. As a scientist, he had always doubted that cliché about hearts skipping beats when a person fancied themselves in love, but now he knew it was true. And it was no fancy either. He knew he was in love. It flowed from him, piercing her eyes with breath-taking effect, making their brilliant green luminescence sparkle in response. They both smiled, contented, as they gazed at each other.

They had recently taken part in the momentous achievement of the first faster than the speed of light space flight. Ethan had fulfilled a dream. Travelling faster than light was something he had dreamed about since, as a boy, he would lie on the lawn gazing up at the Milky Way at night. But it had come at a price. He had lost his closest friend, Jake, to the greed of the megalomaniac, Loki Mason. Loki's adopted daughter Jezebel, the fusion specialist on the project team, had cold-bloodedly murdered Jake to prevent them reaching Iapetus before Loki, so her father could claim the precious astatine deposit there for himself.

His thoughts soured as he remembered the tragedy, but he could not remain embittered for long, not with Jade sitting next to him. They were relaxing on the deck outside Ethan's villa, the spring evening warm as they watched the radiant orange sunset in the west.

Jade became inquisitive. "What will happen now?"

"No idea. But I'm meeting John (General John O'Conner) tomorrow at ten-thirty. I'll find out more then. They have dismantled the team, the ones that remained."

Jade laughed. "We lost the project manager."

Galena Alvarez was the project manager for the undertaking to develop the faster-than-light space drive, or FTL as people called it. Unfortunately — or fortunately, from Galena's perspective — she had met Russian scientist Apep Chernakov. Lonely from a lifetime of being alone, Galena had been surprised to discover a kindred spirit in Apep, who was deeply lonely from years of widowhood. They had connected and become inseparable, so much so that she had moved to Russia to live with him.

"The experience has changed many of our lives, hasn't it?" mused Ethan.

"Yes, it has."

Ethan's comm buzzed. He glanced at the screen and frowned. "That's strange. It's John."

"Well, don't keep him waiting."

Ethan pressed the reply with visual. "Hi. Wasn't expecting you."

John, dressed in an impeccable military uniform, as usual, said, "I wish I were with you from the looks of it. Hello, Ethan ... and Jade, I see."

"Hi," Jade said, raising her voice.

"I'm glad you're both together. Saves me a call. Ethan, I want Jade at our meeting tomorrow, if that's possible."

Ethan and Jade exchanged a surprised glance.

Jade said, "Yes, I'm available, but why?"

"You'll find out tomorrow," John replied with an expression of disguised amusement that only someone trained in the military could display. "Hope you are both ready for a new venture. I must go. There's much to do before I leave the office today. See you both then."

The comm screen blanked. Ethan and Jade stared at each other, baffled by the mysterious call.

"What does he want?" Jade asked, breaking the silence.

"We'll find out tomorrow."

"Guess we will, but why ask for my presence?"

"I presume that whatever we'll discuss involves you too."

Jade sat back with a stare of wondering concern. Ethan looked at her, got out of his chair, stepped behind her and stroked her arms as he bowed over, mischief in his demeanor.

"Don't you dare."

"Dare what?"

"You know what. I've seen that face."

"Then I won't surprise you, will I?" Ethan said as he tickled her into convulsions of laughter. She spasmed as she tried to wriggle away from him. "Don't ... please stop," she gasped in between the uncontrolled giggles Ethan was inducing.

"Well, whatever he wants, we have just each other tonight," Ethan said when he stopped.

Jade jumped out of her chair and started chasing Ethan around the deck, trying to get back at him. They both laughed; two children playing a game of chase. He let Jade catch him, and they both gasped for air as they entangled and then began to kiss passionately like two grown-ups.

2

A NEW VENTURE

Ethan and Jade arrived at the Hilton Los Angeles Hotel at ten-twenty and parked themselves on a lounge in the lobby to wait for John. The lounge was comfortable, designed to instill a relaxed atmosphere, but neither felt particularly relaxed. They were too curious about why John wanted to see them.

Ethan peered around and out the windows. A moderate flow of traffic entered the hotel drop-off zone, with valets and porters busy providing their services. The lobby was quiet. He glanced back at Jade. She wore gray pinstriped slacks matched with a plain white blouse — an outfit that was professional and sexy at the same time. He couldn't get over how much he liked everything about her — what she wore, her hairstyle, makeup, voice, what she did, how she thought, everything. No one had ever affected him as Jade had. Her fresh-from-the-shower smell lingered pristine, new, and redolent, like a field full of fragrant flowers. Ethan smiled at the thought. He was getting poetic again.

"What's on your mind?" Jade asked when she saw the smile.

"Nothing. Just pleasant thoughts."

"Of me, I hope."

"Always."

An elevator chime sounded, and Ethan glanced over to the concourse in time to see John exit the elevator in civilian clothing, resembling a tourist ready to join an organized tour of Los Angeles, minus the sunglasses. Ethan looked at his watch. It was precisely ten-thirty.

Ethan waved to catch his attention as John's eyes scanned the lobby for them. Jade glanced to where Ethan gazed and saw John, too. They both stood as he approached.

"Morning," Ethan said as he extended his hand to shake John's.

"Good morning," Jade added, extending her hand too.

"Good morning to both of you. Hope I'm not disturbing your day too much." John stared at them for a few seconds. "You two make a great couple."

That remark made them exchange a sheepish smile.

"I think we do, too," Ethan said, beaming at John.

Jade couldn't believe what she'd heard. Ethan usually found it hard to express his emotions, especially in public. She beamed with delight when Ethan glanced back at her.

"So, let's go conduct our business, shall we? I have a room booked upstairs. Follow me if you will."

Ethan and Jade followed John as he led them to the elevators. Jade moved closer to Ethan as they walked, her closeness infusing him with contentment. Their relationship had only started, but it felt like an eternity of bliss lay ahead. He could no longer imagine his life without her now. It was an unexpected feeling, considering his nervousness around women. Jade had changed everything for him, though not without the invaluable groundwork Hu had put in beforehand in coaching him in how to speak to women. Not that he had taken the initiative even then. Jade had prompted and hinted for five years before he had found the courage to ask her on a date. She had emitted an audible sigh of relief when he finally did. He wondered if this blossoming relationship was like his parents' relationship before his mother's death.

They reached the elevator, and Ethan returned his mind to the present.

"How has life been since I met you last?" John asked.

Ethan and Jade looked at each other. "We've taken the opportunity to relax and recharge our batteries," Ethan said.

"Good," John said, with no embellishment.

Ethan sensed a note of mischief in John's reply but let matters rest until he was ready to explain the reason for the meeting.

The elevator soon took them to the first-floor meeting rooms. They filed out, and John led them to the reserved room, where Ethan saw that coffee and tea were available on the side table, together with cakes, biscuits, and pastries. It reminded him of their previous session, with a similar view of the Pacific Ocean sparkling in the sunlight.

"Help yourself to refreshments and make yourselves comfortable," John invited, standing back so they could access the table.

Ethan allowed Jade to go first. She poured a coffee from the percolator, added milk and sugar, placed a small chocolate eclair on a plate with a serviette and sat. Ethan poured coffee, grabbed two chocolate chip biscuits, his favorite, and sat in the seat next to her. John took a coffee and sat adjacent.

"So, we can talk here without interruption. I understand you've completed a few more FTL trips with *Destiny*," John said, starting the conversation. *Destiny* was the name Ethan had suggested for the spaceship they had built for the historic undertaking, and it had stuck, everyone calling it that from then onwards.

"Yes," Ethan said. "We've flown a light year out and back, tuning the drive controls as we traveled, but we had no serious issues. We haven't rushed progress, using our time to understand the warp bubble workings and the drive's limits under various conditions. We built a robust ship, and that has helped with the lack of problems. Jake was an excellent engineer ..." Ethan's voice faltered as he said Jake's name.

Jade spoke up to allow Ethan time to recover. "Jake was one of the best spaceship engineers around and a superb pilot in Ethan's opinion."

"I see you're still recovering from the shock of Jake's death," John said, his voice registering sympathy. "Understandable, given your close friendship."

Ethan shook his head and drew a deep breath. "Thanks. I'm adjusting to it as time passes. Anyway, we think *Destiny* is ready for a longer excursion."

"Good to know. I have just the trip in mind. We've been busy, too, wondering how to put you to better use."

Ethan stared at John, then glanced at Jade, who looked a little worried. He returned his gaze back to John.

"And what sort of trip do you have in mind?"

"An expedition. We want you to lead an excursion to Centauri. See if it has any habitable planets."

"What!" Ethan and Jade exclaimed in unison, jumping a little in their seats.

"How long will he be gone?" Jade added, real concern appearing on her face now.

Ethan realized she dreaded being separated from him for an extended period. He didn't like it either. John sat in front of them with a growing smile.

Ethan saw the grin. "What?"

"You won't miss him," John told Jade. "We don't just want Ethan to go."

Jade sat puzzled until she understood the implications of John's words. "You want *me* along as well?"

"Why else would I have invited you here today?"

Jade looked flustered. "I didn't know. Now I do." Her alarm and panic over the separation turned to excitement. She had never stuck her neck out for anything this adventurous before, always limiting herself to her field of expertise: quantum physics. But that was before she'd experienced the adrenaline of the FTL flight. It had given her an appetite for adventure. "Ethan, do you realize what this means?"

"Yeah, more boring flying," Ethan said, considering the time it might take to reach Centauri.

Jade stared at him, astonished that he didn't seem to comprehend the offer's implications. "That's not it, Ethan. We'll be the first humans to travel to another star. The first ... ever. And what wonders will we discover, Ethan?" Her voice grew louder and more excited with each word.

"Whoa, stay calm, Jade! Now you've put it that way, you're right. It's an excellent opportunity."

John sat patiently as a third-party observer, content to let the thought processes and emotions play out. He had an amused smile overlaying a look of pleasure at observing the couple before him as they considered their opportunity and worked through the implications together. He was like a proud parent watching his two children grow into one unit, a unit that he and his superiors wanted to use.

"I think that's a 'yes, we'll do it'," John ventured.

"Of course," Jade said.

"Hold on a minute," Ethan said. "Why us?" The military's ulterior motives concerned Ethan, and he wanted full disclosure of what they were. Something else was worrying him too. He feared for Jade's safety.

John's smile broadened. "I was wondering when that question would surface. Why you? It's easy. You, Ethan, showed exceptional decision-making and leadership on that first flight. Don't kid yourself. We discussed your suitability for the mission at length, and we considered other options. But at the end of the day, we still agreed that you were the best choice. You know the ship backward, and you have the skills to fix problems." John faced Jade. "And you. Well, I could say we didn't want to separate you two, but I won't. That's not the reason. After extensive discussion with many people, we realized we needed a quantum mechanics expert in case you run into problems. You are the finest in your field, so you were the obvious choice. It had nothing to do with your relationship, but that's a bonus."

Jade reddened with embarrassment. "I'm not *that* good."

John's argument still didn't convince Ethan. "We don't know what we might discover there. What if Jade's in danger? I don't want that."

Jade glanced at Ethan and blushed a bright red as she understood Ethan's reluctance to jump at this opportunity. He was worried about her.

Ethan realized what he had said, but his words didn't embarrass him. He persisted, "Well?"

"You'll have the best team you can assemble for this mission. There'll be security from us. You will need other scientists, like a geologist, botanist, biologist, and others. We'll cover every contingency we possibly can. I, for one, don't want to lose what you two have. You are something special. A trait I rarely see in people."

Both Ethan and Jade blushed at the compliment. They looked at each other, wondering whether John was correct. Were they special?

"I'll let you talk about it."

"Yes, please," Ethan said.

"OK. I'll give you as long as it takes for you to decide," adding with a wink, "any time in the next ten minutes. Send me a message when you're ready." John stood up and left the room, giving them privacy.

"I don't know about this," Ethan said, starting the discussion.

"What do you mean? Isn't this what you've always dreamed of? You wanted to venture to the stars, and John's offering you the opportunity. It's the chance of a lifetime, Ethan."

"But what if something goes wrong, and you're in danger?"

"I don't want *you* harmed either," Jade pointed out, becoming emotional. "And I won't let you leave me behind, languishing for months waiting for your return."

Ethan hadn't thought of that. It would be tough on her having to stay home while he endangered his life.

"I'd spend the whole time," Jade added with a cheeky smile, "dreading that you might fall in love with an alien somewhere."

Ethan chuckled at that unlikely prospect.

"All jokes aside, I want to be with you so that we can experience whatever risk there may be together," Jade finished, her expression serious.

Her eyes were so earnest and enticing that Ethan gulped. His pulse increased, and his tension mounted. He was beyond words. Beyond anything he had experienced before as he processed Jade's words. He wanted to express his feelings for her, but it scared him.

His palms were damp. His brow knitted in uncertainty, doubt, worry, desire as he gazed into her eyes. Jade looked back in expectation, defiance. Finally, Ethan got the nerve. "I love you too, Jade."

Jade jerked backward in shock at the unexpected declaration and stared at the floor in ecstasy. This was beyond what her emotions could handle. She sobbed.

"I didn't mean to hurt you."

"You didn't."

"Then what?"

"You said what I couldn't, and you're the shy one."

"Well, everyone's full of surprises sometimes."

Jade glanced up again and wiped away her tears. "I love you, Ethan, and I want to go on this venture with you."

Ethan basked in the love that was permeating the room. He had never experienced the emotional peace and certainty that was reverberating between them. He calmed himself so that he could think with less emotion. "I didn't say I was going."

"Don't be ridiculous. Of course, you'll go."

Ethan thought. "Yeah, you're right." He realized with resignation that it was the only decision he could have made.

"And I'm coming with you."

"I don't have a choice, do I? I can't have you crying blue murder after my alien lovers," Ethan said with an impish grin.

"No, you can't," Jade agreed, punching him, then reaching across to hold his hand but stretching for his face instead, stroking it with affection.

Ethan raised one of his hands, caught hers in mid-stroke and held it, enjoying the intimacy of the moment. "Well, we should get John in and tell him our decisions."

"Our decision," Jade corrected firmly.

Ethan chuckled as he dialed the contact into his comm that John had left. "We're ready," he said when John answered.

"Good," John said.

John walked back into the room a few moments later. He hadn't gone very far away. He sat again, looking at them, assessing their mood. "Did anything happen here apart from decision-making?"

Ethan and Jade reddened.

"No. Of course not," Ethan said.

"Well, what is your verdict?"

Ethan looked at Jade, wondering if she wanted him to answer for her. She nodded. "We both accept your offer."

"Good. I wasn't sure of my options if you'd refused, to be honest."

Ethan and Jade laughed. John laughed, too, when he realized what he had said.

"This calls for a small celebration, even if it's still early. A champagne to seal the contract?"

Jade glanced at Ethan. "Yes, that's marvelous in more ways than one."

John gazed at them quizzically but left his query for another day.

3

WORMHOLE TRANSPORTATION

Ching Hu pounded the punching bag with the utmost strength of her fists, her feet, her knees, any extremity of her body after her day's work. The bag oscillated with the swing of a demented pendulum trying to regain its regularity. She was pounding her frustrations into it, seeking to remove them from herself. Her workout had lasted over half an hour without a break, and the perspiration was now flowing freely. Stopping, she heaved for breath, anger still written across her face, but the tension in her body had eased, thanks to the submissive scapegoat. Her determination remained. She could almost taste the bitterness of the past months. Her only choice was to swallow her failure and tackle the issue from another angle.

The Chinese team working on developing wormhole technology had been trying to generate a useful and stable wormhole of practical size for months now, with only minor success. Nobody could explain why it didn't work. That was the disappointment Hu punched into the bag. Her frustrations were plain in the team meetings too, where she was demanding more effort from the quantum physicists even though she recognized the unfairness of her demands. Their frustration was as obvious as hers. The project manager, Chang Jian Zha, struggled to keep the sessions in order and placate his superiors and party officials at the same time. They perceived failure as resistance against the political hierarchy instead of hitting the limits of the laws of physics.

Hu stood in front of the punching bag, heaving her chest to regain her breath, and started ruminating again. At present, they couldn't generate a wormhole large enough to push through a fart. She amused herself with the vulgarity. Not without a receiving portal. If they positioned a sending portal at one end, and a receiving portal at the other, they generated a wormhole as large as the portal diameters, with a modest consumption of energy. The frustrating bit was positioning a second portal. The power required to open a wormhole large enough was beyond their generation capacity. *We're overlooking something. Maybe?*

An idea blossom in Hu's brain like a new flower greeting the morning sun. She found the period following an intense physical workout her most productive in problem solving and idea generation. Chen Liang was a brilliant quantum physicist, but Hu knew another quantum physicist, Jade Powers. Hu had met Jade when she took part in the first FTL flight with the international team assembled by the Americans, together with Apep Chernakov from the Russian FTL project. Jade had a superior understanding of quantum physics compared to Liang, in Hu's opinion. She speculated on what might happen if they jointly studied the problem. She tossed the notion around in her head for a moment before ingesting it and deciding to raise it at the project team leaders' meeting in the morning. She wondered if her illustrious political leaders would entertain sending a portal elsewhere with an American spaceship that now traveled faster than light. That way, they could at least travel somewhere and collect data on wormhole establishment issues more than their present capacity to gather information over limited distances using conventional shipping. Using the Americans' warp bubble FTL drive ships — or the Russian's hyper-drive ships if they ever develop that technology — to take portals to new destinations for the Chinese technology to open wormhole transportation might be their only choice. They could then develop a network of wormholes. *That may be the cheapest, most energy-efficient means of human expansion into the galaxy*, Hu ruminated.

She grabbed her towel and wiped the perspiration off her face, her anger subsiding with the satisfaction that she at least had a plan to propose for the upcoming meeting. She went off to the change room.

"You gave that punching bag a decent beating today," the gym manager commented as she walked past him.

"It deserved it," Hu said in a black-humored way.

"Hope I never get in your bad books."

Hu gave a good-natured, "Ha!"

She entered the change room and removed her boxing gloves, kneepads, and shoes. She stood still at attention, drawing deep breaths with her eyes closed, allowing the tension to flow from her body as she prepared for her next stage of exercise. She stretched her arms above her head, then placed her hands on her hips and conducted back stretches. Taking more powerful breaths, she calmed her senses before starting her twenty-minute Tai Chi routine. She found it easier to concentrate in the change room than the gym. After completing her exercises, she had her dinner, read, and went to bed.

HU WAS UP EARLY the next morning, jogging around the corridors of the moon base before breakfast, preferring that to the treadmills the gym provided. It felt more natural to her. She completed five kilometers, showered, and ate.

She arrived at the meeting just after nine, late, which was unusual for her as she prided herself on promptness. But she had an excuse. She had used the time to develop the transportation requirements for spaceship capacity portals, their size limitations, and cost of manufacture. She strode into the room armed with that information and her two suggestions.

The others stared at her as she entered.

Hu looked at Jian Zha. "Sorry I'm late. I was working out data for the meeting." She paused when she spotted Jian's haggard face. "You look like hell." They had dispensed with Communist Party protocols of addressing superiors in the meetings, at Jian's insistence. It was extending the proceedings unnecessarily.

"So'd you if you had to placate my superiors." Jian didn't care that Jiang Minzhe was present to report his insubordination to his Communist Party cronies, since he knew Jiang shared the team's frustrations. He was the Communist Party representative and the chemical specialist for the project. "I will note your lateness," he added with a playful smile.

Hu smiled back as she sat down. She looked around the table. Apart from Jian and Jiang, Chen Liang (quantum physicist) and Wong Bingwen (fusion specialist) attended. They all wore dejected expressions; their heads lowered in defeat yet again. *I might project a similar gloom if I had no ideas to suggest*, Hu thought.

"Let's get the meeting underway," Jian started. "Yesterday didn't turn out too well."

Hu noted Jian was careful not to deflate people's enthusiasm any further. The room's atmosphere resembled a tired person trudging up a hill through thick snow, fatigued to absolute exhaustion, finally cresting the ridge, only to face another slope to scale further in the distance.

Nobody spoke.

Hu started the conversation. "No, it didn't. We appear to be hitting too many brick walls."

"Yes, we do. Why do I sense you don't share our depression, as if you have an idea to suggest?"

The others glanced at her, inquisitive at the comment, waiting for a response.

"It's that obvious, is it? Believe me, I felt dejected too last night. The boxing bag in the gym knows."

Everyone chuckled at the jest.

"Then I got thinking. Yes, we can't generate a wormhole with just one generator portal yet. The term I used was 'we can't get a worm-hole large enough to push through a fart.'"

The others laughed, shedding more of their general gloom.

"So, I developed two ideas to share at today's meeting."

"You have our attention," Jian said.

"The first concerns Liang." Hu had decided to try a diplomatic approach because she knew Liang could be touchy. "Liang, is it possible we are missing something?"

Liang sat up straight in his chair. Hu watched him consider what she had said.

"I am doing the best I can. You know I am." He looked affronted by what he interpreted as a slur on his abilities.

"I agree. You are," Hu said, choosing her words carefully. "And you are brilliant at what you do. But I have the pleasure of knowing another distinguished quantum physicist, and my thoughts are that it might not hurt if the two of you could consult each other over this."

Unmollified, Liang stood up, looking upset and ready to argue the point or storm from the room. "Are you implying this person is better than I am?"

Jian waved his hand at Liang. "Sit, Liang. I'm sure Hu doesn't mean that. Let's examine where she is taking us with this."

Liang bowed his head to his superior and sat again.

"Continue, Hu."

"Well, as you know, I had the good fortune to spend time with the American project during their first FTL flight. I met their quantum physicist, Jade Powers. Forgive me, Liang. I don't intend to offend you, but in this precise field, she may have more understanding than you. My idea is to ask her to visit the moon for a few weeks so you can work jointly with her, reviewing our issues. Together, you might develop a fresh approach."

Liang squirmed in his chair as Hu finished explaining her proposal. Everyone was looking at him. Hu saw the misery on his face as he worked through her suggestion. After a few seconds, he admitted grudgingly, "I have read many of her papers. It's true she has much understanding. I guess it is worth trying, Jian. We aren't getting anywhere fast with our current approach."

Hu saw Jian give Liang an intense look, then gazed at her and around the table. "It's a novel suggestion, Hu. What do the others think?"

"If we can get the Party to agree," Minzhe commented first.

"We might progress. Better than chewing away at our budget," Bingwen added.

"I might even have positive news for them afterward," Jian said. Hu watched him pondering her proposal. "I expect I can put forward a proper argument for the proposal. Do we go ahead on this path?"

Hu glanced at the nodding of heads and gave her agreement for completeness.

"OK, I'll make the case to my superior. Hu, you said you had two ideas."

"Yes, I did. We know the Americans have a spaceship capable of faster-than-light travel."

Everyone nodded.

"We can build spaceship-sized portals to produce economical wormholes, provided we have one at each end. We have done it, even if only separated by a few million kilometers."

The others paid her close attention, waiting for her to reach her conclusion.

"My suggestion is to construct two spaceship-sized portals, give one to the Americans to take somewhere far away, open the wormhole at that destination and pass our ship through it. At least we will gather more data on what problems there may be in long-distance wormhole generation and keeping them open."

Silence filled the room. If Hu had a handful of peanuts, she could have tried throwing them into the mouths of those around the table as they sat agape at the suggestion.

Jian broke the spell. "That's another very novel idea."

"We can't give the Americans our technology," Minzhe protested. "The party won't allow it, I'm sure."

"Let me tackle the Party and approvals, Minzhe," Jian said. "The governments have agreed on such matters in past instances. Why wouldn't they consider it again?"

"But the shame that we have failed, sir."

"It is not humiliating, Minzhe. So, we are having difficulties. That doesn't mean the Americans are more advanced than we are. We have been endeavoring to develop a more difficult technology and are having problems. Where is the disgrace in that? If the portals produce stable wormholes, space travel would be even faster than what the Americans can achieve with their warp bubble drives. Consider the prestige in that."

"Well, I suppose so."

"What do you others think?"

Liang commented, "It might be the only way. One-ended wormhole generation may not be feasible, and we need portals transported to the other location first. At least, that is possible. Hu is right. If our government agrees to manufacture the portals, and the Americans take one elsewhere, we will learn more about wormholes."

Bingwen followed. "I just had a brilliant idea. Control of wormhole portals might make an excellent financial return for us."

Jian chuckled. "Aren't we a communist country and above such capitalistic thinking?"

Everyone else snickered, too.

"Regardless, we Chinese can grasp a good enterprise when we see it," Minzhe added.

"So, are we agreed that I forward this proposal too?" Jian said, trying to complete the discussion point.

Everybody nodded in agreement again.

Hu sensed a changed atmosphere in the room than when she had entered. She felt glad. Optimism and purpose had returned instead of depressing drudgery and expectations of another failure when they conducted their next tests.

"Anything else to discuss?" Jian asked.

Nobody spoke.

"Let's end the meeting, then. Hu, stay behind, please."

The demand surprised Hu, but she obeyed. The others filed out, the last closing the door.

"What's up, Jian?"

"You have a small job to do." Jian produced a wicked smile.

Hu knew that grin and didn't like it. It meant she had to do something unpleasant. She tensed. "What's that?"

"You, my comrade, will persuade my superior to run with your proposals."

"Oh!"

4

HUGO

After their decision to accept John's invitation to voyage to Centauri, Ethan and Jade filled their days with planning, recruitment, and seemingly endless other related activities. Time alone with each other was becoming increasingly precious.

Ethan, as team leader, concentrated on recruiting personnel for the project. He included Jade in most of the discussions, though, since Jade had better interpersonal skills than he had.

"So, Jade, do we have the entire list of people to recruit?" Ethan asked.

"I think so, unless you see a hole that we still need filling."

"Well, let's review the list. We need a geologist to understand a planet's geological history and stability and a meteorologist for the climate."

"Right."

"We lack specialists to analyze organic matter, so we need a botanist, a biologist, a zoologist, and a microbiologist."

"But are all of those essential for an exploratory investigation?"

"You're probably right. Let's consider. Can we do with a general biologist and, say, one specializing in microorganisms?"

Jade considered his question. "That should do. We need someone experienced with dangerous microorganisms. Yes, it warrants a specialist. Who else?"

"We will need a medical specialist."

"Right."

"What about an astronomer or cosmologist?"

"Why?"

"To verify the orbital and solar stability of the star and planet."

"Yeah, OK. Who else?"

"That's it for me."

"What about a fusion expert?"

"I suppose we must replace Jessica." Ethan gritted his teeth at the memory. They still hadn't put her on trial yet, a delay that frustrated his sense of justice. She had the best lawyers on the planet defending her case, thanks to her father's money, and they were putting up roadblocks at every opportunity to postpone the proceedings. Loki was in deep water himself, but he had a knack for avoiding trouble.

"I hate to bring this up, but do we need another pilot?"

Ethan thought Jade must have been reading his mind. He glanced at her with a twinge of sadness on his face and sighed. "No, I can handle the ship fine and we have copilots to fly the landers."

"That's everyone, then."

"Good. I'll run the list past John, and we'll get started looking for candidates."

Ethan's comm buzzed. He eyed it to check who it was, but it was an unknown caller. He frowned. "Wonder who this could be?" He pressed audio. "Hello?"

"Hi, Ethan, how are you?"

"Hugo! Where are you? Why are you calling from an unidentified contact?"

Jade smiled at Ethan's reaction. He always became excited when Hu contacted him. It felt like a long-lost sister had reconnected, and he couldn't wait to meet her again. Jade accepted Hu was special to him. She had helped heal many of his insecurities. Jade knew she need not worry, but she couldn't stop herself from feeling a twinge of jealousy regardless.

"I hear you're a hot shot now?"

"Rubbish. Just doing what I'm told. Hang on while I switch to video." Ethan pressed the visual button, and Hu's face came onto the screen. "That's better. Jade's here with me."

"Oh. Hi, Jade. You keeping him honest?"

"Hi, Hugo. As honest as I can."

Jade and Hu laughed.

"So, what can I do for you?"

"Well, it's good Jade is there. It's what *she* can do."

Ethan and Jade glanced at each other, puzzled. "Go on," Ethan said.

"You want to share dinner?"

"Where are you?"

"In LA."

"What! I thought you were on the moon."

"I was, but I had business on Earth, which included talking to you two. So ... must I invite myself again?"

Ethan and Jade chuckled.

"No, you don't," Ethan said.

"What's your suggestion, and when?"

Ethan looked at Jade, who shrugged her shoulders. "We aren't very busy in the evenings at present, so we're available any time."

"Tonight?"

"Fine with me," Jade said.

"Yeah. That's great with us. Where and when?"

"Must I plan everything here?" Hu joked.

"No, you don't. Let's see, do you enjoy Italian?"

"Wow! Haven't eaten Italian for ages."

"Italian it is then. Jade and I go to one near us often. It's nothing special to look at, but we think it serves great food and is authentic, too."

"OK. Suits me. Where and when?"

"The Rubicon Restaurant. Seven-thirty?"

"That's a date."

Jade jerked her head at the last comment.

Hu noticed the response from Jade and smiled wickedly. "Both of you."

Jade blushed but sniggered to herself as she realized what she had done.

"OK. Good. See you then. Can't wait to catch up with you."

"Nor can I."

"Bye, Hugo," both Ethan and Jade responded.

The comm went blank.

"Wonder what she wants?" Ethan asked, his brow furrowed in speculation.

"Doesn't matter, so long as it's not you," Jade replied.

"Do I sense jealousy?"

"Don't be ridiculous," Jade said, defending herself, even though jealousy was precisely what she was feeling.

"Hah! You need not worry, my love. I can only fit one woman into my life, and that's you."

Jade reddened with embarrassed pleasure. "Thank you. You're getting better at expressing your feelings."

Ethan sat back and thought. "Yeah, you're right there." He felt pleased with the achievement. "Anyway, we've got things to do before tonight. Let's get to it. I'll see you later."

They both rose from their chairs in Ethan's office, giving each other a peck on the lips before Jade headed out. Ethan migrated to the chair behind his desk to continue his work.

ETHAN AND JADE walked into Rubicon just before seven-thirty. The owner and headwaiter greeted them as usual, "Buonasera, Mr. Richards and Ms. Powers, how marvelous to see you again."

"Buonasera, Leonardo. It's good to be here. We hope your service is as perfect as ever tonight, so you impress our guest," Ethan said. They were regular patrons at the restaurant, so they had developed a particular friendship with the owner. Ethan enjoyed the atmosphere that the place conveyed. It reminded him of when he had trekked through Italy on vacation many years ago.

"We shall do our best," Leonardo said as he gestured to the table for three Ethan had booked earlier in the day and escorted them to it. It was in the finest position in the house. He seated Jade first, then Ethan. "Would you like an aperitivo while you wait?"

Leonardo had migrated to America from Italy twenty years ago, but he still had the clichéd Italian looks, which added to the restaurant's authenticity. At first, he had shortened his name to 'Leonard' to fit in with America's anglicized culture, but when he opened his Italian restaurant, he found that patrons got a kick out of hearing the Italian name.

"Jade?" Ethan asked.

"I'll try a martini please, Leonardo."

"My usual beer."

"Very well." Leonardo relayed the order to a waiter before returning to the reception counter.

The door opened and Hu, looking as gorgeous as ever, entered, her eyes scanning the premises once she closed the door. Ethan saw her and waved. She waved back and advised the rather handsome middle-aged Italian who came to greet her that she was with Ethan and Jade.

Leonardo raised an eyebrow at the impressive female before him but led Hu forward without giving any other sign of admiration. "Your guest has arrived," he said as they approached the table. "And may I say that your female companions are exquisite, Ethan." As an accomplished lady's man, Leonardo was careful to include both Jade and Hu in the compliment. He knew never to single one woman out in front of another.

Hu giggled. "Your line would've interested me more a few years ago."

"It is never too old for a true Italian." Leonardo ventured to hold Hu's hand and kiss it in the traditional Italian manner before he glanced up with a mischievous smile.

Hu laughed again. "I will keep you in mind."

Leonardo nodded in appreciation.

Both Ethan and Jade rose to greet Hu while the interaction between Hu and Leonardo was being played out. "It's so good to see you," Ethan said.

"It is great to visit you too," Hu replied as she gave him a hug and kissed his cheek. Her eyes were sparkling with mischief as usual. "You too, Jade."

"And you," Jade said, responding with a hug and kiss of her own. "No grand entrances tonight?"

Hu laughed and said, "No grand entrances. I don't have Apep to encourage me."

"No, you don't," Ethan said as they laughed at the memory. "Have you heard from him since our return?"

"Not once Galena swept him off his feet. He's disappeared."

"He and Galena alike," Jade said.

"Well, I hope it works out for them," Ethan said.

"Me too," Hu agreed.

They sat again, and Hu ordered a beer. They chatted about general matters and viewed the menus to select their orders.

Hu asked, "How is life?"

"Personally, or work-wise?" Ethan asked.

"Both."

"We're still very much together. I think our relationship is growing ever stronger," Ethan said as he glanced at Jade for confirmation.

Jade smiled at him and said to Hu, "I agree. I'm getting him sorted out to how I want him."

Hu and Jade laughed.

Ethan didn't think it was funny. "You're not sorting me out." Ethan sat back in a defensive pose.

"Whatever you say," Jade said with a droll expression.

Ethan still scowled, but let it drop. He changed the topic instead. "We're starting a new project work-wise. Our government has asked us to lead an expedition to Centauri."

Hu's eyes lit up when Ethan mentioned the expedition. "Perfect."

"Perfect what?"

"Never mind. I'll tell you later. Continue."

"We are pulling a team together. Interested?"

"I wish. Not this time. I have enough to do. I might still get involved if plans eventuate."

Ethan and Jade eyed each other, intrigued by the comment.

"Are you ready to order your meals?" a waiter asked as he arrived at their table, interrupting their conversation.

"Yes, we are," Ethan said. "Hu, you want to go first?"

They ordered their food, and Ethan requested a bottle of red wine to share.

"What do you mean you might get involved?" Ethan continued the discussion.

"What do you know of our progress?"

"Not much. We've heard that you generated wormholes and have passed objects through them. Only that."

"We've gotten no further than that, unfortunately. We can create wormholes when there's a portal at both ends, but we are having difficulties creating wormholes from one end. Maybe we don't understand the theory, or it just isn't possible. I'm very interested in your latest project because one of my ideas is to get you to take a ship-sized portal far away so we can learn more about wormholes and what affects their creation and stability. You going to Centauri would be ideal for us." A smirk spread across Hu's lovely face. "If you assemble the portal at Centauri, I can enter with fanfare." Hu made as if to bow.

Ethan and Jade laughed. "Apep won't appreciate being left out," Ethan said.

"He will have his turn."

"So, what stops you from generating a wormhole from one end?" Jade asked after the frivolity passed, her interest piqued.

"I am glad you asked," Hu said.

Jade sat back with a wary look.

"We don't know. We can form a micro hole but can't enlarge it. Our quantum physicist can't understand it, which brings me to my second request. I'm wondering if I may pinch your precious jewel for a few weeks, Ethan, and fly her to the moon to review our physicist's work. I promise to take care of her."

Ethan and Jade stared at each other, unhappy at the prospect of separation. Ethan remembered when he was on *Destiny* getting it ready before Jade arrived, and the separation then was unbearable for that brief time, even at that early stage in their relationship.

"Please! For a friend," Hu begged. Her face displayed an impish innocence.

Ethan sighed. "It's up to Jade, although I am the leader of our project, so I suppose I could overrule her if I wanted. I wouldn't want that, both professionally and for my safety."

"Humph. I think I will go just to spite you now," Jade said.

"Oops! I've started a domestic," Hu said.

They grinned.

Jade glanced at Ethan before she turned to Hu. "We aren't busy yet. We still have to recruit our personnel, so my being gone won't affect our timetable, as long as it's only for two or three weeks. I'm interested in reviewing your theoretical work, and I'd be happy to help if our governments agree. It would help us set up the portal, too. I can help with any problems if I understand the details."

"Yes, it would," Hu said, agreeing with the notion.

Ethan looked displeased at the proposition. "You two together spells trouble. I know what you're like, Hugo. I forbid you to corrupt Jade."

"Jade's seen enough of the world to protect herself and you from any corrupting influence I may have," Hu said with a wicked smile, "or don't you want me divulging more of your secrets?"

Ethan became more uncomfortable. "I suppose I trust you."

"I promise to look after her and bring her back to you in one piece."

Ethan sighed in resignation. "I don't have a choice."

Their meals arrived at that point, and they ate their food and drank the wine while they continued their discussion. They talked late into the night before they departed, Hu to her hotel, and Jade and Ethan to his villa.

5

LUNAR JADE

Approval came for Jade's three-week lunar visit to help them resolve their issues, and for the Americans to take a wormhole portal with them on their expedition.

Jade rushed to pack her belongings so she could meet Hu at the airport for the trip to China, where they would board a shuttle to the Chinese moon base.

Ethan watched her pack, unhappy about their separation for three weeks. He felt like a part of himself was leaving, a sensation he had never experienced before.

She looked at him. "Cheer up, Ethan. I'm coming back."

"But it'll be so long."

"They've allowed you to communicate with me while I'm there."

"It's not the same." Ethan knew he was being foolish, but he couldn't help it.

Jade took pity on him and came over, wrapping her arms around his waist in a gentle hug. "You'll be looking after yourself for three weeks," she teased.

"That's not the point. I've looked after myself my entire life," he said, becoming even more miserable knowing that Jade was teasing him. He described to Jade the source of his misery as he reciprocated the embrace. "It's just that after being starved of female support, I found you, and I want nothing to happen that takes you from me."

Jade looked into Ethan's eyes with love and compassion. He realized she understood his difficulties in confiding in her like that. "That is such an honor, Ethan. Thank you." She gave him a warm, long kiss. That cheered him. She released herself from his embrace and continued her preparations.

She finished packing. The quantity of luggage suggested she was leaving for a year, but Ethan didn't comment. He placed the cases in his vehicle and drove her to the LAX Airport. Jade checked in and they talked before she had to enter immigration. They stood away from the main walkway, avoiding others bustling around, holding hands for the comfort the human contact gave them. They both knew that they wouldn't experience that touch again for the duration of Jade's absence. Jade became sad now, too. She realized her departure was imminent, and that upset her more than she expected.

"Am I interrupting farewells?" Hu asked from behind them.

They both started in surprise.

"Yes, you are, but that's OK," Ethan said, worry creasing his brow.

"I will look after her, Ethan, I promise."

"I know you will."

"It's time to go," Jade said after looking at her chronometer.

"I'll see you in immigration," Hu told Jade with a sympathetic smile. "I'll leave you for a moment's privacy."

Jade nodded.

"Bye, Hugo," Ethan said.

Hu departed.

"I'll miss you, Jade."

She nodded, unhappy, and moved close so they could hug each other. She had her head on his chest and sniffed away her emotion. "I'll be back before you know it."

Ethan stroked her hair as she stared into the airport at nothing in particular. She dreaded the separation, as she knew he did. "I'd better go." Jade inhaled again and moved out of the embrace. She looked into Ethan's eyes. They were red and fighting to keep the tears at bay.

He kissed her, hugged her again, and released her. "Stay safe."

"You too. See you soon," Jade said and left.

Jade was glad she had moved away abruptly because her emotions threatened to overwhelm her. She turned just before she disappeared into the immigration hall and waved. Ethan waved back, and she walked past the wall separating them from each other.

"HOW'S ETHAN HOLDING OUT?" Hu asked when Jade reached her.

Jade put on a brave smile. "About as well as I am."

"You're making me feel guilty."

"It'll be fine. It's just hard to separate. I have you to look after me, Hugo. Just us girls." Jade's mood brightened. "That's what worries Ethan."

They both laughed.

Passing through immigration, they boarded the plane.

They talked little during the journey, as each amused herself. Six hours later, they arrived in Shanghai and transferred to the spaceport with the shuttle waiting to take them to the moon. The shuttle left, and they settled in for the trip. They sat opposite each other so they could talk without straining their necks. There was no one else on the flight that trip, either.

Hours into the flight and after sharing a few drinks, Jade asked, "Why aren't you in a steady relationship, Hu?" Like all recently and happily coupled people, Jade wanted everyone to have the same happiness.

When a look of sadness settled on Hu's face, she instantly regretted the question, castigating herself for being both nosey and insensitive.

"Don't answer that," Jade said quickly. "I shouldn't have asked."

Hu looked away. People had asked her that question many times, and she usually gave her stock answer along the lines of 'mind your own business.' But she was suddenly unsure that she wanted to give Jade that reply.

She had bottled up her memories of her first love for so long it was part of her. She saw again his enthusiastic face when he embarked on that last adventure in the wild, her mind having etched the tragedy like an engraved glass plaque. She felt again the shock she experienced when told of his accident, the silence and downcast eyes speaking louder than a load hailer that it was fatal, and he wasn't coming back to her. She sighed and faced Jade.

Jade, who had watched various emotions flit across Hu's face, said again, "Sorry, I didn't mean to pry."

"No, it's time I talked about it again. I had a partner once. Many years ago. Long before I met Ethan, even. He was my soulmate, my love." Hu smiled as she recalled an age of pure joy for her and then continued, "He was a fanatic about exploring the wildest regions of China. He was so excited when planning his next trip and so animated when he returned. His last trek was to follow the Yangtze River from its source to the sea. He left and never ... came back ..." Hu's voice broke as she remembered the wretchedness of her loss.

Jade reached across and placed her hand on top of Hu's and squeezed it for comfort and support. "I'm so sorry."

"... It was a long time ago. Water rapids along the river threw him from his canoe and dashed him against the rocks. I just stopped talking about him after that. The pain was too much, and my friends, out of consideration, ceased discussing it." Hu sniffed and wiped away a tear. "I should have grieved properly then, but I never did. Maybe that's why I've avoided a serious relationship ever since. You are the first person I've talked to about it, apart from the grief counselors. I didn't even tell Ethan."

"I'm so sorry for you and honored that you're comfortable telling me."

Hu slumped back in her seat and sighed. "It's good to talk about it again; it's as if you have unscrewed the bottle and released the pressure."

Jade changed the topic then. Hu relaxed, grateful, as she needed to release the pain in stages. "Tell me about this physicist."

Hu laughed. "It'll interest me to watch you two interact. His name is Chen Liang. He comes from Suzhou. He is brilliant, but he gets too narrowly focused sometimes and can't entertain alternative solutions once he's decided that his idea is the right one. It's infuriating when that happens. His nose was out of joint when I suggested you review his work, so I'm certain he'll resist your delving at first. I'm hoping you'll show him other ways of approaching a problem than his."

"Now you tell me," Jade said.

"I needed to make sure you came."

They laughed.

"Thanks for preparing me. I'll try not to damage his male ego if I can help it. I know him. He's written very enlightening papers in our field."

"Mention that and he'll warm to you."

"What's it like living on the moon?"

"It can be claustrophobic with so many people occupying a limited space. There is little privacy, but you'll adapt. The gravity setting is only fifty percent of Earth's, something to do with conserving energy. It takes time to adjust to it. There is no sun, stars, rain, or wind, and the recycled air smells. They deodorize it, but it's not one hundred percent. You desensitize to it, but the open freshness of Earth is a joy despite its troubles and issues.

"I think you will find the base itself very modern. It has the latest research technology for our work. We can conduct unique particle accelerator experiments difficult to do on Earth, so I am told."

The flight attendant handed out refreshments and meals for them to eat. They continued small talk, but exhausted their conversation and silence descended on them as if the day's sun had set. Jade read, and Hu napped after her meal until they arrived at the lunar research station. It was four-twenty in the afternoon.

Jade felt lightheaded from the reduced gravity, as Hu had warned her, but adjusted. Hu led her through the complex and into the residential section. She showed Jade her living space and how everything worked.

"Thanks," Jade said.

"You're welcome. Sorry I couldn't get you a larger unit, but others are occupying them at present," Hu replied. "I'll give you time to settle in and come by to escort you to the mess hall for dinner, say six-thirty."

"OK. Thanks."

Hu left Jade in the quarters alone. She inspected her surroundings. It was basic but utilitarian, with a small living space, a kitchenette, and an entertainment unit. Through a doorway, she found the bedroom and ensuite bathroom. She unpacked her bag and had a shower to freshen up. An alarm buzzed before she'd finished, and a voice said, "Automatic shower will turn off in one minute." Jade rushed to finish rinsing herself off and got out. *They practice water conservation*, she thought. *I must remember that.* She enjoyed luxuriating under the shower sometimes.

She dressed and pulled her data plate out. Connecting into the network, she followed the instructions in the room, and dialed Ethan using the conferencing clip they both used.

He appeared on the screen after a few minutes. "Hi. How are things?"

"Good. We just arrived on the moon. I've had a shower and put you at the top of the priority list ..."

Ethan sat waiting for two-and-a-half seconds before he reacted, like a news reporter on location hanging out for the next question from the studio newsroom. Her transmission had to arrive on Earth, and his reply return to the moon. The delay annoyed Jade.

He grinned. "... Good. Hope Hu is looking after you ..."

"... Yes, she is..."

"... It's good to see you again. I miss you already..."

Jade smiled in sympathy. "... I miss you too. What have you been doing ...?"

"... I started looking at recruitment lists to find contenders. We have many valid candidates in each field. I'll have my work cut out before I can generate a shortlist for each position to approach ..."

"... Glad it's you and not me ..."

"... You deliberately went to the moon to avoid it ..." Ethan said with a knowing smirk.

Jade laughed. "... You're right. I called Hugo up and told her to save me from it. She came to the party ..."

Ethan chuckled. "... I had better go. Love you, Jade..."

"... Love you too, Ethan..." Jade replied.

The screen blanked. It wasn't time for Hu to come back to collect her for dinner yet, so she busied herself with minor but necessary work-related chores while she waited.

The door controls buzzed. Jade opened it, and Hu was standing there. "Hungry?" she asked.

"Starving," Jade responded.

"Let's go then."

They strolled to the mess hall. She showed Jade around the base along the way. They reached their destination, and Hu walked Jade through the procedure for obtaining a meal. They both got their food and drink. Hu spotted Chen Liang sitting alone eating, so she wandered over to him.

"Mind if we join you?" she asked.

"You back?" Liang asked rather unnecessarily, thought Hu.

"Yes. Well?"

"No, I don't. Sit." Hu and Jade sat opposite him.

Jade could sense Liang distrusted her.

"Let me introduce Jade Powers, Liang."

"Welcome, Ms. Powers," he said with little enthusiasm.

"Jade, meet Chen Liang," Hu said, giving Liang an annoyed glare.

"Hello, Liang. It's a pleasure to meet you. I have read many of your papers. You offer interesting insights," Jade said, trying to get on side with him straight away despite his lackluster mood.

"Yeah, well. It's obviously not enough."

Both Jade and Hu sat in silence and started eating. Jade felt confused about how to handle Liang's hostility. He certainly wasn't disguising his displeasure that Hu had brought in an outsider to review his work. She tried another tack. "What are your thoughts on research into the interaction of string resonances in the fifth dimension?"

Liang stopped chewing. He glared at her with bitterness. "I'm not hungry anymore," he said, got up and left, leaving Hu and Jade open-mouthed and nonplussed.

"Cooperation may be more difficult than I thought. I'm sorry."

"I can understand his attitude in a way. He thinks people are questioning his competence by bringing in an outsider. It makes you doubt yourself. I've had those feelings too, although his reaction is extreme."

"He needs to get over it."

"When are we to meet tomorrow?"

"Ten."

"Let's see how he is, then. He may have adjusted to the inevitable by then."

"I hope so."

They ate in silence, Jade wondering how she would tackle her next meeting with Liang.

She had a reasonable sleep and woke early for a workout in the gym. After vigorous exercise, she returned to her quarters for a shower and left for breakfast. Hu was waiting for her when she arrived at her room again.

"Ready?" she asked.

"Ready as I'll ever be," Jade said, somewhat resigned to her fate with Liang, whatever that might be. "I'll just get my things."

"Sure."

Jade collected what she wanted and followed Hu to a meeting room Hu had organized for Jade and Liang's discussion. Liang was already there, seated, hunched. He looked in a morose and hostile mood.

"Good morning, Liang," Jade said in a friendly tone.

"Morning," Liang replied tersely.

Jade thought he seemed to be fighting his emotions, as if he resented the intrusion, but his manner was childish and not accept-able. She took a gamble. "I've had times when I felt threatened professionally, too, Liang. It's an unpleasant emotion, but the other person just wants to help, and I want to help you make your break-through here. If you can crack this challenge, you will achieve a first."

Liang looked at her intently and suspiciously. Hu was watching, waiting for something to give. The air was tight with tension as Liang mulled over Jade's words and how he should respond. He sighed.

Taking a further gamble, Jade added, "People want to be support-ive, but they don't understand us physicists."

The gamble worked. Liang gave a reluctant smile. "Yeah, you are right. We get too focused sometimes and need someone who talks the same language. Hu does her best, but she's only an engineer."

"Hey! No need to get personal," Hu interjected, relieved at Liang's mood change.

"I wouldn't dare say that to Ethan," Jade agreed.

"It's true," Liang said with a smile, lightening up and relaxing.

"Well, I'll let you two bang your heads together in your own quantum world while I do actual work," Hu said as she left them to their discussion.

"You need us, and you know it," Liang called after her as she walked way.

Liang and Jade settled.

"Why don't you summarize your work so far?" Jade asked.

"OK. Let's see. The basic principles behind wormhole generation are ..."

6

SENNA JACOBS — GEOLOGIST

Senna Jacobs wiped the perspiration from her brow as she helped lift the vast number of core samples into the container for transport back to the research center for analysis. They had been drilling for weeks off the coast of Sumatra to gain samples of the geological architecture of Earth between the Eurasian and Indo-Australian plates and for several kilometers below the join.

It was a laborious process, made worse by the core-sampling drill frequently breaking when the plates moved, causing them to lose the sample. They had to start again each time that happened. They considered giving up, but the last drilling had given them the result they wanted: a core sample from the sea floor to twenty kilometers under the surface. She hoped to examine the geological variation through a major tectonic plate convergence and information on the chronological characteristics of the material driven under Earth's crust by the tectonic movement. It was hard work in an unforgiving tropical climate, but she was thankful for the crew she had. They never complained, even under continual setbacks.

She finally got the specimens she desired and had them locked away in the shipping container, ready for transportation back to shore.

Senna stood up straight, getting the ache out of her body. She addressed her team. "Thank you for your hard work in helping me get these samples. A hotel room awaits us, with a hot shower and celebrations in port for you. My shout. Don't make any trouble is all I ask."

The crew cheered her generosity and eagerly prepared the ship for their journey back to Merak. They would then travel by road to the hotel complex at Anyer for their reward.

The boat sailed the distance to the harbor in an hour, and they arrived at the resort three hours afterward. Senna stood under the cool shower as she cleaned her body and shampooed her hair, styling it into something respectable and feminine for a change. She dried herself and dressed in a white blouse and blue jeans. The day's humidity had relented, and the evening promised to be balmy. She headed for the poolside bar to mix with the others and satisfy her thirst. Several of her team were already there enjoying themselves.

Senna sat on a stool at the bar and ordered a Bintang beer, sipping at it while the sun set in the west. Krakatau stood off the coast, rising out of the ocean. Anak Krakatau glowed like an orange-red neon light. There had been reports of minor eruptions in recent days.

"So, what do you think, boss? Will the kid have a tantrum tonight?" one of her team asked, pointing at the volcanoes.

Senna smiled. "I don't know, even with my geological knowledge."

The hotel stood on the beach, so Senna rose from her stool and walked that way. The waves washed ashore in a gentle rhythmic fashion, reflecting the lighting from the buildings back to her in sparkling scintillation. She paused at the edge of the sand in peaceful solitude.

Anak Krakatau rumbled, and a spray of magma shot into the air, startling Senna from her reverie. *It is having a tantrum tonight.* The volcano settled again.

Senna sat and finished her beer. A hotel attendant came along and asked if she wanted a refill. She said, "Yes." The attendant left and returned, replacing the empty bottle with a full one. *I could just live the rest of my life here*, she thought.

Senna's comm chirped. She took it from her pocket to check and frowned as she read the heading <Centauri Expedition Project – Geologist Position>. It wasn't from anyone she knew. *Is this a crank message?* she thought as she pondered whether to open it. *It won't hurt to see what it says,* she decided and opened the file. It read:

<Dear Ms. Jacobs

This is not a crank message. You do not know me personally, but you may have heard of me. I recently completed the first faster-than-light space flight on the starship *Destiny.* Our achievement was well publicized.

I am putting together a new team for the above-mentioned project. The aim is to visit the star Centauri and explore its planetary bodies. We wish to find out if any are habitable for humans and, if so, to examine their geological stability, among other things.

I have reviewed résumés of potential candidates for the geologist position, and yours best matches our needs.

We will fly to Centauri in *Destiny.*

This assignment provides the opportunity of a lifetime. Please call me on this link if you are interested in discussing the opportunity further.

Regards

Ethan Richards

Centauri Expedition Project

Project Leader>

Senna's heart raced. She read it again to make sure she'd missed nothing. Her palms dampened with excitement. *Stay calm,* she told herself as she took deep, calming breaths.

She rose from the sand and returned to her room to search on the net for the mentioned space flight. She had not heard of it, but then she had been out of reach of the net for several months. A multitude of stories about the momentous event appeared. Ethan Richards was the project's Chief Engineer. Several articles covered other events that had happened on that extraordinary flight: sabotage and murder and confronting a business mogul over a mineral deposit on a moon of Saturn. There was enough verifiable information. She found no report on any recent project or expedition, though. *It might be a secret or too new for media attention yet*, she thought.

As she pondered the articles, she realized the author was correct in describing the project as the opportunity of a lifetime. They'd be pioneers exploring another star. She considered the work she was undertaking at present. As important as it was, it paled into insignificance in comparison. She was sure someone else could take over the study. She paced the floor of her hotel room with uncertainty. It was just after ten. She checked the time differential between Indonesia and America and noted that it would be seven-thirty in the morning on the West Coast of America. The news articles suggested the earlier project was based on the west coast, so she assumed the current one was too. She then recognized that it didn't matter if it was the East Coast. The message had arrived an hour ago, so the person must be contactable. She pressed the link in the file and waited.

"Hello, Ethan Richards here," he said.

Senna was nervous, wondering what to say. "Senna Jacobs calling about your message," eventually came out of her.

"Oh. Hi. I'm glad you called. Just wait a moment. I'll get the video going."

Shuffling and other noises emitted from the speaker. The visual display then flickered, revealing a man. He looked in his early thirties, had a full head of dark brown hair and brown eyes. He was clean-shaven, and his face was handsome to Senna. *I wonder if he's taken.* She could only see him from the shoulders up, but he had an athletic build. Senna placed herself on visual.

"I wasn't sure when you'd receive my message. The report suggested you were out in the Indian Ocean collecting core samples."

"I was, but you're in luck. We finished today, and the entire team is back at the hotel celebrating."

"I'm sorry for interrupting your festivities."

"Don't be. If the news is true, it's worth the interruption."

"Believe me, it's true. Let me give you more detail. The American military has asked me to assemble a team to investigate Centauri for possible habitable planets. I'm excited at the prospect and eager to gather the team quickly. It will be the longest test of our new FTL drive, my baby. When Jade Powers, the project quantum physicist, and I started considering the people we needed, we realized we had to have a geologist to inform us about the geological stability of any planet we study. I've looked at many résumés of the world's leading geologists, but yours stands out as someone who uses lateral thinking to find original ways of doing things. You have experience in meteorology, too, which satisfies our policy of selecting people able to cover another field of expertise."

"Thanks for the compliment. Can I ask a few questions?"

"Fire away."

"How long will the trip be?"

"That depends on what we find there. To give you a rough approximation, it'll take twenty days to reach Alpha Centauri and twenty days to return to Earth. I expect at least a month there, so we'll be absent for three or four months."

"Only twenty days?"

Ethan chuckled. "Yes, twenty days. I can't believe it myself sometimes."

"Who else is on the team?"

"You are the first to respond, so only Jade and me at this point. Eventually, we hope to have a fusion specialist, an astronomer, a meteorologist, a biologist, a microbiologist, a medical specialist, and of course, a geologist."

"Oh. What authority will I have?"

"I'm the team leader, so you'll report to me. Besides that, you will have complete freedom with your responsibilities on the geological side within reason. So, are you interested?"

Senna grinned. "You bet!"

Ethan smiled too. "When could you begin?"

"As I mentioned, we just finished collecting our core samples. We need to study them to see what they tell us, but I can pass that job onto someone else. I could start in a few weeks."

"Good. Don't rush too much. We won't be leaving for at least a month or two. You will be invaluable with the preparation activities, though, and for team bonding. I'll send through more information and other documentation for your employment in the project and clearances."

"I can't wait!" Senna said with exuberance.

"You'd better get back to your festivities. You'll have two reasons to celebrate now."

"Yes, I will, and thanks."

"You're welcome."

The screen blanked.

Elated at her stroke of luck, Senna wanted to tell someone. She returned to the poolside bar hoping some of her team remained. She would announce it to whoever was there. Going downstairs to the bar, she ordered another drink. A few men were, to Senna's disgust, coupled up with the local women, buying them drinks. That wouldn't dampen her excitement. She called the party to order.

"I have news to announce," she said when they quietened. "I have a job opportunity."

There were murmurs of disappointment and disapproval from the gathered crowd.

"I'm going to Alpha Centauri to study any planets we find there."

Discontent changed to incredulity and approval, whistles coming from them, and then a chant of "Skull, skull, skull!" erupted, urging Senna to drink the rest of her beer in one gulp. She laughed and tried to satisfy their request. She placed the lip of the beer bottle to her mouth and started drinking, gulping the amber fluid as fast as she could. To her amazement, she finished the bottle and replaced it on the bar. The others cheered her success.

She surveyed the crowd, content with the day's outcome, before emitting the loudest belch she could remember ever producing.

∿

7

MAX ROBERTS — FUSION SPECIALIST

Max Roberts reclined in his chair at the European Organization for Nuclear Research complex, known as CERN, near Geneva in Switzerland. He rubbed his eyes to remove the tiredness of staring at the computer screen for hours. He was looking at operational cost reports and felt bored and in a rut. There was nothing further to achieve in his current role as the fusion specialist there. The position was now routine and a pure management role. He reminisced about his younger years when he was green and eager to meet ground-breaking challenges. Not that he was averse to new endeavors, but they rarely presented themselves. Research at the particle accelerator was just tidying up on discoveries already established.

Max had landed the job at CERN five years ago, coming over from England. He had been educated in London, where he'd discovered he had an affinity for quantum physics, with a particular interest in the practical side of fusion reactions and power generation. Now, at forty-one and with no partner or family, he felt he wasn't getting anywhere anymore. Maybe he needed to change careers and go in a different direction.

He was contemplating this crossroads when his comm chimed.

He opened the message without checking the sender or heading, reading it to distract himself from his current melancholy, but his interest increased the more he dissected it and understood. It was a message from someone called Ethan Richards, seeking a fusion specialist. Had this guy read his mind?

When he had finished reading the message the second time to make sure he had read it correctly, Max sat up straight, flabbergasted. He couldn't believe his luck. It seemed Ethan Richards really had been reading his mind. The FTL space flight from Iapetus to Mars had headlined the news feeds and technical periodicals, and Max had daydreamed of being involved. He thought it was six months ago. Now they intended traveling to Alpha Centauri, and they wanted him to join them. He reclined with a childish grin on his face, deep in fanciful speculation of adventure and mystery.

"You okay there? You look zoned out," a colleague said from his office doorway.

Max returned to reality. "Yeah, I'm fine, Manfred. I think I just got a job offer."

"Where?"

"Fusion specialist on a spaceship traveling to Alpha Centauri."

"You're joking!" Manfred said with a disbelieving smirk.

"No. It's true. Have a look for yourself."

Max showed him the message on his comm. Manfred read it, doubt turning to impressed awe.

"You taking it?"

"Don't know. I should get more details first, but it beats sitting around here shuffling paperwork."

"Sure would. Lucky bastard! I knew something would come your way. You're wasted here."

"You didn't."

Manfred gave a sheepish grin. "I may exaggerate, but it's true this job's too mundane for you."

"Thanks. At least someone appreciates me."

"Anyway, here's another report."

"Thanks so much. Go away before I hit you with it," Max said. He feigned to throw the document back at him, but Manfred ducked beyond the doorway.

"Lots of luck," Max heard Manfred say as he left.

Max returned to his dreaming and wondering what he should do. He decided it wouldn't hurt to talk to the sender of the message. It was just after 4 pm. After checking the time disparity, he realized it was seven in the morning for Ethan Richards. Deciding to wait two hours before he called, he researched the earlier project and the history of Ethan Richards in particular. The more he read, the more excited he became and the more he desired the position. He even stayed late at work — something unheard of with his present mundane job.

Six o'clock came, so he pressed the link in the message and sat staring at the screen, anticipating the connection.

Ethan's image appeared. "Hello, Ethan Richards speaking."

"Hi. I am Max Roberts. You sent me a message earlier."

"Yes, I did. I'm pleased you called. Has it piqued your interest?"

"It sure has. Can you explain the project and what my position would be in more detail?"

Ethan nodded his head, expecting the question. "Have you heard about the faster-than-light space flight undertaken six months ago?"

"I saw it on the newscasts. It was an impressive achievement."

"That it was. Well, we are ready for an actual trip now to another star. The American military wants us to go to Centauri and investigate any habitable planets there. I am putting together a team to take there and complete that mission."

"What happened to your original fusion specialist, then? Wouldn't that person be first choice?"

Ethan's jaw tightened. This was one line of questioning he didn't want, both because it was painful to talk about Jessica and he didn't want to put off anyone by dwelling on what had happened before. "She is otherwise occupied, so we're short a fusion specialist. I've been sifting through many résumés, and yours caught my eye, especially since one of your fields of expertise is quantum physics. Your present job seems a waste of your considerable talent. Do you mind my asking why you took it?

Max shrugged. "It seemed like a good idea at the time." Ethan's perception surprised him. "I had occupied my prior position for a while and wanted something different. I knew the role wouldn't challenge me, but I needed a change."

"Fair enough. Are you ready for another change, then?"

"What would I be doing?"

"You'd be responsible for the power supply reactors, the FTL drive reactor, and the muon particle generator. You'd work with Jade Powers, the quantum specialist, looking for alternatives to the astatine that we use for the muon particle generation and trying to understand why astatine works so well and why it doesn't decay when not on Earth."

Max's eyes lit up with the excitement swirling in his stomach. He was getting a rejuvenated life, like watering a withered plant. Needing no time to decide, he said, "I'm hooked."

Ethan smiled. "I assure you, it's the most interesting thing you'll do, even without your actual job duties."

"It'll be more impressive that sitting here filling out paperwork."

"I'll send through more information on your position and other administrative details. I expect we won't be leaving for at least six weeks, so you'll have plenty of opportunity to place your affairs in order, but I'd prefer you here as soon as you can complete your current duties."

"Fine. Can't wait to get on board."

"I will see you soon then."

The screen went blank.

Max reclined with a beaming smile.

CELESTE GRÜBER — ASTRONOMER

Celeste Grüber looked at the display readouts of the Gran Telescopio Canarias (GTC) telescope on the Canary Islands. It was late at night. She was studying star systems, searching for signs of orbiting planets. It was a long and laborious exercise that required much patience. She gazed at several galaxies and nebulae that appeared on the telescope in the position they had moved it to that evening. She relished the sight of the galaxy structures and the glow of the nebulae. Another of her duties involved operating the Hoyle Space Astronomical Center at the L4 Lagrange point of Earth and the moon.

Celeste still enjoyed her job at the observatory, where she'd been for four years now since completing her PhD in astronomy at ETH Zurich in Switzerland. She had gained enough experience to provide a useful contribution without extensive supervision. The discovery of exoplanets and trying to figure out if they could support life from significant distances away from Earth excited her. She was getting itchy feet, though.

Celeste had grown up in Munich, Germany, as the first child of three and part of a typical German family. Her intelligence, however, was plain from an early age, so her parents worked extra hard to give her an excellent education. She contributed when she was old enough by gaining part-time jobs. Celeste loved her parents and wanted to pay them back someday. She was now making a name for herself, which made them proud. They would boast about her to everyone they met, much to Celeste's embarrassment.

She continued reviewing images from the Sirius star constellation, needing to search for any planets orbiting either Sirius A or Sirius B. They had discovered none up to that point, other than unaccounted for gravitational anomalies with the binary star.

Her comm buzzed. It was one-thirty in the morning and odd for anyone to message her so late. When she opened the message, she saw it was from someone called Ethan Richards, and he was looking for an astronomer. She read the message with the same bemusement and growing excitement of the other recipients.

Celeste reread the message to make sure she had interpreted it correctly. She sat back in her chair, butterflies fluttering in her stomach. Someone had headhunted her for the position. That was unbelievable. What had she done to qualify her above the other brilliant minds and practitioners in the field? She was still young, being just 29. Could she really research in person what was only possible to view with Earth-based telescopes?

Glancing at her time charts, she worked out Los Angeles was nine hours behind her time zone, so it was four-thirty in the afternoon there. She pressed the link in the message to call the sender before she lost her nerve.

Ethan came onto her screen after a few seconds. "Ethan Richards here." His face looked strong and competent but preoccupied.

She was nervous and unsure of her words until she regained her senses. "Oh ... Hi. I'm Celeste Grüber. I'm calling about the message you sent me."

Ethan stopped what he was doing and gave Celeste his full attention. "Excuse me, I was thinking about something else."

"That's OK. You must be very busy."

Ethan looked at Celeste for a moment. His eyes seem to drill into her soul, making her squirm. He smiled. "I'm sorry. I don't want to make you uncomfortable. You appear nervous."

"I ... this ... oh, I'm making a mess of everything, like I always do. You'll reject me now."

"Stay calm, Celeste. I didn't just read your résumé and your profile. I understand your reaction. You remind me of myself. Young, thinking you need to impress to get ahead and unsure of yourself." Ethan chuckled. "I know just the person to straighten you out, but she's working on another project. But I presume you want more information about my message. I'm putting together a team to go to Centauri and explore the possibility of habitable planets there. We need an astronomer."

"Don't you have plenty of astronomers on Earth?"

"Sure. But when I was reading their résumés, one thing stood out. Most astronomers are conservative, only wanting to refine their research and make a name for themselves without overstretching their abilities. Then I read your résumé. I spotted a freshness, someone willing to go outside her comfort zone to satisfy her curiosity. I'm looking for that inquisitiveness, apart from a brilliant astronomer, which you are."

Celeste squirmed, being uncomfortable hearing so much praise. She was usually on the receiving end of a reprimand for allowing that inquisitiveness Ethan admired to lead her into bending the rules at the Observatory. "Thank you," was all she could think to say. She felt so nervous and foolish that she forgot why she had called him.

Ethan waited, then said, "Well?"

Celeste reddened with embarrassment. "Well, what?"

"Are you interested?"

Celeste became flustered, fearing she would blow it unless she said something, anything. "Yes, yes, I'm in if you'll still have me after you've met me."

Ethan chuckled again. "I'll have to work on you. Better still, I'll get Jade working on you."

"Who's Jade?"

"She's the quantum physicist for the project and a very perceptive person. You'll like her."

"So, you want me?"

"Definitely. How many times need I tell you?"

Celeste produced a smile that highlighted her inherent charm. She relaxed in front of Ethan's eyes as the seconds elapsed. Her pulse slowed. "Thank you so much. I can't think of a better contribution to science."

Ethan grinned, too. "I'm glad my instincts were right. You are ideal for what I want for the expedition. I'll send more information and paperwork through and hope to see you over here soon."

"You will — and thank you again."

The screen went blank.

Celeste rose from her chair and danced excitedly around the room until she was puffed from the exertion but still elated. She'd make her parents so proud. She had to call them, impatient of the wait till morning.

Once she sat again, Celeste contemplated her extraordinary opportunity, then headed for the telescope-positioning control panel. She dialed in the coordinates for Centauri, despite knowing they would reprimand her for it when the day shift started. The telescope moved and locked in on the new position. For the rest of the night, she observed her future goal.

9

DAVID SUMMERS — METEOROLOGIST

David Summers walked into the Meteorological Headquarters in Silver Springs, Maryland, USA. He was in an acerbic mood. It was three-twenty in the afternoon of his day off, but a crisis was brewing, one that would have been averted if they'd listened to him.

I warned them a week ago. They just nodded their heads and continued as if nothing would happen. Now it's happening, and everyone is in a panic. They should have listened. It's like talking to a brick wall. He had informed his managers that two large hurricanes would form simultaneously off the east coast of America, an event that was rare, and would converge and combine into one super hurricane, causing significant damage, and the government needed to act to prepare for it. His superiors had ignored his advice, and now the hurricanes were bearing in on sizeable population centers on the coast, with no time for emergency arrangements. The Bureau had called in their meteorologists to watch and make recommendations about the movement and severity of the hurricane so they could inform the relevant authorities.

The bureaucratic indifference that the agency exuded toward its staff and the public exasperated David. He wondered why he still worked there.

Weather forecasting had advanced in accuracy with larger and more powerful computers, better prediction models, and smaller atmospheric cell sizes. They predicted further into the future with greater certainty, thanks to David's work and the contributions of others worldwide.

David wished he could go somewhere where he was his own boss and people looked to him for advice instead of just throwing his reports into the trash or the review-later pile.

"What is it now?" he asked his panicky supervisor.

"The cells are converging, and we're unsure how large the resultant hurricane will get."

"Didn't I tell you that last week?"

"It's developing even larger than your prediction."

David sighed, but the fresh information intrigued him. *Had his model underestimated the severity of the approaching storm?* "Let me have a look."

He walked into the weather-monitoring center for the USA with its floor-to-ceiling display on one wall showing the latest radar readouts from the satellites in space. It stunned him when he studied it. The hurricanes were monsters, and they hadn't joined yet. Even he felt a surge of panic; his heart raced, and his palms dampened, which was very rare for him. After the emergency ended, he would need to review this storm's details to discover where the modeling had failed. He looked at the approach paths and rotational speed of the two cells. They were approaching the coast from the north and east. Sitting at a computer terminal, he brought up one of the forecasting programs and mapped the directions and cell details for the approaching storms. He ran the model, which took a few minutes. His eyes widened when he saw the displayed results. It showed the cells converging just off the Florida coastline and the united hurricane continuing to travel east into the Gulf of Mexico, crossing the coast around New Orleans, with Houston as its destination. The model presented wind strengths and precipitation predictions, too.

"Boss!" he called out.

His boss came over to him, and David pointed to the screen.

"This'll be a disaster," his boss said, his face creasing with worry as he interpreted the readouts.

"Afraid so."

"Confidence level?"

David looked at the figures and brought up two related screens. "Ninety-five percent."

"I'd better tell the others the unpleasant news," his boss said, getting his handkerchief from his pocket to wipe the perspiration from his brow. "Can you keep monitoring and let me know of any changes?"

"Yeah, OK," David said, annoyed at the menial task his supervisor had given him. He sat back and thought. *We'd have prepared for the disaster if they'd listened to me when I told them.* The modeling predicted as he had forecast, although the severity parameter equations needed recalibrations.

His comm buzzed. He grabbed it from his pocket and looked at the subject line. It made him raise his eyebrows in surprise. He opened the message and read it. It was from a guy called Ethan Richards — now, that name sounded familiar — about an expedition to Alpha Centauri. They were looking for a meteorologist.

The message contents surprised David, especially where exactly they had retrieved his résumé. *They keep tabs on you everywhere.*

He had heard of the faster-than-light space flight six months ago and wondered how they might use the technology. Now he knew. He pondered the offer. Apart from reporting to this Ethan guy, he'd be his own boss. He could take revised versions of the models and adapt them to map whatever they found. He'd have inferior computing power than they had in this establishment, but he presumed they were looking for rough predictions initially.

As he perused the center, he saw people looking busy. He realized he shouldn't be too harsh on them. They were trying to avoid a disaster and would labor for many hours yet. Several had worked their normal day already. Nothing was changing much with the forecasts he had made, either.

Once he slipped into a quiet room, he pressed the link to dial the comm number and waited. He wanted the details, at least.

Ethan came on the display. "Ethan Richards here."

"Hi. I'm David Summers. I've called about the message you sent regarding the Centauri expedition."

"Oh. Thanks for calling. I hear you are having a tremendous storm over your way at present."

"Yeah. It's converging now. I told them that would happen — but, as usual, they don't listen till it's bleeding obvious and then it's too late to do much to avoid the consequences. This could be the largest hurricane we've ever had."

"Hmm ... well, I hope it's not too disastrous. So, what can I tell you?"

"Just explain the expedition details and what my role would be."

"As I said in the message, I'm putting together a crew to go to Centauri to explore for habitable planets–"

"Any reason for thinking any would be habitable?" David interrupted.

"Well, there are a few promising ones, and there may be others. Part of the assessment involves assessing the planet's climatic conditions for suitability. That would be your job."

"Who else would work with me?"

"As far as meteorological analysis, you are it. There will be other specialists involved. We need to assess many criteria to decide if a planet is habitable. We'd rely on you to offer a comprehensive profile of the planet's weather throughout the year."

"That's quite an ask."

"That's why you were top of the list. If you're not up to it, I'll chase the next candidate."

"You don't get rid of me that easily, buddy. I didn't say it was beyond me, but now I know why I was your first choice. If I'm the best, how come people don't listen to me more?"

Ethan assumed the question was a joke and chuckled. "So, are you interested or not?"

David couldn't see why he still procrastinated. This was the chance of a lifetime. He could make a name for himself. "Describe yourself."

Ethan pondered his reply before he answered. "I'm straightforward. But I hate being messed with, and I don't like surprises. I'm not the right person to give you the answer to that question. I'm biased."

"How long is the project?"

"My current estimate is three or four months."

"What happens to me when we return?"

"That depends. I'm sure we'll have a mountain of data to analyze. And there'll be other expeditions now we have FTL travel. It rests with you. It could be your only expedition, or you could make it your career."

David considered the last statement. That was the crux of his decision. Did he want a long-term commitment? It would be his first time. His mind often wandered after a while, making him yearn for new challenges. Somehow, he sensed this was different. They wouldn't exhaust the multitude of planets to examine and analyze for habitability if he played his cards right. He might even bring the science of meteorology to the next level, studying multiple worlds and how atmospheres behave in diverse circumstances. As he stared at Ethan, he decided. "I accept."

Ethan smiled. "Good. I'll send you more details and the paperwork we need to sign you up to the position. I hope you can get through your current storm."

David laughed. "That is out of my hands. They should have listened to me when they could change the outcome. Now I just watch it and tell them where it will hit worst."

"Well, good luck anyway, and expect to see you soon."

"Me too."

The screen went blank.

David couldn't wait to leave this dump and get started.

10

ZANE FOREST — BIOLOGIST

*Z*ane Forest sighed as he finished another lecture at MIT for second-year graduate scholars. It was late afternoon. He didn't understand why he continued lecturing. He was atrocious at it, and the students offered him the same blank expressions every lecture. But it was a necessary sacrifice in the academic world. He just wanted to delve into his biological research into the *Mesopelagic* and *Bathypelagic* fish species in the deep sea. Their survival mechanisms intrigued him, and more species were being discovered each day with the unique bathyspheres developed for the exploration.

He walked back to his office with his lecture notes, depressed about his fate in life. With no sign of his future changing, he wondered why he stayed in his current position. He realized that even his research was falling below his high standard. *Where is the enthusiasm I once possessed?* He arrived at his office and slumped at his desk, placing his notes on it as he did so. The desk almost groaned under the weight of the piles of research papers, conference proceedings, and textbooks already there.

As he gazed out the window, he realized he had been more alive years ago when he researched entire ecosystems, linking the interconnections between each species and how they kept each other in balance. He had had no responsibilities and roamed freely without a care. Then he'd married and settled down. Once the children came along, he needed a steady income in a fixed location to give them a stable environment. So, he had taken the teaching position at MIT. *The rot set in then*, he thought. That was when he atrophied, both intellectually and in his marriage. Once the children grew up and left home, his wife did too. She just packed her bags and fled, saying that she needed a life. His lecturing nailed him to MIT as if he had been super-glued there, and he couldn't move, couldn't adjust to something else. That was ten years ago. *No wonder I'm restless.* He needed to live again, just as his wife had done. She had done what he couldn't. He just wasn't sure how to kick-start himself to search for alternative employment.

His comm buzzed. He didn't like comms, didn't like the abruptness of their demand for attention. These harbingers of change interrupted the peacefulness of his world. It was interrupting his reverie now. He considered ignoring it but had nothing better to do, only finishing the next day's preparation work before returning to his lonely home. He picked the comm up from the desk and read the heading: <Centauri Expedition Project – Biologist Position>.

Zane frowned with curiosity. What on earth was the Centauri Expedition Project? And what could it want with him? He opened the message and read it.

Zane put his comm on the desktop. His heart raced. *Why would he choose me? There are thousands of other biologists. There must be plenty better qualified than me, but he selected me.* As he became increasingly fidgety, he wondered what this offer might mean. He had been complaining that he needed a change. Standing, he walked to the window and gazed out over the quadrangle, where students lounged on the grass like cats basking in the late afternoon sun, talking and laughing without a care in the world.

He glanced back at the comm, wondering what he should do. Could he leave this slovenly existence and gallivant across space to the stars? What if he called this Ethan, and Ethan discovered he wasn't as brilliant as his résumé implied? Where had he sourced the résumé, anyway? Zane sighed. *Do you want to die regretting a lost opportunity or investigate this expedition further?* He decided he would call and find out. He returned to his desk and sat down. His hand shook as he picked up his comm, clicked on the link, and waited.

Ethan came on the screen. "Hi, Ethan Richards here. What can I do for you?"

"Hello, I'm Zane Forest. I received your comm message and need more information."

"Hello, Zane. Yes, an interesting proposition I have given you, don't you think?"

"Well, it looks intriguing, but why do you want a worn-out university lecturer on your team? I mean, there must be plenty better at the job than me." Zane started feeling foolish and fidgeted with a pen on his desk. He self-consciously replaced the pen on the desktop again but picked it up straight away when his hand's inactivity became intolerable.

Ethan assessed Zane's response and watched Zane's hands as they played with the pen. Finally, he said, "Zane, I gave much thought to choosing you. You do not give yourself enough credit. I have read your recent papers and the papers you wrote years ago when you were looking at ecosystems and how they interacted. That got my attention. Those earlier papers were brilliant. I don't understand why you abandoned that for a lecturing position. I've found no one else who understands the intricacies of ecosystems better than you do."

Zane felt proud and humiliated at the same time. "I needed to make sure the kids had a stable upbringing."

Ethan looked at his notes on Zane. "Well, the kids have well and truly flown the roost. What's stopping you now?"

The challenge in Ethan's voice flustered Zane. He wasn't sure how to respond. "I suppose I'm too comfortable doing what I am doing. My research work is challenging."

"Nothing like you used to do, though. Am I right?"

Zane sighed. "Yes, you are. The work I conducted years ago was exhilarating."

"I'm offering you an opportunity to conduct that research again but on a planetary scale should we find a planet with an ecosystem on it."

"What is the chance of that?"

"You tell me. We know planets exist in the habitable zones."

"Flora is a possibility, I suppose. The question might be how it compares with Earth-based biology. So, what would I be doing?"

"What you just said. You'd investigate whatever we find and compare it to our biological ecosystems. Solving issues like, 'Is it harmful to us? Can we eat it?' and other such questions. You won't be alone. We're sourcing a microbiologist to study pathogenic issues specifically and how that may affect humans and other Earth-derived species of plant and animal."

"Oh. Who will that be?"

"I don't know yet. I'm still reviewing the prospective candidates."

"Oh." Zane didn't know what else to say. It was too much to absorb, too much potential change, too fast. He had lectured for twenty years now. He became fidgety again.

"What do you think?"

"It would be interesting," Zane said slowly, "and it would be different than my present duties."

"Shall I send further details?"

Zane was indecisive. It wouldn't hurt to investigate the details. He could still decline the offer if he felt he was inadequate. Finally, he said, "Yes, send what you have. I'll read through it and decide."

"Good. You will enjoy this, Zane. Trust me."

"We'll see."

"I need to go. Good talking to you. Hope to see you soon."

"Yeah, OK."

The screen went blank.

Zane sat back and thought. He couldn't believe the fortuitousness of the message. It was as if Ethan was reading his thoughts and understanding his predicament. He would read the details that Ethan sent through and seriously consider it. Maybe he was ready to make a leap again, the leap he had rejected when his wife left him.

11

MARIE LORRAINE — MICROBIOLOGIST

Alarms blared and lights flashed as Marie Lorraine isolated the Biohazardous Organisms laboratory. "Who the hell breached the decontamination protocols?" she shouted into the microphone at the staff in the lab. A detector had detected a hazardous compound and raised the alarm. Marie was furious. They now needed to close the laboratory for days while they decontaminated the affected section, and she dreaded the paperwork imposed on her to report the incident. Luckily, the standard procedure required personnel using the lab's disinfected section to wear hazardous-material protection suits, or she would have had a major disaster on her hands, with the potential for death if the wrong pathogen had migrated into the sterile environment.

No one talked, fearful of admitting guilt. *I can't blame them*, she thought, still fuming. *I'd have their gizzards for breakfast.* She calmed, realizing anger wouldn't change the outcome.

Marie understood the risks were high in the research she conducted, and she took the assessed safeguards highlighted in the laboratory's hazards risk analysis policy very seriously. She imposed the procedure ruthlessly. It was a procedure that kept people safe.

Something leaking across to the sterile side mystified her. She eventually had everything locked in a secure condition. The others had already evacuated the laboratory through the decontamination and sterilization room. She was the last. She rose from her console seat and stretched. Spectators stared with goggle-eyed perplexity from the observation window of the enclosed room. She shrugged her shoulders in annoyance, wondering what they were doing. She suggested they had work to do, and they dispersed with haste, knowing her personality. They feared being in the vicinity when she exited.

She headed for the decontamination and sterilization section and sealed the entrance behind her, stepping into the sterilization chamber first. A massive dose of UV light irradiated her when she started the decontamination cycle, followed by a downpour of antibacterial solution designed to kill every microorganism that might have lodged in her suit. The suit protected her from the UV radiation that infiltrated every nook and cranny. Next was the decontamination chamber where a shower of pure water washed the solution off her. The dry-off chamber blasted hot, dry air onto her, removing the moisture. Stepping from that, she headed to the suit disposal section and stripped off to her underwear. She shoved the suit into the recycle chute and donned a pair of overalls before entering the airlock to escape into the outside world. The outer door of the airlock opened, and Marie stomped to her office to tell her superiors of the incident. Everyone she passed avoided her in fear. The culprit responsible had better prepare for the consequences when she discovered who it was.

Back in her office, she had time to calm herself, although calmness wasn't in her DNA. She was always an intense person. She commed her boss and told him of the issue and her intention to investigate how the breach had happened. The laboratory needed to be cleared and safe before she could re-enter it and understand what had occurred. She called her workforce to an immediate meeting. Getting out of her chair, she stomped to the conference room, serious business written on her face.

Her staff filed in with eyes looking in any direction but hers. A few quietly acknowledged her, but most remained mute as they entered. Her entire personnel finally arrived. "What the hell happened?" Marie asked, her tone as calm as she could make it.

No one responded. Marie stayed silent, staring at each of them. After a time, a laboratory assistant worked up the courage to speak. "I'm uncertain, but one of the manipulator's arms may have torn as it was transferring a specimen from one container to another."

"You're not sure?"

"Ye... Yes, I'm not sure."

"Do you know which arm?"

The assistant considered the equipment layout, working through the designation convention. "3B."

Marie calmed herself. If that was true, her staff were blameless. She needed to inspect the maintenance records to verify the arm's last checks. "Very well. If that's the case, I need maintenance in here. Does anyone have any other information?"

The group stayed silent.

"If I discover anything pointing to a breach of procedures during my investigation, the person involved had better have an airtight excuse. Anything else?"

A collective sigh percolated throughout the room as the assembly realized they had satisfied their boss for now, and she wouldn't demand a scalp from them unless the revelation proved false.

"OK then. You can go."

Everyone left the room. Marie paced it, thinking. She at least knew where to search when she returned to the laboratory. Her comm buzzed. She took it from her pocket and frowned, as she didn't recognize the sender. It was from a person called Ethan Richards. The comm didn't consider it suspicious, so she opened the message and read it.

The potential interruption to her life surprised Marie. With nothing else to do before the laboratory's decontamination, she pressed the link and waited. A face appeared after a brief delay.

"Hello, Marie. I'm Ethan."

The friendly greeting caught Marie off guard. "Hello, Ethan. What's with this message? I've got a hundred and one things to do."

Ethan chuckled. "You live up to your reputation."

"What do you mean?" Marie asked as she tidied an annoying dislodged strand of hair.

"Oh, our background checks say that you are abrupt and straight-forward."

Marie relaxed. She smiled for the first time. "Sorry. We've just had a pathogen breach in our laboratory, and I'm in the middle of cleaning up the mess, but your message has me intrigued."

"So, it should. It is an exceptional opportunity for you. You have an interesting and demanding job, but what compares with discovering an entire world of pathogens to study and declare safe or otherwise?"

"Oh? What do you mean, world?"

"As my message said, we intend to travel to Centauri to look for habitable worlds. If we find promising ones, and remote-sensing indications suggest we will, it's essential we find out whether there's anything there that could harm us or any species we introduce to the planet."

Marie gave Ethan her full attention. "That sounds interesting. How long is the expedition?"

"I don't have firm dates yet, but we need another month to prepare for departure. It's difficult to give a definitive period of absence. That depends on what we discover when we get there, but I estimate four months. You are one of the last to join should you accept my invitation."

"Hmm. Forward the details to me. It sounds interesting enough."

"I can do that. Do you have more questions at present?"

"Not now, no. I might have more when I read through what you send."

"OK. I'll leave you to your cleaning up then."

Marie raised her eyebrows and sighed in annoyance at being

reminded of her responsibilities. She smiled, "Thanks." The screen went blank. The offer overwhelmed her, with the incident report looming on the breach at the laboratory. But Ethan was right. It was an opportunity that couldn't escape her grasp. *I'll review the details first*, she thought as she prepared to return to the lab and her investigation.

12

CONSENSUS

J ade sighed as she stared at Liang in defeat. They had worked together for two weeks with little to show for it.

That's too harsh, Jade thought. *We've made significant progress in our understanding of wormholes and how they form. Things we didn't know before we started. It's just we haven't been able to solve Liang's problem. We've achieved the opposite result. One-sided wormhole creation on a large scale is impossible without immense energy.*

"We've come to a dead end," Liang suggested.

"If our current theory is solvable, we can't prove it. Yes, we are at a dead end."

Liang had learned to relax working with Jade, adjusting to the need for cooperation and mutual respect. "You have great skill, Jade," he told her.

"We both have come a long way. You've taught me much too," Jade replied.

Liang smiled at the compliment.

Hu walked into their research study just then. "What've you two mad scientists devised?" She smirked in amusement as she looked from one to the other.

Jade looked at Liang. Liang looked at Jade. Jade let Liang speak when he was ready.

"Consensus," Liang said.

"Well, I'm glad that you've been able to achieve a philosophical understanding of our differing political systems, but I meant our minor wormhole problem," Hu said, smiling satirically.

"So was I, Comrade Hu," Liang answered.

Jade chuckled at the interplay. "Liang has come a long way in his social skills if nothing else. He's got you worked out, Hugo."

Liang grinned with pride. "I must know why you're called Hugo," he said to Hu.

"That is a capitalist top secret. You die if I tell you."

"I will take the risk."

They laughed.

"Seriously, what can you report?"

Jade gestured for Liang to answer, which he did. "I was always right. Creating a one-sided wormhole is not possible except for a tiny one, at least not with our current understanding. Jade has been most stringent in making me clarify my theories and has been very useful in her enlightenment. She is brilliant." Liang grinned sheepishly. "But I am clever too."

Jade laughed. "Let me explain, Hugo. Liang was getting very depressed over the last couple of weeks, concerned he wasn't performing in the way your superiors demand of a Chinese scientist. It took an effort to convince him to have confidence in himself. Liang's a more grounded person now than two weeks ago."

Jade could see Hu look at Liang with pride and increased respect. She saw the change just by the response he had given.

"Well, I'm disappointed you haven't solved our problem but happy you have a fundamental understanding of why there's no solution," Hu said.

"You could say that our technologies complement each other," Jade replied. "We go to unexplored places with one of your portals, and you power it up and come through, providing a fast link between the two locations afterward."

"I hadn't considered it that way. You get the fun bit, though."

"I disagree. We do the hard work of finding someplace, but once you set up the wormhole, you secure the discovery and explore it."

"You have a point, too. You are both sure of your conclusion?"

"Yes," Liang said. Jade nodded in agreement.

"One last thing is necessary, then. Your last supper ..."

Liang stiffened in alarm.

"I'm joking," Hu said.

"Do not joke about such things, please."

"Sorry, but I was serious about the meal. You've finished, so I should get Jade back to Ethan before he falls apart. We must celebrate with a feast together before she leaves."

"Yes. We need to laud the strength of science."

"That's wonderful," Jade said. "Ethan is holding out fine, though. He's been very busy."

"Our comm link cost has skyrocketed over the last couple of weeks," Hu joked.

Jade reddened, even knowing that Hu was joking. She had spent a significant time talking to Ethan while visiting the moon, with the permanent Earth-moon channel being the only means of communication.

Hu laughed again. "Our scheduled management meeting is tomorrow morning. Both of you will need to report your findings. After that, you should be able to go on the next available shuttle."

"That sounds good. As much as the moon has interested me, I'll be happy to stand under the Earth's sky again," Jade replied.

"Yes, one misses the open air after a while."

"Anyway, Liang, we should wrap up here and prepare for Hugo's banquet."

"The feast will be delicious," Liang agreed, nodding.

"I might even find a bottle of wine to share," Hu said. "I'll see you at six in the small dining room." Hu left.

They enjoyed the banquet that night, celebrating Jade and Liang. It was a welcome reward for their hard work over the past two weeks.

Jade fronted up to the team meeting the next morning with the rest of the Chinese project team assembled as usual. For Jade's sake, the meeting was in English, although they often reverted to Chinese without realizing it.

Jian conducted the regular business before he brought the agenda to Liang and Jade's review results. "Now, Liang and Jade, please report your final recommendations in your two-week study of wormhole behavior and what is possible for us to achieve."

"Chairperson Jian, I would be happy to report our findings," Liang responded, "but it's only fair for Comrade Jade to have the honor."

Jade looked at Liang, amused. *That's the first time someone has called me comrade.*

Jade stood, as was customary for team members when they reported. "Chairperson Jian ..." Jade started by using the formal title to show respect for the team. "... Comrade Liang and I have been working on every facet of wormhole theory that we considered important to resolve wormhole creation from one side. We conclude it's impossible to create a large wormhole in this way with our current level of understanding and technology. So, we recommend your team pursue implementing the two-portal approach you have already achieved." Jade sat.

"Thank you for your report, um ... Comrade Jade. Are there questions?"

"This is a disgrace," Jiang Minzhe blurted, anger and passion expressed on his face and in his tone. "This is capitalist propaganda and trickery."

Jade looked on, appalled at the outburst. She felt hurt and astonished that Minzhe had accused her of such an act. His judgment that she would sabotage their project confused her. She gazed at the table's surface, dejected, but caught Hu watching her in sorrow and growing anger.

"This is ridiculous, Jian," Hu said. "Minzhe's accusation is nothing more than political maneuvering. I've kept a close watch on this review, as it was at my recommendation. They've done nothing but work at one hundred percent of their abilities to resolve this roadblock. I know Jade, and Minzhe's accusations are a slur on her integrity. I demand an apology on Jade and Liang's behalf."

Jade glanced up and saw Hu was furious. It was only the second time Jade had seen such extreme emotion from her — the first being her sorrow when relating the loss of her partner. Hu always gave measured responses.

"Please let us stay calm," Jian said, perplexed by the developing drama. Hu's reaction was much more than ordinary. He stared with authority at Hu and then Minzhe. "Now, Comrade Minzhe, on what basis do you make such an accusation?" Jian asked in a level voice.

Minzhe squirmed in his chair as he became the center of attention. "Well, isn't it obvious? They made no headway. The American has steered Liang away from any enlightenment."

Hu responded as best she could through gritted teeth. "First, Jade is Australian, not American. Second, if you will recall, Liang was making no progress — which, as it turns out, was no fault of his. I am sure Liang is observant enough to detect anyone manipulating the review's direction."

Liang raised his hand, requesting to speak. Jian indicated that he could. "Comrade Minzhe, by suggesting that Jade has sabotaged the investigation, you are accusing me of sedition against the state. If you have evidence of such treason, instead of vague ideological conjecture, I wish you to offer it. I am insulted that you consider me someone who would betray his country."

Minzhe became distressed with the pressure placed on him to give proof of his accusation. Jade sensed it would be humiliating for him to retract now, knowing the extreme measures used in Chinese culture to save face. Minzhe finally spoke again with a humbled and chastened voice. "It's possible I was premature in my assessment, Chairperson Jian. I ... apologize if I embarrassed or insulted you."

"I note your apology to the members of the project team, but I agree with Hu here. You owe Jade a personal apology for questioning her integrity in this matter."

Minzhe stared at Jian in defiance. Jian had no problem with staring him down, being senior to Minzhe. Minzhe then gulped and looked at Jade. "Ms. Powers, please accept my humble apology for any inference that you are not an honorable person. I did not intend that. In my exuberance with our superior Communist culture, I suggested an ideological motive for the lack of progress in the scientific research Liang and you were conducting. I may have been mistaken. Again, my humble apology."

Jade knew Minzhe was seeking to back off without saying he was wrong. He was trying to save as much face as possible. She looked at Hu and saw that the apology didn't satisfy her either. Jade left things as they were and accepted the recant. "I accept your apology, Comrade Minzhe. There are no ill feelings. You are free to state matters as you see them." *As citizens of a democratic society*, Jade thought, wishing she could express the words.

Minzhe nodded.

"Now that we've addressed ideological concerns, are there further questions?" Jian asked, glancing at Minzhe with challenging eyes.

Bingwen put up his hand. "Chairperson Jian, I have a question."

"Speak."

"Jade and Liang, you confirm single-ended wormhole generation is not yet possible. What is your recommendation for our progressing this project efficiently?"

Jade glanced at Liang, wondering who he wanted to answer the question. Liang indicated Jade should reply. "Bingwen, that is a good question. Liang and I achieved wonderful insights into your current dual-ended wormhole technology. Liang has developed the observations with little prompting from me." She gazed at Liang when she made the compliment, acknowledging his work. "We've improved the present theories further — they will allow wormhole formation more efficiently and with more stability under greater distances. You should concentrate on developing this technology to commercial practicality. You should still support research on single-ended wormholes as fundamental theoretical studies, though."

"So, it's still a possibility?" Minzhe butted in, his interest roused.

"We never said that it was impossible. We just said that, with our current understanding, we do not know how to achieve single-ended wormhole generation at present."

"How do we transport wormhole portals to the other end, then?"

Jade looked at Hu and back to Bingwen. "I believe Hug... Hu has already suggested a means. With the prevailing political climate between our two governments, we can work in collaboration. We can take a portal to its destination, where you assemble it and create the wormhole. There's no need for us to understand the portal's technicalities other than its assembly and commissioning. If China deems the technology a commercial secret, one of your team could supervise the construction."

"This is excellent news," Bingwen replied, happy they had a way forward that allowed equal, if not superior, political standing.

The room fell silent. Jian scanned the participants. "If there're no further questions, I offer a formal thanks to Comrade Jade for making time in her hectic schedule to assist us. I understand you are working on your own project."

Everyone except Minzhe clapped as a sign of their appreciation. Minzhe joined in the acknowledgment at the end.

"Thank you, Chairperson Jian. It has been a pleasure. We are assembling a team to go to Centauri. Ethan Richards is busy pulling the team together at this moment. I believe we are to take a portal with us, so you might join us."

"Yes, that is the plan. How are the arrangements progressing, Hu?" Jian asked.

"We were intending to disassemble our existing portal, but we now prefer constructing a new one instead, one that has modular components and assembles easily. It will be ready in six weeks to package up and load into the spaceship. I don't know how it aligns with the American project yet. I have not communicated this with Mr. Richards. The link has been busy of late."

Jade blushed. The others looked at Jade and laughed.

"Keep us informed, and I suggest communication with Mr. Richards as a matter of priority," Jian said.

"I will," Hu replied.

The meeting broke up, and everyone went their ways except for Hu and Jade.

"I am sorry about that," Hu said when they were alone.

"It was unexpected," Jade admitted. "I saw a side of you I haven't seen before, though."

Hu reddened. "I usually control myself, but I could not allow such an insult to my friend to go unchallenged."

Jade felt a deeper connection with Hu over her revelation. "Thank you. That is much appreciated." Jade expressed a warm smile.

"You're welcome. I debated jumping the table to throttle him."

Jade giggled at Hu and responded. "Ethan told me about your skills. You would've created quite a mess."

"Yes, in more ways than one. The thought still gives me a buzz."

They laughed again.

"I had better get you back to your puppy, then."

Jade howled. "I can't wait till I tell him that," she said when she calmed herself.

Hu said, "You do that," with a beaming smile on her face.

They stood up, gave each other a hug, and left together.

Jade returned to Earth the next day.

13

VISITING THE FAMILY

On the way back to Los Angeles, Jade detoured to visit her family in Hoffnungsthal, near Adelaide, South Australia. She had not seen her mother and father for ages and was eager to spend a few days with them and her siblings living nearby and catch up with the local gossip. She rented a vehicle to travel from the airport to their home. She wove her way up the winding roads and through the hills behind the city. With her side window open, the scent of apple blossoms wafted through to her from orchards near the road. She eventually drove into the sleepy country town, which had changed little for decades, and up the main street. Hoffnungsthal only came alive at Christmas, when it was lit with colored lights to greet the festive season. She turned onto the road where her parents lived and stopped in front of their house, still cream brick with a gray-black-tiled roof as it always had been. The lingering aroma of cut grass on a freshly mowed lawn filled the air. She paused for a moment in the car to reminisce about her childhood.

She alighted from the vehicle, headed for the front door, and pressed the doorbell. Jade heard movement as someone approached, and the door opened to reveal Bernice, her mother. She wore a blue flower-patterned dress and had tidied her hair, which was no surprise to Jade.

"Oh Jade, darling, come in. Come in. How are you?"

"I'm good, Mum," Jade said as she entered the house and gave her mother a hug and a kiss on the cheek, smelling a hint of lavender-scented perfume as she did so.

"Your father is outside in the garden. He's always pottering out there."

They both headed for the family room scattered with lounge chairs. Bernice opened the sliding door that gave access to the back-yard and yelled, "Jade's here, Clyde. Come inside!"

"I'll be right in," Jade heard him reply.

She looked around the room. They had upgraded it since her last visit with new furniture and other knickknacks, but it was still the same room where she had tussled with her siblings in play and some-times anger, as they hurt one another and demanded retribution. She smiled to herself at the memory.

"Do you want a coffee or tea? It's time I put the kettle on. Clyde will want one when he comes in."

"Coffee would be good, thanks."

The sliding door opened, and Clyde entered. He wore an old red-and-white checkered shirt and faded blue denim jeans streaked with various dirt stains where he had been squatting on the bare earth. "Hi, Jade. We weren't expecting you so soon."

"Hello, Dad. The plane was early, and I had a fast run out of the airport," Jade replied as she walked over to give her father a kiss on the cheek.

"Not too close. I don't want to get you dirty."

Jade smiled. "I won't."

They parted. "I'll go clean up. How about a cuppa, Bernice?" he said, raising his voice.

"Kettle's on," Bernice called from the kitchen.

Clyde disappeared through a door leading to a bathroom.

Jade was alone, so she sat in a chair nearby. She looked at the coffee table in front of her, stacked with the latest paper magazines.

They'll never modernize to electronic journals and papers, she thought fondly. She realized they needed to stay in the past for the stability it gave their lives.

Her mother came from the kitchen with a tray full of mugs of steaming hot drinks: coffee for Jade and tea for herself and Clyde. It also held an assortment of cookies on a plate including Jade's favorites, Tim Tams. She placed the tray on the coffee table and distributed the drinks to where everyone would sit. She and Clyde always sat in their favorite chairs. The plate of cookies sat in front of Jade.

"You don't eat enough."

Jade smiled. "I eat fine, Mum," she said as she reached across to help herself to a Tim Tam.

"It must be that young man of yours then, chasing you everywhere."

Jade laughed at the comment. "Ethan would love you to tell him that."

"We'll make sure we feed you here, even if it is only for one night."

Jade gave her mother an adoring and loving smile. "I'm confident you will. Lucky I'm not staying longer, or Ethan won't recognize me."

"And when are we meeting this Ethan of yours?" Clyde asked as he re-entered the room. "It's about time we had a talk."

"Oh, Dad, we've been too busy."

"Why? What are you up to now?"

"We are preparing for a space flight to the star Centauri, four light years away."

"How are you traveling that far in one lifetime? Is that what that new gadget he's developed does?"

"Yes, Dad. We only need three weeks."

"You look after yourself. I don't like it. You're so far away. What if something happens? How would we ever find out?" Bernice asked with creases of worry on her brow.

"I'll be careful, Mum."

"You should bring him here so he can educate me on how it

works," Clyde said. Clyde was interested in understanding new technology when someone bothered to explain it to him, even if he never intended to use it.

"So, what's been happening here?"

"You know nothing happens here of interest to you young ones. Allen Siegel broke his leg, falling off a ladder. He should be more careful at his age. Oh, Madden got some floozy pregnant. Didn't he used to have a crush on you?" Bernice said.

Jade blushed at the memory. He had been a pleasant-looking teenager, and she had contemplated letting him take her on a date. She was glad she hadn't. She'd heard he was a womanizer and wild. "You exaggerate, Mum."

"I hope you can relax while you're here."

"I'll try. Just don't keep bringing up terrible memories."

Jade's comm rang. She got it from her pocket and opened it. It was Ethan. She was undecided whether to answer the call there or retreat to somewhere more private but ended up taking it where she sat. She pressed the visual button, and Ethan's face appeared. "Hi, Jade."

"Hi. It must be late over there. I'm at Mum and Dad's."

"I've been working and just called quits for the day."

"Let's check out this man of yours," Bernice interrupted.

Jade gave an embarrassed giggle at the comment but relented. She turned the screen so that both her mother and father could see Ethan.

"Hello!" Ethan said with a raised voice and a self-conscious smile.

"Hello, Ethan," Clyde said. "I finally see your face. We started thinking you were in Jade's imagination. You must have a beer with me soon."

Ethan chuckled. "When we finish this, I promise to come and meet you."

"By the way," Jade butted in, "my father is Clyde, and my mother is Bernice."

"Hello, Bernice. Hi, Clyde."

"Hello, Ethan," Bernice said. "You're everything Jade said you were."

Ethan searched for Jade, but she wasn't visible. He blushed. "She exaggerates sometimes."

"I do not," Jade said, from out of Ethan's sight.

"We'll let Jade have you back. I presume you have business to discuss," Clyde said.

"Yeah, well, thanks. I'll see you then and keep that beer chilled."

"Hope to see you soon, too," Clyde replied.

"Goodbye," Bernice said.

Jade beamed with love and pride as she turned the screen back to herself.

"How did I do?" Ethan asked.

"Idiot," Jade joked with an exasperated roll of her eyes as she rose and moved away for more privacy.

Ethan gave a sheepish grin.

"How are you, honey?" Jade asked when she was out of her parents' earshot.

"I'm OK, but I'll be glad when you're back, and I don't just mean to wrap my arms around you. Things are getting hectic, and I can use another pair of hands. I'll manage for now, though. I want you to enjoy your time with your family."

"You look tired. It'll be good to get back. But I'm not sure I should if the work's going to be that hard ..."

"I have something special waiting for you," Ethan said with an impish grin.

"You're wicked," Jade replied with a giggle.

"I just wanted to check you landed safely. I better go. Miss you."

"I miss you too." Jade hesitated but then said, "I love you."

Ethan smiled with pleasure. "Love you too."

The comm screen went blank. Jade returned to her parents.

"That was a quick conversation," Clyde said.

"Clyde!"

Jade blushed. "I'll be seeing him soon."

"What are your plans for the rest of the day?" Bernice asked.

"Whatever is happening around here will do. Are the others coming over for dinner?"

"Yes, the entire gang'll be here. I don't know where they'll sit, mind you, but we'll manage. Clyde's the cook tonight — he's doing a BBQ for us."

"Good. I haven't had a decent BBQ for ages."

They talked for a long time. Clyde started the BBQ when the family arrived, and they caught up with events while they ate. Jade then retired to bed. She had an early start as she was catching the first plane back to Los Angeles.

14

REUNION

Ethan drove to the airport early. He heard his coworkers snicker behind his back as he left the office, but he didn't care. It had been three weeks since Jade left, and he wanted to see her when she exited the customs hall.

He waited with the other people welcoming loved ones or picking up arriving passengers. A constant buzz of noise reverberated through the concourse as people talked while they watched. Ethan looked at his chronometer. *Where is she? The plane landed ages ago.* He got fidgety and rocked on his feet.

At last, Jade appeared at the exit, scanning her surroundings. Ethan tried to attract her attention without getting too much of it himself, but she didn't see him. He waved his hands more aggressively. She finally recognized him when she looked at the face of the person frantically waving his arms. She smiled. At that instant, the sun filled the airport with light and warmth for Ethan. He adored the smile and the woman owning it. Jade rushed toward him, halting in front of him just long enough to place her hand luggage on the floor, and then wrapped her arms around him. Ethan felt her warmth again. He was complete. He pushed her away enough for him to kiss her on the lips. They parted — too soon, in Ethan's opinion.

"Hello, gorgeous," Ethan said.

Jade radiated pleasure. "I'm glad to be back so you can pamper me again."

"You don't get off that lightly for deserting me."

Jade laughed and kissed him.

"Let's get you home," Ethan said once they had fulfilled their immediate need for intimacy. He collected Jade's luggage and started wheeling it from the terminal. Jade walked by his side.

"How was your visit to your parents?"

"Too short as usual, but I appreciated I could make the detour. They did too. You'll have to come next time — so they don't pester me. They can pick on someone else now."

"That's making me want to go," Ethan quipped.

"They'll love you. Mum will dote over you till you are sick of it."

"Maybe I'll get attention for a change."

Jade patted him on the arm. "That attention enough?"

Ethan smiled. They stopped for a moment, and he glanced at her, marveling once more about how this woman had changed his life. He didn't know what to say.

"What?" Jade asked.

"Nothing." They started walking again, and he concentrated on that instead.

They reached his vehicle, and Ethan packed away the luggage and drove them back to his place. Jade still had her own apartment, but they agreed she shower and freshen up at his villa, which delighted him. Once they got to his place and unloaded the bags, they shut the door on the outside world and embraced. Each trying to remove the other's clothes first, they inched into the bedroom like two butterflies dancing in courtship before consummating their love.

They showered an hour later, dressed, and went to the office to continue the mounting tasks to prepare for the expedition.

"I should warn you. You might get a few snickers when we arrive. I did when I left."

"I can handle that."

They arrived at the office complex at JPL, the same buildings they had used for the original project. As predicted, the staff whispered a few suggestive comments when they walked in, but the culprits soon pretended to be busy when Jade glared at them. They went to Ethan's office.

"When are the new team members arriving?" Jade asked.

"They'll get here in dribs and drabs over the next few weeks. I still need a medical specialist."

"I can help you with that. What else are you doing?"

"Just trying to requisition the supplies and everything we need for the journey. It's a nightmare. I hate the bureaucracy ... and the paperwork!"

Jade chuckled.

15

ANGELO SOULA — MEDICAL SPECIALIST

A ngelo Soula stretched his neck back and pinched the bridge of his nose as he walked out of the operating theater, trying to shed his exhaustion. He had just completed a complex operation to clamp an aneurysm deep inside the patient's brain and was bone-tired even though the computer-controlled surgical equipment they used had done the physical work. The operation had been intricate, requiring delicate procedures to access the problem. It had taken just over thirteen hours, and Angelo's confidence in a complete success was high. He removed his surgical gown and scrubbed his hands in the preparation room before heading out to the waiting relatives, who would be anxious to hear positive news about the outcome.

He walked into the reception room. The husband looked up with worried expectation. He rose and came over to Angelo. "How did it go?"

Angelo sighed and gave a professional smile. "It's too early to say before she regains consciousness. But the operation went well, so she has excellent prospects of a complete recovery."

The man exhaled in relief and gratitude. "Thank you so much, doctor."

"We won't know for sure until she wakes. Two or three hours. I will check on her then."

The husband's expression changed to one of concern for the doctor. "You look tired."

Angelo chuckled. "The woes of a surgeon, I'm afraid. Rest now, and you'll be able to see Claire soon." He walked away, returning to his office in another part of the Mayo Clinic in Rochester, Minnesota.

Angelo was one of the leading neurosurgeons there, having taken on tenure in research and surgery over the past five years. He never forgot to keep up to date with general practice, though, regularly visiting impoverished countries to serve the people in those communities with their everyday medical problems. It kept him grounded in the true role of a doctor, and it humbled him when he received deep gratitude from the recipients.

He headed to the small refrigerator in his office and searched the contents for something to eat. A quantity of carrots and celery sat there, and cheddar cheese. He cut off several slices of cheese, placed them on a plate, and grabbed a carrot and a celery stalk. He located a few crackers from a packet nearby and parked behind his desk, the stick of celery in his mouth as he took an absentminded bite and munched. It was dark outside, being after three in the morning. It had been sunny and early afternoon the last time he'd looked out a window. He pondered the operation and felt at peace. Every executed procedure had gone to plan, promising a successful recovery. There was nothing more he could do now to change the outcome.

Helping people had always been in him, and he had an innate talent for diagnosis. The medical profession had been the obvious choice for him as a young man when it came time to choose a career path.

Angelo had just finished eating his snack when he remembered he had switched off his comm for the operation, as was his habit. Moments after he turned it on, it buzzed. The message was headlined <Centauri Expedition Project – Medical Practitioner Position>. Intrigued, he opened it and read:

<Dear Dr Soula

This is not a crank message. You do not know me, but I am putting together a team for the above project. We aim to travel to the Centauri star system to explore their planetary bodies for human habitability. One of our needs for the expedition is a medical professional to look after the team's health issues, particularly from novel diseases of unknown origin. A biologist and microbiologist in the team can isolate and classify any organism involved. We need a person of your talent to treat any crew succumbing to illness.

On reviewing résumés of potential candidates, you are the most suitable for the position.

This is a marvelous opportunity for you should you accept my offer.

We will fly there in the starship *Destiny*, which recently completed its first faster-than-light space flight. Our achievement was well publicized, so is verifiable.

Please call me on this link and let me know if you are interested in discussing this opportunity further.

Regards

Ethan Richards

Centauri Expedition Project

Project Leader>

The message had all his attention, but why they needed a specialist of his caliber confused him. He was a neural surgeon, not an infectious diseases specialist.

He could do nothing at present. It was only one in the morning on the West Coast, so he made a mental note to research more in normal working hours.

He retired to the couch in his office and reclined on it for a power nap, stirring as a nurse woke him just over two hours later to inform him that the patient had woken. The scene wasn't unusual for Angelo or the nurses on duty. He stood and stretched, thanking the nurse for letting him know. Wasting no time, he headed for the intensive care unit to check the product of his work. Claire was conscious and coherent, which were excellent signs. He completed his checks and made notes on the tablet hanging at the end of the bed. He then informed the nurse to allow Claire's husband a brief visit and left.

It was still too early to call about the message. As he had nothing else to do, he headed home, showered, and ate breakfast. He could have gone to the golf club to swing his clubs with whomever he could find wanting a round, but he had no inclination, so he caught up on the latest general practice research in the periodicals he had been falling behind in reading.

Angelo woke with a start. He must have dozed in the study from the sunny morning warmth. As he glanced at the chronometer, he saw it was approaching midday. He could now call and learn the expedition details and why they needed someone like him. He opened his comm, pressed the link and waited.

A face appeared on the screen. "Hello, Ethan Richards here."

"Hi, it's Angelo Soula calling about your message."

"Oh. Thanks for calling back. How are you? You look tired."

"I'm fine. I had an exhausting and difficult operation overnight and napped while reading this morning. I just woke, so I might look a bit bleary-eyed."

"Hope the operation was successful."

"Yes, it was, but I'm intrigued why you want a neural surgeon on your trip."

"It's simple, I believe. As I explained in the message, we are embarking on an expedition to the Centauri system to seek potential planets for human colonization. When we were reviewing the personnel we needed on the team, we identified a need for a medical specialist. Now, I know you specialize in neural conditions, which may or may not come in useful, but that isn't why I selected you. First, you still conduct general practice activities. We will need this field of medical experience on the expedition. But it was the second charac-teristic that caught my attention. You often diagnose rare and diffi-cult-to-detect medical issues, resulting in successful interventions. That ability to quickly and correctly analyze the trouble is an essen-tial criterion for the person we want."

"I think I understand your thinking. How long is this expedition?"

"We expect three to four months, maybe longer, depending on what we find when we get there."

"You mentioned a biologist and a microbiologist in your message. Have you selected them yet?"

"Yes, we have. The biologist will be Zane Forest, and the microbiologist is Marie Lorraine."

"The first name is unknown to me, but Marie's reputation precedes her. She has conducted brilliant work in understanding infection pathways for pathogens."

"Yes, she has."

"I understand she has a candid personality, though," Angelo added.

Ethan smiled at Angelo's effort to be diplomatic. "Her candor, as you put it, may help keep us alert. Are you interested enough for me to send further details through to consider?"

Angelo mulled over the proposition in his mind for a moment and then decided. "I've been planning my regular leave for my charity work. It'd be a pity to miss that, but there's always sick people to cure, I suppose. It's longer than I'd prefer — but yes, send through more details. I'm certainly interested."

"Good. I'm sure you'll find the experience most exhilarating should you come on board. It may help in gaining an even better understanding of human physiology."

"Yes, we can always learn more there."

"I'll send the material to you then and hope to hear affirmative news."

The screen blanked. *What an extraordinary opportunity!* Angelo thought.

16

TEAM BONDING

It took Ethan an immense effort to pull together the team he wanted. The experience exhausted him. However, he was pleased his first-choice candidates had all accepted his invitation. His assessments of their characters had been correct in that regard, at least.

The team members assembled at the JPL site a few weeks after they accepted their positions. Ethan had arranged an orientation camp to help everyone bond into a cohesive and functioning group of people. He hoped they would start bonding. He knew some members were shy and needed prodding to emerge from their shells enough to make their skills plain to the other team members.

They gathered at a remote resort set up for such activities, isolated from the usual distractions of life. The first day was spent on icebreaker exercises. Ethan sensed everyone was still closed and guarded, the trust not yet established between them.

"How do I encourage the others to bond?" Ethan asked Jade as they lay in bed that night.

"Give it time. They've only just met. I'm interested in seeing their competitive streaks and watching their behavior when they think their reputation is at stake."

"Maybe we'll see that with any takers on my run in the morning."

"Maybe."

"You coming?"

"Can't let you hog all the glory. It'll go to your head."

"Ha! Sure."

Ethan lay in thought, wondering how he would control such a diverse group. "I'm scared. I haven't led a large team before this."

"You'll be fine. Besides, I can help, and someone will shine in leadership, too, so you can share the load. That's one of the purposes of this camp, isn't it? To test what makes them crumble under pressure."

"You're right, as usual. What if it's me, though?"

"I've seen you face off a maniac shooting deadly missiles at you. You won't crack."

Ethan smiled and gave Jade a kiss. "Better sleep. Good night."

"Goodnight."

Ethan and Jade rose at six the next morning for their ten-kilometer run, something they did every morning when they had the time. One prerequisite of the camp was giving everyone a chance to exercise if they desired, although Ethan pointed out to the team that he expected them to pursue physical training that suited them while they were there. They needed to continue exercising on their voyage to prevent muscle atrophy, so they might as well get started.

They stood at the rendezvous point, waiting for whoever would join them. Before long, Senna, Marie, David, and Celeste converged on them from their separate cabins. They greeted each other.

"We've downloaded the circuit into your fitness wrap. It'll warn you if you veer off course, but I'm told that the track has distinct markings. It is ten kilometers, so you can complete it as you wish. Jade and I will just keep a steady pace."

The others nodded in acknowledgment.

Ethan and Jade started jogging, and the rest followed. Senna and Marie lagged at a speed that suited them, and Celeste and David pushed ahead. Ethan had no concern. He thought the split was interesting. *I wonder how it will finish.* Jade and he knew they ran at the same pace from experience, and he enjoyed jogging alongside her.

Three-quarters into the run, Ethan noticed Senna and Marie had picked up their pace and were catching them. That pleased him. It showed they would put in the extra effort when needed in his eyes. The two caught up and maintained the group's speed, puffing from the exertion but displaying dogged determination.

As they rounded the corner to the home straight at the end of the run, Ethan and the others saw Celeste arguing with David. Celeste was short and petite, unusual for someone of German origin, Ethan thought. Her breasts, being large, appeared out of proportion to the rest of her body. Ethan hoped David hadn't made inappropriate comments to that effect.

They approached Celeste and David. Marie and Senna bowed, clutching their knees, trying to regain their breath. Jade quickly recovered hers, as did Ethan. "Is there a problem here?" Ethan asked both Celeste and David in between breaths.

David gave Ethan a nonplussed look.

"Nothing I can't handle myself. He's just being a jerk," Celeste said.

"I only mentioned she ran well," David said with hurt innocence.

"Yeah, right," Celeste retorted with daggers in her eyes.

"Let's let it go for now, OK? If either of you wants to discuss anything, I'm always available to listen, or I'll suggest someone for you to talk to if you're reluctant to confide in me. That goes for any of you." Ethan looked at Senna and Marie with his last comment.

David and Celeste appeared satisfied with Ethan's suggestion.

"Let's go freshen up," Ethan said. "By the way, Senna and Marie, I'm pleased with your determination to catch up and match our pace. You didn't have to."

"We both set ourselves the challenge and kept egging each other on," Marie said, wearing a delighted expression. Senna looked on with pride.

They returned to their cabins. Ethan held back, studying David momentarily. *We did thorough background checks before I sent out the offers. Still, I'll get John to dig deeper into his history. Just to make sure.* Jade glanced at him with a questioning gaze. He smiled and started toward her and a refreshing shower.

"Any ideas about the issue?" Ethan asked Jade when they were alone.

"I don't know. Something upset Celeste."

"Not a good start."

"Give it time. Everyone needs to acquaint themselves."

~

~

~

"WHAT HAPPENED BACK THERE?" Marie asked Celeste when they were alone. Marie was a perceptive person. She had learned and honed her observational skills as the head of the pathology team where she worked to make sure no incompetent assistants joined her team and took shortcuts to save time or didn't follow procedure. The lives of people were at stake. Marie had monitored the behavior of the various team members when she arrived. She saw Ethan could be awkward but, all up, he was competent and accomplished and took his job seriously, as did Jade. She had taken an instant dislike to David when they first met but couldn't figure out why. David had upset Celeste, and it was clear it still ate at her.

"Nothing. It was just something ridiculous. I shouldn't have gone off like I did."

"It didn't look like nothing to me. Don't bottle it up, or it'll keep eating at you." She sensed Celeste was a shy person.

Celeste fidgeted and looked embarrassed, avoiding eye contact as she decided what to do. Then she looked over at Marie. "He was harassing me about the project's need for an astronomer when they had him. He felt he knew enough for what Ethan needed on the expedition."

"Did he now! Well, that's intriguing information. I wonder what other gifts he has that make the other team members redundant?"

Celeste giggled at the absurdity of Marie's question and smiled a radiant smile. "I don't know — maybe they should just send him?"

Marie beamed too. "Don't misunderstand me, but you have a gorgeous smile."

Celeste blushed with embarrassment. "Thanks. That's what my mother keeps saying. Keeps asking why I'm still without a man."

"He'll come along sometime. As for David, well, I've seen his type. Thinks he knows everything. Ethan wanted you for a reason, and it wasn't so David could boast of his brilliance. Ignore him the next time he tries baiting you."

"Thanks."

THE NEXT DAY, Ethan watched as the others filed into the recreation hall dressed in casual sporting wear, as they'd been advised to do. The coordinator stood waiting, using the time to talk to Ethan about various aspects of the bonding camp. The team members chatted while waiting for the coordinator to explain their tasks to them, falling silent when a stranger to most of them walked into the hall in similar attire.

Ethan raised his voice. "Everyone, I'd like you to meet General John O'Conner of the Pentagon Special Forces. He'll watch this next exercise and offer feedback. Please welcome him."

When the polite applause subsided, John said, "It is a pleasure to meet the team that Ethan selected — see what I'm getting for my money, so to speak. As Ethan said, I'll watch this task. I won't take part as I make a lousy team member. I prefer a chain of command. Please continue, Ethan."

"I'll hand us over to the mercy of Jason, our coordinator," Ethan said and walked over to join the rest of the group.

"Hello, everyone," Jason said, "I hope you have an enjoyable time at the camp even though I'll tax your skills, energy, and acumen. The following exercise involves getting you across the stream flowing through the camp. Sounds easy enough. You have a few rules, though." Jason gave the group a mock-ominous smile, which made them laugh nervously.

"First, you have several items to help you with your task: nine planks, a rope, a length of twine, a grappling hook, and a strip of rubber.

"Second, come the rules. Everyone must cross the stream without getting wet. So, if someone falls in, anyone making that crossing must return to the bank they started from and retry. And I will remove one plank. A plank disappears each time you complete a crossing and on each failure. I decide when a crossing has failed with no negotiation. At least one foot — and no more than three feet — must contact a plank when traversing the stream.

"Last rule: everything must end up on the far bank, except the planks I removed.

"If you plan well and have a perfect implementation, you will complete the task with ease, but the more mistakes you make, the harder it gets. Understand?"

Ethan heard a general murmur of excitement and consternation as the team absorbed the instructions. "Questions?"

Everyone glanced around and back at Ethan. Several shook their heads.

Senna asked, "Does it include all the rope?"

David rolled his eyes, which Ethan saw and noted.

"Everything must end up on the far bank," Jason said, avoiding a direct answer.

"OK. Thought I'd make sure," she replied, embarrassed.

"Anything else?" Jason asked.

When nobody spoke, Ethan said, "I want to add that, just because

I'm the expedition leader, that doesn't make me the natural or best leader for this exercise."

"That's true," Jason confirmed. "OK. Let's move to the stream and start."

They left the hall and headed to the waterway, two hundred meters distant, some discussing the challenge and the options as they went to execute the task. Others strolled, pondering it quietly.

They ended up standing around the materials left at the shoreline.

"Well, it's obvious," David said, as if knowing the solution, and they only needed to do it. "We take one rope end across, tie it off, and pull ourselves over on the planks."

"How do we do that? We can't walk through the stream," Senna said.

"We tie the end to the grapple hook and throw it over the water," David replied.

"It's a long way. I can't toss it that far," Max said.

"And don't forget that we lose a plank for each failure," Marie added.

"Must I think for everyone?" David asked.

"Call that thinking?" Marie snapped.

David bristled at the barb, staring daggers at Marie.

Marie relented for the sake of team harmony. "But yes, your idea might work."

"We have this strip of rubber," Celeste said. "Could we use that as a sling and catapult the grapple across the water?"

"Good idea," Ethan butted in, trying to encourage Celeste.

Celeste grabbed the rubber strip and unfolded it to see how long it was. There were five meters available. She saw two small trees two meters apart, near the shoreline. "We can tie it around those two trees."

David stared at her with disdain but shrugged his shoulders.

"What's wrong with that?" Celeste asked David.

"Nothing," David replied curtly.

"How do we guarantee the grapple catches something? We'll lose a plank if it doesn't," Jade said.

They nodded, acknowledging the dilemma. The stream was fifty meters wide, and trees and large rocks populated the bank. Senna headed to the edge of the water and paced beside it, staring at the other shore, pondering the issue.

"We should decide how we intend crossing so we know how many failures we can have," Zane said. "I'm not pessimistic, but we should count on at least one failure, so we can't just grab our own plank and file across the water. Remember, he removes a plank at each try. In that case, someone may need to return to get the others."

"Why not? Anyone who stuffs up gets left behind," David said.

Marie rolled her eyes.

Ethan said, "Then we fail as a team. The aim is for everyone to reach the far shore. If we don't do that, we lose."

"We can't put two people on one plank. There would be four feet, and that's not allowed. We'll need at least two planks per crossing. We can lose one and return with the other to collect more," Jade said.

"Why can't one hold a foot in the air?" David asked, shrugging.

Marie looked at Ethan like she was getting fed up with David and his smart comments and suggestions. He didn't impress Ethan with his manner, either. He seemed to want the others to acknowledge how intelligent he was without question.

"Don't be so obnoxious, David," Marie said.

"What's in your bonnet? I don't see you coming up with ideas," David replied.

Angelo had been drawing on the ground while the bristly exchange was occurring. "Two crossings at a time won't work," he said. "We'll run out of planks. We need three people on two planks. That satisfies the no-more-than-three-feet rule. One person can return on a plank to collect two more. If we don't lose a plank, we'll have one left. That's our contingency."

Everyone except Senna, who still stood in contemplation, looked at Angelo and his scribbles on the ground.

"See, that's two at a time." Angelo pointed at two columns of numbers. "We'll strand four on this side." He gestured to the next two columns, alongside the first two. "This is three crossing and one returning."

"That's good thinking," Ethan said.

"If one person crossed first and secured the rope, then groups of three cross on two planks, we'd have two spares," Jade said.

Angelo strained in thought. "You're right."

"OK. It looks like we have a plan for getting everyone across," Marie said. "We still need the grapple to hold when we throw it over the water. Although I suppose we can have one failure and still have a plank up our sleeve."

Senna returned. "Our best bet to get an anchor hold is to lob the grapple over those forked tree branches." She pointed to the tree in question. "When we pull the rope, the grapple should catch in the fork."

Everyone gazed at where Senna pointed.

"That looks achievable, but how accurately can we aim it?" Marie said.

"I used to be an archer when I was younger. I think I could produce the accuracy we need," Zane said.

"Really?" Marie asked.

Zane nodded. David looked on, a sulky face developing. Ethan had been studying the interchange so far, and the team dynamics intrigued him. A buzz of anticipation and excitement circulated as they saw a full plan maturing that might just work.

"So that just leaves retrieving the rope afterward," Marie said.

"That's easy," David said.

The others groaned.

"Let him speak," Marie said.

A surprised look appeared on David's face at Marie's unexpected support. "Thank you. It is straightforward. I was in the Scouts when I was a child. We tie the rope so that it unties with a tug on the open end. We secure the twine to it and take the roll with us. When everyone is across, we yank on the twine, the knot comes undone, and we pull both across the river."

"What if the twine breaks? We'll lose," Max said.

"The twine looks thick enough to handle the stress. I'll test it now to make sure it works," David said.

"That's good, David," Marie said. "We have a plan." Marie looked at Ethan for approval.

"Heh. I'm not the leader here. You're doing a great job, Marie, but if you need confirmation, yes, it's a workable strategy, and we have a contingency if something goes wrong."

Marie smiled. "Well, let's get to it then. Where do we start?"

"We need the rubber positioned so I can get the right trajectory. Can two of you help me with that?" Zane asked.

Senna and Jade volunteered to help him.

David left to conduct his test on the twine. Max helped him.

That left Ethan, Marie, Angelo, and Celeste with nothing particular to do until the action started. Angelo and Celeste left to attach the grapple to the rope to prepare for its catapulting.

David tested his idea with success, and Zane was ready to use the sling after ten minutes. Zane had a few trial pulls on it to see how it behaved. He decided he needed extra strength to produce the required force for the projectile to fly the distance.

"Are we ready, then?" Marie asked, assuming command of the exercise with an air of expertise. Ethan watched and liked what he saw.

"I'm ready," David said. "My test was successful."

"I'm ready, but I need extra muscle to pull back the rubber," Zane said.

"OK then. Let's do it," Marie ordered.

David tied the loose end of the rope to one tree with the sling setup and coiled it so it wouldn't tangle when the grapple shot toward the far shore. Zane positioned the grapple in the middle of the rubber, estimating the center of gravity of the steel so it traveled true to its course. David and Angelo volunteered to help extend the sling to give enough thrust for the grapple to reach its target. The others stood back in anticipation, watching Zane, David, and Angelo as they started pulling back on the rubber. Their muscles bulged as the rubber reached its limit, the tension in the sling reflected in the faces of those watching.

"Let go on a count of three," Zane said between gritted teeth. He checked the angle one last time. "One ... two ... three."

They let go in perfect synchronicity. The grapple launched in the preordained arch the angle and force had placed on it. Everyone's hopes rested on the destiny of the massive arrow they had flung. It looked like the grapple would penetrate the space between the forked branches, but it fell short at the last instant. Everyone watching gave a cry of disappointment at the failure.

Jason came over and removed a plank.

Zane looked in desperation at Marie.

"You have your aim right. You just need to get more flight," Marie said, encouraging him.

The group's behavior and how they pulled together impressed Ethan. *Even David is pulling his weight now*, he thought.

"We still have one spare plank," David said. "We'll pull the rubber back further, and you can aim higher."

Zane glanced at David, considered his words, and nodded. They retrieved the grapple to their shore. David coiled the rope. They pulled the grapple back again. Zane adjusted the angle. The three pulled back until they were straining with everything they had. "One ... two ... three."

Everyone held their breath as the grapple flew. It rose to the apex. The rope uncoiled at a monstrous speed. The projectile started its descent. Everyone watched and hoped, prayed, for success. It passed through the tree fork, and everyone shouted in delight at achieving the first part of the plan. David slapped Zane on the back in congratulation. Zane stood straight, proud of his effort.

David dragged the rope for the grapple to catch an obstacle for anchorage. The grapple reversed to the tree fork. They held their breath again. The rope tightened as David kept pulling. They had their tether line to pull the first person across the stream. David tied off the rope to keep the tension and tied the twine to the end.

"Who wants to go first?" Marie asked.

"I will," Senna volunteered. "I can take the roll of twine with me and unroll it as I go. David can untie the rope then, and I'll secure it before the rest of you cross."

"Do you know how to tie a rope properly?" David asked.

Senna glared at him with disdain. "Of course I do."

"Just asking," David said, breezily ignoring the rebuke.

Marie looked at the others. They said nothing, so she shrugged, "OK then."

Senna grabbed a plank and the roll of twine. She found a stick and placed it through the center hole of the reel, so it unwound by itself as she moved. She placed the plank in the water and carefully balanced herself on it while she gripped the rope. When she felt she was stable, she started pulling on the rope. The plank glided through the water, and the twine unwound as she pulled. The stream flowed gently, so there was little turbulence to upset her balance. Tense with hope, the people on the shore watched her.

"That's it, Senna," Marie said at one stage. "You're halfway."

Ethan could see dogged determination in Senna's profile. He saw that she had had practice in balancing. She may have learned gymnastics or something similar. Senna stepped off the plank when she reached the far shore and pulled it from the water. The others cheered her success. She unwound more twine, so it was loose, and tied the rest off so that the current wouldn't pull the roll into the stream.

"Which plank can I take?" Jason asked.

Marie conferred with the others. They decided. "The one Senna used," she said.

Jason had Senna put the plank aside.

Senna examined the rope. "Can you give me slack, David?" she shouted across the stream.

"OK." David headed to the knot he had made, untied it, and let the rope loosen.

Senna grabbed it on her end and dislodged the grapple from its position, letting it lower to the ground. She untied the rope from the grapple and pulled it from the tree fork. Then she re-secured the rope around the trunk at a reasonable height. "Is that OK?" she shouted across to David.

David drew the rope tight and studied the general height of the catenary across the stream. "Yes, that should be good." He tied off his end with the same self-untying knot he had made earlier and reattached the twine.

"OK then. Which three want to cross first?" Marie asked.

Zane, Jade, and Max volunteered. Max grabbed two planks and placed them in the stream. Zane got on first while Max held them steady. Jade stepped on the board next. Max stood on while the other two held the rope. They started pulling themselves across the river. The planks wobbled five meters from the bank and parted until they were doing the splits and fell into the water.

"Return to shore," Jason ordered with an amused grin.

"That was inevitable," David said.

"Why didn't you tell us then?" Marie asked, annoyed.

David chafed to retort but refrained.

Max, Jade, and Zane rejoined the others, wet up to their waists. Max and Jade held the two planks, and Jason took one of them. Ethan sniggered at Jade, who returned a peeved expression to him in response.

"How do we prevent that from happening?" Marie asked.

The others discussed it amongst themselves until Angelo suggested, "Why don't we tie the planks together with twine? That way, they can't separate. They'll behave like one plank."

"That's a good idea," Ethan said.

The others agreed. They had nothing to cut the twine with, so David found a stone and smashed it against another rock until it split with a sharp cutting edge on the split line. He untied the twine and asked Senna to give him slack. Once he retrieved six meters, he severed the twine with the rock and retied it to the rope. He cut the off-cut in half, got two planks, and bound each end together with the twine. "How is that?" he asked.

"Good," Marie said. "Let's try again."

"We had better take the rubber across since we don't need it anymore." Ethan strolled over to it and removed it from the trees. Coming back, he gave it to Max. "Here."

Max wore the strip to prevent it from interfering with them or falling off as they made the crossing.

Max, Jade, and Zane straddled the boards again and started pulling themselves across the water. They successfully crossed the river.

David repeated the tying of the two planks together for the other four planks, with Senna supplying him with the twine.

"Who's next?" Marie asked.

Angelo and David volunteered. Ethan suggested, "Why don't you go, Marie? Celeste and I can bring up the rear."

"OK," Marie said.

David, Marie, and Angelo got onto the planks, steadied, and started ferrying themselves. Angelo got a wobble at his end seven meters from the bank, and they fell into the water. David gave Angelo an angry stare.

"Back to shore," Jason announced.

They waded ashore, David hauling the planks along with him.

"What happened?" David asked, annoyed.

"I don't know. The plank moved, and I couldn't re-balance myself."

"I wouldn't want you operating on me if you're that unsteady."

"That's enough," Marie butted in, dissipating the rising tension. "Let's try it again. Will you balance better in the middle, Angelo?"

"Yes, I think so."

"Which plank can I have?" Jason asked.

They needed the remaining two planks for Ethan and Celeste, so they instructed him to remove one from the far shoreline. David, Angelo, and Marie straddled the plank and started across again. They heard a giant splash upstream of them as they moved. Moments later, several broad waves headed toward them, which unsettled the planks. David lost his footing that time and pulled the others into the water.

"Damn, what was that?" David asked, angry, as he grabbed the planks.

Angelo gazed on with satisfaction, happy it wasn't his fault this time.

"A rock must have fallen in the stream," Marie said, annoyed at their bad luck.

They got to shore, and Jason asked for a plank. David untied the remaining two planks and gave him one of them.

"We have a problem now," Marie said. "There're five people and three planks."

They considered the situation for a moment. "We're limited to three feet on each plank, so we need to carry one on our shoulders," Ethan said. "The women are lightest, so who volunteers?" Celeste was lightest at forty-two kilograms, but Marie was only slightly heavier at fifty kilograms.

Celeste became fearful. "Take Marie. I can cross on my own."

"But you are lighter," David protested.

Celeste cowered at his tone.

"It's OK," Marie said. "I couldn't make the crossing on my own. So long as you're confident you can, Celeste?"

"Yes, yes," Celeste pleaded.

David placed the planks in the water again. He and Angelo got on them. They rotated the planks to make them side on to the shore. Ethan helped Marie so that her shoulders were on David's and her midriff was on Angelo's shoulders. They struggled to hold her while still maintaining their balance but succeeded. Ethan got on and held Marie's thighs on his shoulders. They started pulling with their awkward load. Things went well, although they had to stop and steady themselves at one stage. They finally crossed, unloaded Marie, and came ashore, where the others were cheering their ultimate success. Celeste was the final one to cross.

"Your turn now, Celeste," Marie shouted.

Celeste appeared frightened and tentative as she grabbed the plank. She got to the shore and froze.

"What's wrong?" Marie said.

"I'm scared. What if I slip?" Celeste replied.

David rolled his eyes. "That'd be right. I told her she was useless."

Ethan picked up the barb. "That's enough. She has her skills." He turned to Celeste. "You'll be fine. We lose if you don't try. If you fall in, you fall in, but at least you will be trying. It's up to you, and I know you can do it."

Celeste gazed at Ethan with little confidence, but, in the end, she found her resolve. "OK."

"Don't look at the water. Concentrate on the rope and shoreline," Senna offered.

Celeste nodded. She placed the plank in the stream and stepped onto it nervously. She took a deep breath and began pulling, fixing her gaze on the others. They voiced their encouragement as she approached. Just past midstream, she started losing her balance and wobbled. Fear entered her eyes.

"That's it," David said, expecting the inevitable.

"Look straight at me," Senna encouraged. The others tensed in anxious anticipation.

Celeste bristled at David's remark, and resolve came over her. She found her poise again and continued. She gained more confidence as she approached the shore. She stepped off the plank, grabbed it, and placed it on the ground with satisfaction. They cheered her success and slapped her back in camaraderie. Celeste gave David a steely glare and looked back at the others with pride.

"Just one task left, David," Marie said once the congratulations dwindled.

David seized the twine and pulled. The rope didn't budge. He reddened in embarrassment and tugged harder, but still with no success. The others waited, impatient. Ethan saw Celeste eager to give David a barb, but checked herself, not wanting to replicate David's behavior. After consideration, David untied the rope on their side and tried again. The knot untied with ease, and he pulled the rope and twine across, completing the task.

They jumped in the air, excitedly congratulating each other on their success. Jason and John had crossed the stream over a bridge in the meantime. "Congratulations," John said. He gave Ethan an amused expression, which Ethan knew meant, 'We have much to discuss.'

17

FINAL PREPARATIONS

They filled the weeks following the orientation camp with almost frantic preparations to transfer to *Destiny*. All the while, Ethan kept a sharp eye on David. He and John had considered removing him from the expedition after his performance at the team-building exercise but had decided to persist with him. They needed his skills and didn't have the time to recruit anyone else at this late stage.

Ethan was in his office reviewing yet another report when his comm buzzed.

"Hello, Ethan. How are you today?" Hu's exquisite face said from the screen.

"Hi, Hugo. I'm decent. Bogged in reports and other rubbish but bearing the drudgery."

"And Jade?"

"Good. She says she enjoyed herself on the moon. Anything I should know?"

Hu laughed. "No. We didn't have any wild parties if that's what you're asking."

"What can I do for you?"

"I wanted to update you on the portal preparations and that you have an extra passenger."

"Really? Who is it?"

"Me."

"Oh, that's great! Hope the same problems don't recur. Why?"

"We considered what we needed to achieve and decided it was vital someone from our team be at the other end. Liang isn't the right person. He's more useful on the lunar base, so that left me."

"Draw the short straw?"

"Ha! No way. I want to be part of your achievement. I volunteered."

"Jade'll be pleased. You'll meet the rest of my troop, too. They're a good bunch, mostly. What's the plan?"

"When you fly to the moon to load the portal, I'll board and join you for your grand venture."

"I hope it will be," Ethan said, concern creasing his brow.

"What's wrong?"

"Nothing. I think I'm catching Galena's disease and worry about everything."

"You need me to sort you out."

"Ha! You could say that. You always had a way of getting me back to my senses."

"Yes. It'll be great seeing you and Jade again."

"When will you be ready?"

"We're in the last stages of disassembling and packaging the portal. We should be ready in two weeks."

"That'll fit in well with our schedule. We'll be ready to leave then, too."

"OK. I'll keep in touch. Say hello to Jade."

"Hope to wrestle with you soon."

Hu snorted. "In your dreams."

Ethan laughed, and the screen went blank.

Ethan glanced at his chronometer and realized a team meeting was about to start. He collected his items for the meeting and headed for the conference room.

Ethan entered the room. Jade sat there waiting. She looked up when she heard him enter. "Hi," she said with a smile and a sparkle in her eyes.

"Hi," Ethan replied. "I've been talking to Hugo. She gave me an update on the portal preparations, and she'll be joining us."

"I thought they were getting us to put it together."

"They wanted someone at our end to supervise and optimize the portal's settings, so Hugo was the obvious choice."

"That makes sense. It'll be good to have her again on the *Destiny*. The old team together."

"You could say that." Ethan sat, sadness filtering across his face. Not quite the whole team.

Senna and Celeste came into the room, still discussing a current news item. They said hello to Ethan and Jade and parked themselves. Zane and Max walked in next, greeting everyone as they entered. David sauntered in, inspecting the others as he did so as if he was assessing the competition's mood. He had reverted to that tendency ever since the camp, but Ethan couldn't pinpoint why. Marie and Angelo came in last.

"About time," David said, with a probing grin.

Marie darted dagger eyes at him but decided not to take the bait.

Ethan decided not to make a comment, either. He started the meeting instead. "I called this meeting today to get an update on equipment procurement. We should be ready soon to transfer to *Destiny* and make our final preparations for departure. Max, please start."

"Sure. We fully charged the reactors, and they are functioning at maximum efficiency. We just need to collect more astatine before we leave the solar system. When can we do it?"

"We may have time to run a quick trip to Iapetus soon," Ethan said. "It depends on everyone else's status. Let's review that afterward."

Max nodded his agreement.

"Angelo?"

"You already had the medical bay well equipped. I've brought other items for the journey as a precaution, and they are on board."

"Good. Zane?"

"The sampling equipment will be here tomorrow. We've packed the other things already. I've renovated one cabin into a storage room for samples to bring back with us for further analysis."

"Sounds good. Keep me posted about any delays. Senna?"

"The seismic gear and drilling rigs are on board. I have mineralogy mapping apparatus to analyze the planet's available ores too. It will transfer to the ship on the next flight. Everything else is in order."

"Uh-huh. David, what's your progress?"

David sighed his impatience. "The weather balloons were ready ages ago, and the satellite equipment is now on board. The probes are up there, too. I have everything else right here." He held up his tablet.

"Right," Ethan said. David was so difficult to control. No wonder his meteorology center bosses, while praising his workmanship, had little positive to say about him otherwise. "Marie?"

"The isolation room on the ship is complete and fitted out to my specifications. A mobile sampler will arrive in a few days. I'll be ready after that," Marie said in her usual professional manner. "I've changed the landers to include decontamination chambers and external storage lockers." She was deadly serious about her work, although Ethan had seen her relax too, becoming a barrel of laughs on those occasions. She was a natural-born leader from what he observed of her behavior. Both he and John had agreed they should nominate her as second in command of the team, although they had informed no one yet, except for Jade, who had voiced wholehearted agreement with the choice.

"That sounds under control," Ethan said. "Celeste?"

Celeste looked worried. "The spectrometry equipment has arrived, but I can't locate a suitable magnetometer. I've looked everywhere," she said, pleading for help.

"That'd be right," David muttered under his breath, just loud enough for Ethan and others nearby to hear.

Ethan was getting fed up with him. He glared in David's direction.

David stared back with a 'what did I say?' expression of innocence. Ethan said, "Any suggestions?" still glaring at David. David decided he was suddenly busy with something else.

Most had blank faces, unable to help. Senna said after consideration, "If you can give your spec, Celeste, I can ask around my circles."

Celeste nodded. "I can do that," she said, gratitude etched on her face.

"Give me the specification too," Ethan said. "I'll check the military."

Celeste's eyes widened in surprise. "You have that much influence?"

Ethan chuckled. "It pays to know someone like John."

"OK. I will," Celeste said.

"Jade, how are the general supplies going?"

"That's under control. The last shipment arrives in two days."

"Good. Let's see. There are two items arriving in the next two days. Everything else is in order except Celeste's magnetometer."

"How long would it take to ship if we can locate one, Celeste?"

"As long as they can release it from its current duties, we should be able to load it straight away."

"OK. It's looking like we have time for that run out to Iapetus."

"Why? What are we waiting for?" David demanded. "Can't we get this show on the road?"

Ethan gritted his teeth. "I have told you we will help the Chinese with their wormhole project by taking a portal with us. That's ready to load in two weeks. We can travel to Iapetus in just over a week, giving everyone a suitable opportunity to establish yourselves on board."

"What about me?" Celeste asked, worried. "Shouldn't I stay behind and chase up the magnetometer?"

Ethan looked at Celeste for a moment, nibbling his lip. He especially preferred her along, as he felt she needed the experience and wanted to train her on a few ship functions useful for her to learn. He sensed a dormant talent in her timid frame and wished to tap it if he could.

Jade spoke. "I know that look. I can stay here and chase that up for her, Ethan."

Ethan turned to Jade, surprised by the offer and disappointed by her impending absence. Jade smiled. "You'll survive without me for a week."

The others chuckled. Ethan smiled back. "I suppose I'll have to bear the pain. It's settled then. Jade, you do that. Celeste, I want you with us. You have things to learn."

Celeste raised her brow in surprise, morphing into a pleased and determined look. "OK."

"Last, we'll have another passenger on board when we pick up the portal. She is Ching Hu, the chief engineer for the China project."

"Not another freeloader?" David grumbled.

Ethan stared David out, who finally looked away. "You'd do well if you had half her brains," Ethan said. He winced inside after he said it, realizing it wasn't the right thing for a team leader to say, but David was getting on his nerves. *Hugo will see through him.*

David darted a fiery look of anger at Ethan but said nothing. The others stayed silent in the tense moment.

"She's coming with us and supervising the wormhole test work at our end," Ethan said. "Questions?" No one had any. "OK. Let's get on with it then."

Everyone exited the room except Jade. "You could have dealt with David better."

"I know. It just came out. He's getting to me."

"Think of how you handled Loki."

"Loki was different. He was only a megalomaniac. David's a downright smartass who thinks he knows everything."

"Well, you can't let him get to you. That's what he wants."

"Yeah. I know. It'll be interesting how long Hugo takes to put him straight."

Jade giggled. "Let's hope she's gentle."

"I'm not sure I want that." Ethan gave a wicked smile. They both laughed. "Let's go have something to eat."

18

QUICK TRIP TO IAPETUS

Ethan and the others, except Jade, boarded *Destiny* and sped to Iapetus to collect more astatine for the expedition. Ethan had mentioned to Jade that he wanted to teach Celeste, and he now intended showing Celeste his intentions. She hadn't stretched her abilities, and he wished her to take on much greater responsibilities than just astronomy.

He had her sit in the spare seat next to him in the command chair. She looked so nervous and unsure about why she was there that he wondered whether she would rise to meet the challenge.

"How are you feeling?" Ethan asked.

Celeste glanced at him, worried, not knowing why he asked. "I'm OK."

"Have you ever flown anything?"

"Only in VR games. Why?"

Ethan gave Celeste a wicked grin. "I want you to fly this ship back from Iapetus."

"What! I can't do that. It's not possible."

"It is possible. You can do it, and you will do it. Don't worry. I'll be right here if you get into trouble."

"But why?"

"You have untapped talents that need tapping."

Celeste looked unconvinced but said, "I'll try, I suppose."

"Good. We are about to turn the ship soon. Bring up your screen, and I'll talk you through the controls."

Celeste placed the spare screen in front of her and brought up the ship's control page. She studied the diverse readings and buttons. Ethan saw her concentration, which pleased him. He started describing the controls with her and what their functions were. He showed her how to enter commands for the different automatic code sequences. She comprehended the concepts quickly, asking relevant questions as he explained things.

Ethan looked at his watch. "OK then. It's time to turn the ship around and start decelerating."

"I'll get out of your hair then," Celeste said as she started packing the screen away.

"Where are you going? You'll do the maneuver."

Celeste's eyes bulged in surprise. "I couldn't do it. I haven't even touched any of the controls."

"No time like the present to start. Don't worry. I'll be here to stop you from making any mistakes. I've shown you the controls for it. You just have to run the sequence."

Celeste stared at him, not convinced she could take effective control of the ship, but her demeanor changed when she saw Ethan wasn't budging. "OK, then." She reopened the screen and brought up the page. "Do we announce it?"

"You can, but I wouldn't. That way, you can always blame me for any mishap," Ethan said, grinning.

Celeste smiled and returned to concentrating on what she was doing. She located the turnaround menu, punched in data for the speed of rotation and other settings, sighed, and pushed the rotation button. The ship reacted to the command and the EM drive reduced power to idle. The side thrusters turned the vessel, the drive increasing to the original energy setting afterward. No one felt the maneuver. "Ship rotated," she said to Ethan as she faced him with a beaming smile of satisfaction in her achievement, her cheeks etched with creases of happiness.

Ethan smiled too. "Well done. Play with the controls whenever you like, to get familiar with them."

Ethan and Celeste rose from their chairs and left the command center. It took another two days to reach Iapetus. Ethan flew the lander to the moon, taking Max and Senna with him. They collected the astatine without any mishap and stored it in the lander's cargo hold. Ethan estimated they had gathered several years' worth of astatine. He returned to the ship and allowed Celeste to fly it from orbit around Iapetus and direct *Destiny* toward Earth under his oversight. She did an excellent job, in his opinion. Others were in the command center as she performed her duties, and her dexterity at the controls impressed them.

As Celeste finished the final settings for the flight back, she turned to Ethan and asked, "What's this screen?" She brought up the laser cannon screen.

Ethan remained nonchalant as he replied, "Nothing to concern you. I hope I won't need to use that again." He changed the screen to the astrogation display.

It took them another four days to return to Earth's orbit, including the time it took to drop off the astatine on Mars to prevent it from decaying. So far, no scientist, Jade included, had found the reason for astatine's rapid decay on Earth and not elsewhere.

They shuttled to the planet surface, where Jade was waiting for them at the spaceport site at JPL. The team was full of excited chatter as they left the lander. Ethan exited with Celeste and brought her to greet Jade. "Meet your new pilot," he said.

"Really?" Jade asked with delight.

Celeste gazed at the ground, embarrassed by the attention. "I'm sure I have lots to learn yet."

"But ...?" Ethan asked, waiting for a response.

Celeste stared at him. "... but I really enjoyed it." She broke out in a grin, displaying her satisfaction in her achievement.

"Your magnetometer has arrived."

Celeste's eyes sparkled. "That's great."

Ethan placed his arm around Jade, and they went back to the offices.

19

LUNAR PICKUP

Last preparations complete, everyone settled on board *Destiny* for departure, the first leg being to the moon to pick up the wormhole portal and Hu.

Ethan, Jade, and Celeste were in the command center. Ethan allowed Celeste to pilot the ship from the orbiting platform around Earth, so she was in the command chair. Ethan sat to her left, observing. Jade parked in another nearby chair, looking on with interest. She had mentioned to Ethan earlier how impressed she was with Celeste. She had taken to her added responsibility and his delegation of that part of his duties with enthusiasm.

Ethan glanced at Jade, catching her looking sad, but the expression was fleeting, and she smiled again. Ethan surmised that she had been thinking about the first pilot that had sat in the seat Celeste occupied, Jake Brodie. Such a thought led automatically to thoughts of Jake's murder just before the maiden FTL part of their voyage. The recollection saddened Ethan, too. Jake had been a dear friend. Ethan resolutely returned his thoughts to the present.

The ship left the controlled flight space, and Celeste increased the acceleration to gain cruising speed, reaching the moon in four hours. They could have had a shorter journey, but Celeste wanted to take her responsibilities slowly until she familiarized herself with the controls. Ethan appreciated that line of thought.

Celeste's command of the vessel impressed the others, too, except David, who, jealous that Celeste was centerstage, predicted she would panic and put the entire ship in danger. When Ethan was told about the comment, he let it pass as just another example of David being his obnoxious self.

They neared the moon. Celeste placed a communication through to announce their imminent arrival. "Comm call to the Chinese Wormhole Project from Celeste Grüber of *Destiny*. Arriving at the designated staging point. Directions for a parking orbit needed."

Moments elapsed before Hu appeared on the comm screen. She looked surprised when she saw Celeste. "Hi. Ching Hu here. I am pleased to meet you, Celeste. I see Ethan has shirked one more of his duties."

Celeste gasped at Hu's comment but then grinned when she realized Hu was joking.

"That's enough cheek from you, Hugo," Ethan said from beside Celeste, raising his voice.

Celeste raised an eyebrow at the name 'Hugo.'

"Long story," Ethan explained. "Hu might tell you sometime, but her friends call her Hugo."

"Oh. Well, I'll stick with Hu until she tells me otherwise. I was wondering why you were so quick to teach me to pilot this ship."

They laughed.

"I'm sending you the orbital coordinates for parking," Hu said. "It's near the packaged portal. We can use the space tugs to ferry the parts through your lander bay and into the storage compartment."

"Acknowledged. Coordinates have arrived. I'm adjusting my trajectory, and we should park in ..." Celeste looked away to study a display and turned back, "... twenty minutes."

"Check, and you can call me Hugo."

Celeste beamed at being included in Hu's exclusive club of friends.

"Is Ethan still there?" Hu asked.

"Sure am," he said.

"I want to shuttle on board when you park. Is that OK?"

"That's fine with me, but you had better ask the pilot."

Celeste laughed. "Yes, that's fine with me, too."

"Good. Might catch you in half an hour."

"We'll have the welcoming party ready," Ethan said. "Estimated time to store the portal?"

Hu contemplated her response. "There are seven packages to move into the ship. We prefer zero gravity in the bay and storage compartment to make handling easier. The attached package G-grids will carry them. We should load everything in five hours."

"OK. It gives me a timeframe for departure. Thanks."

"You're welcome. I'll keep Celeste informed of any updates."

"That'll be good," Celeste said, and the screen blanked. She sat back, satisfied with her work.

Ethan rose from his chair, exchanging a glance with Jade, who nodded in agreement. "You don't need me, Celeste. I might go to the lander bay and wait for Hugo. I may as well open the storage hatches while I'm there."

Celeste gave Ethan a smile. "Thanks for showing confidence in me. But you might have warned me."

"About what?" Ethan asked, alarmed he had overlooked something.

"That Hugo is so stunning and elegant and friendly ... well, she's perfect."

Ethan laughed.

"Yes, she has that effect on people. But don't let that fool you. She is one of the most accomplished individuals I know and one of the most dangerous if you get on her wrong side." He turned to Jade. "You want to come and welcome her?"

"Sure do."

Ethan and Jade left the command center to Celeste and traveled to the lander bay. Ethan headed to the storage compartment doors' control panel and pressed the button to slide open the enormous doors leading into the store. The large cargo was stored in this space so they could seal it separately from the lander bay to segregate the components from the comings and goings of the landers and prevent any accidental movement of parts. The doors stopped moving in the open position. He returned to Jade and waited with her for Hu to arrive.

The lander bay doors parted, and a shuttle maneuvered to enter. The shuttle landed, and the cabin door opened. A few moments later, Hu emerged, scanning her surroundings. She broke into a smile when she spotted Ethan and Jade and quickly descended the steps and walked over to them.

"Welcome aboard," Ethan greeted as he kissed her on the cheek, which Hu returned.

"Great to be here again," Hu said. "Hi, Jade." She gave Jade a kiss on the cheek, too.

"Good to see you again," Jade said.

"I like your new pilot," Hu told Ethan.

"She's our astronomer, but I decided she could expand her outlook. It's taken a degree of coaxing to convince her to take on the role, but she's doing well."

"She sure is. She looked the slightest bit timid when I first appeared on the screen, but she settled with complete competence."

Ethan chuckled. "You'd intimidate anyone."

"I do not," Hu protested. "Anyway, I'll retrieve my gear and help load the portal. The first package should arrive in half an hour. I will stay here and supervise the loading."

"OK. Come to the command center when you're finished. I'll be there," Ethan said. "I'll get your pack taken to your room." He called one technician over to complete the task. "See you soon." He left with Jade.

The portal transfer took a shorter time than Hu expected, and she entered the command center after four and a half hours. She was hot and perspiring from the manual labor in the storage compartment's confined space. Her hair, disheveled from the effort, still held its shape because of its short length.

"Looks like you could enjoy freshening up," Ethan said as he glanced up to confirm who had entered. He had taken over from Celeste, who was having a well-earned break.

"Sure could," Hu said.

"Let's find out where you are." Ethan searched his tablet to check the cabin allocation. "There you are. You're in 1703." Sadness crossed Ethan's face. It had been Jake's cabin.

Hu recognized the number, too, and gave Ethan a somber smile. "Are you and Jade in your old rooms?"

"Yes, we are. We're maintaining an element of propriety while on the journey."

"OK. I will go freshen up. I could use something to eat too."

"We'll meet you in the mess for lunch."

Hu left, and Ethan returned to monitoring the ship. Now that they had everything, they could set their course for Centauri. Ethan felt a sense of excitement as he contemplated the fact that they would soon be the first interstellar human explorers.

20

DAVID MEETS HU

E than powered up the EM drive and set a course for Centauri, which was sixty degrees south of the solar plane. It was late afternoon. He set the thrust at 4g to power away from Earth and would change to FTL in the morning. They could relax and celebrate the momentous occasion in the meantime. He wondered what occupied the solar outskirts at such an angle to the plane. From his recollection, no one had asked the question. Few large objects occupied the space to collide with them. After checking everything was stable, he locked the controls and advised the Commander-On-Duty(COD) that he had control of the ship and to inform him of any problems. He told them to record the visual feed of the space they passed for future analysis and reference.

He left the command center and headed for his cabin to freshen up before visiting Jade. After an exhausting day, he needed his full concentration when Celeste and he transferred to the FTL drive. She hadn't seen it before, so he wanted to give her a thorough review of the controls and how they worked. He was sure the opportunity would excite her.

Celeste's rapid progress filled him with a sense of pride that he could play a part in stretching her capabilities further. He was pleased that she had met the challenge head-on and succeeded. He was pleased with himself too. It was the first time he had attempted a mentoring and development task. Indeed, he wondered how he had ever achieved his current position, given his lifelong difficulties dealing with people, especially women. He was glad he had pushed himself to where he was, though. It was where he belonged. He had dreamed of it so often and now he was reaching for the stars, a genuine pioneer.

He shook himself from his reverie and concentrated on where he was going. The elevator arrived at the accommodation level, and the doors opened. He headed for his cabin, took a quick shower, and dressed casually. He made for Jade's cabin and buzzed her, but she did not answer. Calling her on her comm, he learned she was in the lounge with Hu, so he left to join them there.

Ethan came into the bar and spotted Jade and Hu at one table, talking. They were the only ones there. Ethan had issued a notice announcing departure drinks that night for anyone interested. He got a drink and sat with the two of them.

"Hi. I see the tourists have made themselves comfortable," Ethan jested.

Jade laughed. "You poor, overworked slave. You should have said something. I would have wiped your brow."

Hu erupted into laughter, too.

Ethan gave Jade a mock insulted expression. "You should be more attentive to my needs. Where is everyone? I was hoping to introduce Hugo to the others."

"It's still early. They'll be here soon. They don't want to make a poor impression on the boss."

"Too late for that. I discovered their skeletons at the camp."

Celeste, Marie, and Max walked in as Ethan finished talking. Celeste spotted them and started walking over, waving for the rest to follow. "Hi. Hu ... go, it's great to see you in the flesh."

"It's good to see you, too."

Marie and Max stared at Celeste, puzzled. Celeste detected their consternation. "Let me make the introductions," she said.

Ethan raised a surprised eyebrow at her lack of shyness. She was like a butterfly emerging from its chrysalis. He glanced at Jade, who smiled in appreciation. Hu nodded for Celeste to continue.

"Hu, meet Marie, our microbiology expert, and Max, our fusion specialist. Marie, Max, Hu."

Marie lifted an eyebrow. "I didn't know you'd already met her. You're surprising me, Celeste. Anyway, it's a pleasure to meet you, Hu."

Max stood with mouth wide open, speechless. He had never encountered anyone so attractive.

"You'll catch a fly in your mouth if you don't close it," Ethan commented drily.

Max came out of his trance, blushing in embarrassment. "I'm sorry. Please forgive me. I've made such a goose of myself."

Hu's eyes were dancing with amusement. "Don't worry, you're not the first to react like that. I don't bite, and I'm a fun person once you get to know me. It's a thrill to meet someone so honest."

"The pleasure is mine, but I need a drink to relax after this." Max laughed nervously.

"Let's find a drink then," Celeste suggested. The three headed for the bar.

Jade bent across to Ethan and asked under her breath, "What have you done to Celeste?"

Ethan chuckled. "She's something, isn't she? John and I both sensed a latent talent in her, and I am glad it's blooming. Do you approve?"

"Certainly."

Angelo, Senna, and Zane were the next to arrive. They spotted Celeste and the others at the bar and waved a greeting as they joined them. Marie pointed toward Ethan, and they glanced around and waved. After getting their drinks, they came back to Ethan's group. They found seats and positioned them so they could converse as a group.

"Some of you have already met Ching Hu," Ethan said, "but I'll introduce her to the rest. Hu, meet Senna, our geologist, Zane, our biologist, and Angelo, our medical specialist." They greeted each other, Hu's eyes glinting as she noted each person's reaction to her presence. "That just leaves David to meet when he comes."

"He mentioned he'd be a minute when I bumped into him," Zane said. "He wanted to catch up on something."

The group was busy talking when David strutted into the lounge. Ethan saw him scan the room, his eyes quickly resting on Hu. His demeanor changed to one of seduction. Ethan groaned. He suspected he knew how events would end but had no power to avert the impending disaster. He was interested in how Hu would handle the interaction, too.

Hu caught Ethan looking at David and looked for herself. Her expression morphed from joyfulness to wary watchfulness, like a predatory cat eyeing a dangerous threat. Ethan knew she had sized up David instantly. David walked over to them. "Well, hello," he said, leering at Hu with what he thought was charm. "I don't believe we've been introduced. I am David Summers, and you are ...?"

"Hi. I am Ching Hu, a member of the Chinese Wormhole Project team, here to tend to our portal assembly," Hu replied with polite indifference.

"We'd better make sure you feel at home," David replied, his tone giving the words an innuendo that made the other women gape at such an overt display of machismo.

David doesn't realize the hornet's nest that he'll kick if he's not careful, Ethan thought.

"I'll get a drink, and we can acquaint ourselves better," David said as he left.

Hu looked at Ethan, an eyebrow raised in disbelief. Ethan shrugged as if to say, 'There's one in every crowd.' She then displayed a calculating expression that Ethan rarely saw but knew exactly what it meant. He pleaded with her with his eyes not to make trouble. Hu reassured him with a pat on the shoulder as she rose to get another drink herself. She walked over to the bar and ordered another glass. The body language said everything. David lent his back on the bar in a flirting stance, and Hu turned half away from him, disinterested. He started talking to her anyway. She remained polite but distant. David received his drink and stayed to continue flirting, oblivious to the fact that it was one-sided.

"I can't watch this," Ethan said to Jade, nodding his head at the impending disaster between Hu and David. "David will get his ass kicked if he's not careful. He's misunderstanding Hu's body language completely."

Jade looked. Amusement appeared on her face. "I am curious about Hu's abilities now."

Hu received her drink, which she held when David said something to Hu that Ethan couldn't hear but which got Hu offside in a big way. Her eyes glared daggers, but David didn't notice. As she turned to return to the table, David placed his hand on her shoulder. Ethan closed his eyes. Hu wrapped her free arm around the one David had on her shoulder, and with one quick motion, almost faster than the eye could see, she sprawled David on the floor, leaving him bewildered at what had just happened. His drink spilled everywhere. Hu made a harsh comment to David and walked away, not a drop of her drink having escaped her glass in the maneuver. The group stopped talking and looked at the commotion, mouths agape. Hu came back and sat down.

Ethan opened his eyes again. Hu was still furious, angrier than he had seen her for a significant time. "Sorry, but I did warn you about him."

Hu glanced over at David and said, "Gweilo!" She returned her attention to Ethan. "There's one in most groups. I can handle them."

David rose, glowering. He brushed the spilled drink off himself and ordered another. After calming himself, he walked back to the group as if nothing had happened. Ethan noticed he made sure he stayed as far away from Hu as possible. They had no further disturbance for the rest of the evening as they socialized, albeit with David uncharacteristically reserved.

21

TO CENTAURI

Ethan and Celeste perched in the pilot seats the next morning, preparing to engage the FTL drive. Celeste sat in the command chair.

Suddenly she turned to Ethan with an imploring look. "I can't do this," she said.

"You'll be fine," Ethan said. "You're just having an attack of nerves. Nerves are good. They stop us from being cocky, which is far more dangerous. And I'm here to prevent you from making a mistake. Just do as I have shown you, and everything will go smoothly."

Jade walked in, eager to watch the transition to the speed of light again. Ethan glanced over at her, beseeching her support.

"Can I help?" Jade asked.

Celeste gaped at her, moon-eyed with tension and worry. "I'm afraid I'll do something wrong."

Jade placed her hand on Celeste's shoulder and gave her a soothing look. "You have the best teacher at your side to instruct you — and you have excelled so far, haven't you?"

"If you say so," Celeste replied. She took two deep, calming breaths to help her concentrate on what Ethan had taught her. She glanced at Ethan. "Are we ready?"

"Whenever you are," Ethan said.

Celeste looked at the screen and pressed the button to activate the FTL drive start-up sequence. It powered up and changed status to standby after several minutes. In the meantime, other crew members had herded into the command center to watch the momentous occasion. Earth and its sun were invisible from the forward viewing window. They had left these far behind overnight. Only stars were visible.

"Where are we going?" Senna asked.

"See the star straight ahead? That's Alpha Centauri," Celeste said. She glanced at Ethan. He nodded, so she engaged the FTL drive and increased power. The EM drive reduced power simultaneously. Speed rose, as did Celeste's excitement. They were traveling 0.9c within a few minutes at the low power setting she had selected and increasing. They reached the speed of light and continued to go faster. "We are now going faster than light," she told her colleagues, who stared in amazement. Celeste raised the power further, and the spaceship moved faster still. Celeste and Ethan had agreed beforehand that they would settle the vessel to 80c as a cruising velocity. Ethan had completed several runs at that speed, and it had produced no problems. Celeste brought the ship to the required speed and locked the controls to keep it. She looked at Ethan with pride.

Ethan slapped her on the shoulder. "I knew you could do it."

"Thank you."

Jade gazed with satisfied amusement at the teacher-student relationship in front of her.

"What do we do for the next twenty days?" Max asked.

"I have enough astronomy for a lifetime. No one has seen the stars from our destination before," Celeste said, anticipating delight. The eagerness to engage in her passion was obvious on her face.

"I'm not sure what else you're going to do, but I've organized a strict exercise schedule for us starting in two hours," Ethan said.

Everybody protested and most filed out in quick succession, grumbling as they left.

"You know how to spoil a party," Jade said, staying behind with Celeste.

Celeste laughed.

"I need to keep you fit and active," Ethan said. "Otherwise, we'll be lethargic and slow in thinking. Any exploration will be pointless until we get fit again."

"Good to see you are considering our wellbeing," Jade jibed.

Ethan stared at Celeste and back at Jade. "You're lucky Celeste and the others are here, or you'd be in trouble."

"Promises, promises," Jade riposted, giving Celeste a wink as she moved to leave the control center. Ethan followed close behind her. He had a twinkle of lust in his eyes.

HU WORKED out hard in the gym. It had been a week since they had gone FTL. She was punishing the punching bag to abandon with her fists and feet and sometimes even her head. Perspiration covered her body and dripped from her brow. Her movements reflected a ballerina's precision to the music of the dance playing in her mind. The noise of the gym door opening broke her concentration. No one else was there. She glanced around and saw David walk in wearing gym gear. She increased the intensity of her workout as the bag bounced like a piñata beaten by a stick and ready to burst at the next jab. David approached Hu and waited for her to finish her performance.

She sensed he wanted to talk, so she stopped, gasping for air from her effort. "What do you want?" she asked, sensing a repentant temper in his stance. She got the towel that was resting near her and wiped her face.

David didn't speak straight away. Hu wasn't sure whether from fear or humiliation, but she waited. "I wanted to say I'm sorry for my behavior. I was a jackass and treated you poorly."

Hu studied him intensely. He seemed genuine in his remorse. "I forgive you," she said. "You've just seen what I could have done to you," she added, trying to lighten the mood.

"Yes, I have," David said, studying her before averting his eyes.

"Is this of your own volition, or has someone advised you to apologize?"

He looked offended by the accusation.

"That's OK. I got my answer, and I'm glad that this of your own will." Hu smiled. "Let's start again, shall we?"

He relaxed at the suggestion, "Let's."

"How are you at boxing?"

David stiffened in alarm.

Hu laughed. "I won't hurt you; I promise."

"Well, I'm not very good."

"I'll teach you."

David still looked unsure. Hu pondered whether he thought she was searching for an excuse to pummel him again.

Finally, David sighed. "Yes, OK."

They both went to get gloves and sparring headgear.

22

CENTAURI

The days dragged on as they sped toward Centauri. They were getting bored with the inactivity. The odd bickering and disagreement flashed, much to Ethan's consternation. Jade brought to his attention that he should expect occasional flare-ups with so many inactive and confined in an enclosed environment for an extended time.

"We're almost there. Only another couple of days, Ethan," Jade said.

"I can't wait to arrive and start doing something myself."

"You'll be complaining that you're too busy next. Enjoy the relaxation when you can get it. Has Celeste made any planetary observations yet?"

"We're still too distant to get any usable data with our instruments. She's receiving better information on the stars, though. We'll pass Proxima Centauri tomorrow and that might have a habitable planet, but Celeste believes our best bet is around Alpha Centauri A or B. We can always go back to Proxima for a closer look later."

"So, another two days of having you to myself?"

"You wish. The others might be idle, but the drudgery of running the ship never stops."

"I can't interest you in any other activities?"

Ethan took in her suggestive comment. She laughed. He pounced on her and gave her what was on her mind as they cavorted to abandon in his cabin.

Two days later, the team assembled in the command center to get a close-up view of their destination. They were two hours away from Alpha Centauri and passing through the binary star's Oort cloud. Celeste busied herself collecting more detailed intelligence on the system now that they were close enough to gather meaningful information for the expedition. Ethan piloted the ship so Celeste could concentrate on her work as they neared the stars. They flew to Alpha Centauri A first to explore the region surrounding that star, as it was the most promising. Celeste recorded magnetic information with the magnetometer, even though the distance made any useful results scant. She wanted data on the magnetic field structure as they approached.

"Can you see any orbital bodies yet?" Ethan asked her.

"There appear to be two gas giants orbiting both A and B at forty and thirty astronomical units. They look to be in highly eccentric orbits, which doesn't surprise me. We're still too distant to receive any visual of the inner worlds of either star." Celeste sat at her astronomy workstation in the command center.

"Any details for those planets?" Senna asked.

"We are too far away. When will we go back to the EM drive, Ethan?"

"I was thinking at thirty AUs. We can slow to 0.1c and then decelerate at 5g to reach one AU from A in three and a half days," Ethan said from the command chair, studying the screens in front of him, searching for large objects to avoid. He placed the planned trajectory to the star on the primary screen for everyone to see. He intended to approach the system on a parabolic path to align with its orbital plane.

There was a slight grumble of discontent amongst the others as they realized they had to wait still longer for more excitement. A few considered wandering off, except they wanted to experience exiting light speed.

The ship approached the thirty AU distance, and Ethan started decelerating. It slowed and reached 1.0c. A blinding flash occurred as the warp bubble released the photons and other grains it had captured along the way. The team gave a shout of fearful surprise.

"Sorry. I forgot to tell you about that," Ethan said apologetically. "The warp bubble collects tramp particles as we travel and releases them when we re-enter sub-light speed." He continued to reduce the velocity until they reached 0.1c and then shut off the bubble drive and started the EM drive to decelerate the ship.

Celeste began collecting more detail now that they had slowed. The window view was clearer, too, even though they oriented away from Alpha Centauri A. The viewing screens displayed the scene toward the star. She studied her displays with immense interest. One gas giant was too distant, being opposite the suns, but the other gas giant was approaching fast, and it passed them at twelve million kilometers at its closest approach. The detail was already showing. She transferred the image over to the primary screen for everyone to see. Those present gasped in wonder at the spherical spectacle. Purple-colored bands with large swirling clouds of gas cavorted across the planet. The designated North Pole region had an octagonal standing wave surrounding it.

"What causes that shape?" Max asked.

"We believe the different rotational periods of the outer cloud and the inner core. We can replicate it to an extent in the laboratory," Celeste explained. "Saturn has a similar one, but that is hexagonal."

Two large green spots appeared on the screen. One, at sixty degrees north of the equator, covered twenty degrees of latitude and longitude. The second was thirty degrees north and half the other's size.

"Are there any moons?" Jade asked as the sphere noticeably grew larger with their approach.

"I've picked up five so far of various sizes. I'll show where they are with pointers." Celeste's hands moved over the keyboard, and red arrows appeared. They pointed to small circles of light in orbit around the planet. The panorama mesmerized the audience.

"Can we see any inner planets yet?" Ethan asked.

"I'm not sure. We are still too far out. I'll see clearer tomorrow."

Thirty minutes later, the gas giant passed the ship and then receded fast. Once the external excitement was over, the team members drifted from the command center back to their mundane activities.

Ethan caught up with Hu a few hours afterward as she was leaving her room to go to the equipment storage compartment for her daily inspection of the wormhole portal parts to check that they hadn't moved or suffered damage. He walked with her. "Have you given any thought to setting up the portal?" Ethan asked her as they entered the store.

"A little. We can locate it near a planet. As you know, we have one in close orbit around the moon, which doesn't cause any spacetime distortion when we open a wormhole."

"Wouldn't that depend on the power you need to consume, though? You'll use much more energy to generate this wormhole, won't you?"

"We will, but our calculations and measurements suggest only minor changes will occur. It depends on which planet you explore and around which star, although we are within a reasonable distance of each. I'd prefer you close by in case I need you."

"Good thinking," Ethan said, wrinkling his brow, pondering. "It may be desirable for both of us to have you nearby. I'll organize a meeting for tomorrow to produce a plan for the portal construction and other matters since we're approaching our destination and can start what we came here to do."

"That sounds great," Hu said.

They both spent another half hour looking at the portal parts and left. Hu headed for the gym, and Ethan detoured to the Engineering deck to review the day's operations.

∿

ETHAN SAT in the conference room attached to the command center at ten the next morning, waiting to start the meeting he had organized. Jade was with him, chatting about nothing important. Marie and Hu walked in and greeted them before they sat. Max, Zane, David, and Senna followed soon after, with Angelo in tow. Celeste was the only tardy one. She arrived five minutes late. Ethan considered starting without her, but he needed her at the meeting because she was setting up vital recordings.

"Sorry I'm late," Celeste said, flustered and blushing.

"Someone has to be last," David said. For once, David was just making a factual statement and showed a neutral expression.

"I was preparing my detectors to scan for any planets in Centauri A's inner system. It took longer than I expected."

"That's fine," Ethan said.

"Anything that provides stimulation other than exercising and reading is fine with me." David sounded bored.

"Let's get the meeting underway, shall we?"

Everyone nodded.

"I've called this meeting for two reasons. The first is to develop the portal setup details, and the second is to review our activities once we arrive. Does anyone have other issues to discuss?"

The others made no comment and waited for Ethan to continue. He noted Celeste's incessant checking of her comm, which distracted him. "Hu, please lead the discussion here and give us your thoughts on the portal assembly."

"Sure. As I mentioned to Ethan yesterday, I want the portal near the world we explore. That way, we are nearby, and I can use *Destiny* as a base of operations without constant traveling. Considering that, I believe it should be in the habitable zone and orbiting the planet at two hundred and fifty thousand kilometers. I'm not sure where you intend to locate *Destiny*."

"I was thinking five thousand kilometers when we are on any planet," Ethan said in clarification. "But we must unload the portal parts. So, we'll stop at the portal location first. Otherwise, *Destiny* may be too far away to commute."

Hu creased her brow. "You're right. Could we use a shuttle while we assemble it?"

"How many of my engineers and technicians will you need?"

"Six should be enough."

"Hmm. It'll get squashy." Ethan sat in contemplation. He then said, "How long will it take to build?"

"A week unless we strike problems, which I don't expect."

Ethan scanned the others. He frowned as his eyes passed over Celeste, who remained distracted by her comm. He decided. "I know I won't be popular, but we'll stay near the portal until it's working."

Murmurs of disapproval and dissent spread through the group.

"We're stuck in here for another week?" David growled.

"Yes, more than likely. What did you expect? Letting everyone descend to a planet willy-nilly when we arrived?"

"Can we take a shuttle closer to reconnoiter the world and make preliminary observations?" Senna suggested.

"Yeah, that would be useful," David said, mollified by the possibility.

"That should be possible," Ethan agreed.

"Yes," Celeste blurted loudly, forgetting where she was. Everyone looked at her expectantly. She glanced up and turned bright red. "Sorry."

"Well, spit it out," Hu said, bemused.

"I programmed the controls to alarm me when it detected a suitable planet. It just gave me an alert." Another quiet ping came up while she talked. Celeste peered at her comm. "Correction, two suitable planets."

The group started chatting excitedly amongst themselves, forgetting about the meeting.

"Hmm-hmm," Ethan interrupted. "Shall we return to the point? That's great news, Celeste, but can you concentrate on the meeting?"

Celeste blushed again at the reprimand. "Sorry."

"So, we'll stop at the portal location while Hu builds it. We'll help Hu with any issues she might have while we wait there. We can schedule trips to it looks like two planets now to check their compatibility for human habitation and to make preliminary plans for excursions to the surface once we move closer."

The group nodded.

"Let's circle the table and see what everybody else's agenda might be over the next days. Jade?"

"I have little to do. I can help Hu if she needs it and powering up the portal will be of interest when it happens."

"OK. David?"

"It depends on what trips we take to the planets. If we fly within atmospheric proximity, I could drop meteorological probes to gather data on the climatic conditions at various locations. I can use that information to model the weather."

Ethan made a note. "That seems a worthwhile reason to organize a flight. Let's plan that."

"We can take surface images, too, to get a picture of their geology," Senna added.

Ethan jotted another note. "Celeste, where are the planets?"

Celeste produced a sheepish grin. "I'm uncertain but, against your instructions before ..." she bowed her head in embarrassed repentance, "I extracted that information, and they're on our side of the star."

Ethan gave a stern stare. "That's why I asked. So, we could visit both planets within a reasonable time while we are waiting?"

"Probably."

"Let's work on that, then. I'll start looking at flight schedules and trajectories, and David and Senna can prepare their equipment."

"I'd like to get more detailed data on the star," Celeste said. "So, I should release a probe to crash into it."

"OK. You can start organizing that," Ethan said. "Max?"

"I don't have any plans. I can lend a hand to whoever requires help."

"Me too," Zane said.

"Angelo?"

"Nothing for me unless anyone needs a doctor."

"Hu's said enough," Ethan said, prompting a feigned aggrieved look from Hu. "Marie?"

"Will your probes be descending to the surface in one piece, David?"

"That's the intention."

"Is there space for a microanalyzer in the capsule?"

"That depends on its size and weight, but it's possible."

"If we can fit a microanalyzer into David's capsules, Ethan, I can sample for any micro-biological matter."

"Sounds reasonable. Well, that's everyone. We have actions to progress. Is there anything else?"

No one said anything further.

"OK. Let's get on with it, then."

The meeting broke up, and the team went their separate ways.

23

THE PORTAL

They arrived two hundred and fifty thousand kilometers from one of the habitable planets and entered orbit around it. Celeste continued studying both worlds as the ship arrived in the inner system. The closest one seemed the most promising choice for habitability. It was toward the outer edge of Centauri A's habitable zone. Celeste named the planet Chiron in honor of the wisest centaur in Greek mythology and the other planet Chariclo, after his wife. She mentioned it to Ethan and the crew, and they liked the designations, so the names stuck.

Hu jumped into action when the ship reached orbit. She organized and directed crews to get the components out of the vessel, and construction started. She glanced over at Ethan, who was grinning at her. Smiling back, she walked over to him.

"Why are you smiling?" she asked.

"You are in your element."

"It's hard sitting around doing nothing for three weeks."

"Yeah, I know the feeling. How are things going? Do you need help?"

"Not at present, or we'll fall over each other. We've almost removed everything from the ship, and I have a crew positioning the first sections now, ready for connection."

"Tell me if you need anything."

"I will." Hu returned to her work.

She donned a suit, equipment belt, and jetpack and darted out the lander bay door to check the construction. The workers were using magnetic guides and small chemical thrusters clamped to the parts to align them so that they would move into place smoothly. She looked on with satisfaction at their progress. They were working faster than planned.

Max had volunteered to help with the assembly, having experience with reactor installations in the past, and he needed to disperse his boredom. Hu jetted over to him to see how he was doing. "How are things here, Max?"

"Under control. Not much to it. You've packaged it well, so everything fits like a Meccano set."

Other workers were positioning two parts into their locating slots behind Max. One part jammed against the other from misalignment. It slipped and violently collided with another minor part, catapulting it toward Max and Hu. Hu spotted what had happened out of the corner of her eye and moved to start her jets to collide with Max and get them both out of the way of the approaching missile. But she couldn't get into motion in time, and the projectile smashed into Max, sending him gyrating into space. Hu heard a cracking of bones through her radio when the collision occurred and feared the worst. She radioed for help and activated her suit thrusters to chase Max and stabilize his position. She needed to reel him in to check his injuries. Fortunately, no depressurization alarms emanated from his monitoring system, so his suit was intact, but his condition was unknown. The monitors showed he still lived.

Hu arrived next to a rotating and receding Max and grabbed one of his legs, which started sending her into rotation as well until she used her thrusters to slow them both to a stationary position against the background again. She then employed the jets to stop the outward trajectory and reined them both back to the portal and help.

She stared through the faceplate of Max's helmet. He looked unconscious, and blood globules floated around and splattered his face. A shuttle arrived nearby. Hu hauled Max toward it and into the entry airlock. The lock cycled to pressurize, and the green light flashed. She whirled her helmet off and his. The inner hatch opened, and two people looked at her.

"Help me get him inside and take his suit off," Hu commanded, frantic with worry. They jumped into action and dragged him into the passenger compartment, laying him on the floor.

The pilot opened the door. "The doc is on the line!"

"Can you punch it through to my comm?" Hu asked.

There was a slight static and then, "Hello, Angelo, here. What is Max's condition?"

"I'm not sure. A flying object hit him. He is unconscious but still alive. I heard cracking when the part struck him, so I presume multiple fractures, at least. I haven't removed his suit yet."

"Hu, I understand you're a calm person. Take a breath and settle yourself. We will work through this."

A moment of resentment flashed through Hu's mind until she realized he had sensed her agitation, so she did what she was told.

"OK. Can you get the emergency medical kit? In there, you'll find scissors to cut his suit off," Angelo said.

Hu asked a helper to get the kit. She grabbed it, found the scissors, and started cutting the spacesuit away from Max's body. She spotted misaligned limbs as the suit peeled away. Her gut wrenched at the trauma, and she had dreadful concern for Max's life. They removed the suit from him.

"OK, Angelo. I see obvious fractures, but what do I do now?"

"There's a biometric scanner in the kit. Switch that on, link it to the shuttle communication network, and pass it over Max's body. I'll receive the scanner readout at my end, and we'll know more then."

Hu retrieved the instrument and did as Angelo had instructed her. She passed the scanner over Max's inert body. When she had finished, she said, "Well?"

"Give me time," Angelo grumped.

Only seconds ticked by till Angelo spoke again, but for Hu, it seemed an eternity as she stared at Max's unconscious body.

"OK then," Angelo said. "The bad news is that he has serious fractures and injuries. The good news is that no major organs have been affected, and he should recover once we can treat him."

"Thank God." Hu sighed in relief.

"When will the shuttle return?"

Hu looked at the others. One left for the pilot to check. "Another ten minutes," he called.

"You hear that?" Hu asked Angelo.

"Yes, I did. Just keep Max comfortable and make sure he can breathe. I'll stay online for you in case his condition deteriorates. Two of my staff will wait at the lander bay for you and ferry him through to me."

"OK."

Angelo chuckled. "Not that I wanted this to happen to Max or anyone else, but at least I have something to keep me busy now."

"You're sick," Hu said, her mood improving.

"I know," Angelo agreed. "And how are you?"

"I'm shaken. It just missed me. And I feel guilty that someone injured himself working for me. I must give an account to Ethan."

"An understandable reaction, Hu. Find me if you want to talk more."

"OK. Thanks, and I'll keep that in mind."

The shuttle landed. The cabin door opened, and two orderlies rushed on board with a stretcher. They placed Max on it and trolleyed him to the elevator. Hu accompanied them. Ethan sped from the elevator as they exited the shuttle and strode over to them. He stared at Max and then Hu. "I just heard about the accident. Are you okay?"

Hu nodded. "A little shaken. But I'll survive. A different story for Max, though."

"Angelo says he'll pull through once he gets medical attention."

They reached the elevator, and the orderlies entered with the stretcher. Hu and Ethan followed. They reached the sick bay and

Angelo instructed the nurses to place Max in an operating cubicle.

Angelo came over to Hu and Ethan. "I'll let you know his condition once I've patched him up and stabilized him."

"Do you need me?" Hu asked, keen to stifle the guilt she felt.

Angelo studied her. "No. You rest. You did a good job getting Max back in one piece. I'm here if you need to talk." He patted her on the shoulder in support.

Hu smiled wanly. "Thanks."

"I'll come with you," Ethan said to Hu as they both headed out to leave Angelo to do his business. "Keep me informed," he said to Angelo as they left. "Are you sure you're okay, Hugo? You look pale."

"I'm so sorry, Ethan," Hu said with guilt and sorrow. "This is my fault. I shouldn't have rushed the assembly."

Ethan stopped walking, as did Hu. He looked at her nonplussed. "I don't believe what I am hearing, Hugo. How on earth can you be thinking such nonsense? We both reviewed your construction schedule and agreed it was proper and achievable. I don't know the details of what happened yet, but I'm sure it wasn't because you tried to rush things. You can't punish yourself because of a chance occurrence you had no power to prevent. You didn't place Max in that exact location at that exact time to hurt him."

Ethan's words of support lifted a terrible weight from her. She placed her forehead on his shoulder and sobbed and then chuckled.

"What's so funny?"

Hu raised her head and looked at him. "It's usually me giving you a tirade over your self-pity."

Ethan smiled. "Well, I know someone who's been an excellent mentor," he said as he patted her shoulder. "And a wonderful friend."

Hu stood still for a moment longer as the friendship soaked into her. "I suppose I'd better retrieve the part we lost."

"You're going to your cabin and resting for a while, doctor's orders. I can organize that. What are we looking for?"

Relief engulfed her. "I'm not sure. The technicians can tell you. It has a beacon on it."

"OK. I'll find it. Go to your cabin now. I'll have Jade imprison you if you disobey."

Hu laughed. "I don't want that. Thank you."

"You're welcome."

Hu went to her cabin in submission to Angelo's and Ethan's orders. She felt tired. After lying down for a quick nap, she woke up over four hours later, surprised she had slept so long. Cleaning herself up, she headed for the sick bay to check on Max's condition.

Angelo wasn't there, so she approached an attending nurse. "How is Max?"

"He's stable, and he should make a complete recovery. The bones need time to mend, but there's no permanent damage."

"Thank God for that. Is he awake?"

"No, he is conscious, but we gave him a sedative, so he rests."

"OK. I'll come back later." Hu walked out.

Hu returned to the routine of constructing the portal, the drama of the incident receding into memory but not entirely forgotten. She paid Max regular visits to check on his progress. His condition improved as his injuries mended, but he was still bedridden.

After another week, they completed the portal ready for testing, which she could conduct from the ship with a microwave link to the controls mounted on the portal itself. She brought up the control screen for it on her data tablet and gave the instructions for power to flow into it. The portal was in view on one of the ship's screens that she had directed the crew to display, so she could keep it in sight while she worked through the commissioning sequences. They magnified it to see the ring details. After a few minutes, lights started blinking on the portal, which made Hu smile with pleasure. Everything was progressing as expected. She turned on the controls to power up the reactor and placed it into idle once its startup had finished.

Ethan came over to the spare station where she sat. "How are things going? I can see lights flashing."

Hu faced him and smiled. "It's going well at present. I've just powered up the reactor and am ready to direct energy into the portal ring. I'm working through the checklist to confirm no red alarms are active."

"Mind if I stay and watch?"

"Be my guest."

Ethan grabbed the seat of an adjacent station and sat. He swiveled the chair so he could view the screen and what Hu was doing on her tablet.

"Here goes," Hu muttered. She punched in a command, and a ribbon of light started progressing around the portal as the reactor directed particles into the portal torus. Lights lit each segment until she had a dull ring of green light. "We have portal integrity," she said to Ethan.

"So, what's the plan?"

"I want to produce a small wormhole and send a message through to our base on the moon, telling them I am ready. I'll specify a time for them to start the portal on their end. Then, we'll energize both units and hopefully create a wormhole large enough for a shuttle."

"Hopefully ...?"

Hu laughed. "Well, we haven't tried from this distance before today."

She directed her attention back to the tablet and started ramping up the power. As she passed thirty percent, an explosion emanated from the portal, and the power cut off as part of the inbuilt trip sequence. Both Ethan and Hu jumped at the unexpected event.

"What was that?" Ethan asked.

"I don't know," Hu said, worried. She looked at her tablet and the monitoring readings for the portal. "Something blew on it, but I don't know what. It's strange. There must be a loose connection, or a part installed incorrectly. I'll need to have a look."

"Mind if I tag along with you?"

"Sure. I could use an extra set of hands."

Leaving the command center, they headed for the lander bay to claim a shuttle to transport them to the portal.

They approached the portal and stopped where the destruction was plain. A splintering mangle of metal broadcast the epicenter and power of the detonation. Hu's visage of worry reflected her mood as she examined the damage. "We won't know the full extent of the damage until we go out and examine it," she said the Ethan.

"Let's suit up and check it then," Ethan replied. He stood and strode from the shuttle's cockpit, heading for the spacesuit locker.

After dressing and exiting the hatch, they floated from the shuttle and toward the portal, the distorted remnants of the damaged segment in sight ahead of them. Approaching the framework with their jetpacks, they got a magnetic lock to the portal when they came within range and drew themselves closer until they touched it.

"A bit of a mess," Ethan said.

Hu jerked her head to see if he was serious or joking. He was serious. "Yes." She started sifting through the wreckage with her gloved hand, trying to find the source of the failure, if it still existed. A puzzled expression settled on her as she worked through the connections of the huge cabling exposed by the blast. Something was amiss. She frowned.

"Is everything okay?"

"I am not sure. These cables are wrong. Please pull away this flap of metal while I check the design on my tablet."

"Sure."

Hu removed her tablet from the pouch of her suit and brought that part of the portal design they were looking at onto the screen. She studied the schematics and their physical manifestation in front of her. She reached in and tried moving the cables with her free hand, Ethan pulling back the sheeting with all his strength while she did that. She noticed his strain and retracted her hand from harm. "You can let go."

"Thanks. I was thinking I needed to work out in the gym more. What have you found out?"

"That cable connection is loose. What worries me more is the connections are incorrect. I'd blame incompetence or complacency, but the connecting lugs are different sizes to prevent that error from occurring. The only explanation is that someone reamed out one hole so it would fit on the other lug." Hu looked at Ethan with a sense of déjà vu nauseating her as she remembered earlier experiences.

"Loki can't still be after us, can he? Anyway, he'd chase me, not you," Ethan commented, concern wrinkling his brow through his visor.

"How do you know he's not? He might want the portal to fail, so you can't return."

"He can't be that vindictive."

"Who knows? He has power and influence. I don't think so, either. This looks like a shortcut by someone too lazy to check the design drawings."

"You'd better chase up the technician and have him explain himself."

"I will but how do we prevent it in future?"

"We can't."

"I suppose not. What should we do?"

"We can only stay alert, and remove any incompetent worker from the job. Otherwise I'll start thinking I'm jinxed."

Hu smiled and chuckled at the comment. "You and me both. Let's get this fixed. It only looks like superficial damage to the outer skin. We may have to find ore on those planets and produce spare parts, though."

"OK. Let's do it."

24

TRIP TO CHIRON

While Hu continued building the portal, Marie, David, and Senna prepared for their excursion to skim the atmosphere of Chiron and conduct their measurements. Jade went along, too, since Hu didn't need her help. Ethan wanted someone there to make executive decisions, if they needed them, and he trusted Jade most to do that, even though he had confidence in Marie's competence, too. He knew Marie would defer to him if she was uncertain or the problem was outside her experience. They placed their equipment aboard the lander and were on their way.

The planet grew on the display as they flew closer. They discerned the unmistakable blue tinge mark of oxygen in the atmospheric halo surrounding the orb. Auroras displayed their characteristic patterns at the poles as the solar winds of Alpha Centauri A interacted with the magnetosphere. Swirls of water-bearing clouds mottled a surface of browns, greens, and whites. This excited Marie, as the green signified lifeforms on the world. The screen no longer contained the entire planet as they approached. They came into close planetary orbit at five hundred kilometers. Circumnavigating the globe, they made one revolution to familiarize themselves with it and decide where to release the probes.

Senna filmed the surface with the instrumentation she brought along to get multi-spectral images of the planet's exterior for her to analyze later. "There's a lot of water," she said.

"Yeah, makes it hard to pinpoint where to drop the probes if we want to collect them afterward," David replied.

"See that mountain range there? It is extensive. It suggests a massive fault line," Senna added, excited at the view.

Their vision obscured when they entered the night side of the planet. Senna had an infrared scanner set up so they could still view in that bandwidth and get the temperature differences between various surfaces, particularly between the uniform warmth of the water surface and the more variable temperature of the landmasses. They completed their circuit of the entire planet.

"So, David. Where do we drop the probes?" Marie asked.

"Give me a chance, will you? Senna, can you produce a chart of the globe from the orbital observations we just made?"

"Sure. Let me massage the data." Senna pulled out her tablet and loaded the footage she had taken onto it. She opened a clip and, within a few seconds, had a full map of the planet. "There," she said as she handed the tablet to David.

"That was quick." David took the tablet and studied it. He took several minutes to work out where he wanted the probes dropped. Senna showed him how to mark the locations on the map. "That should do it, for starters." He passed the tablet back to Senna. He had marked six sites in which to drop the probes.

"It's where you want them to land?"

"Of course," David replied.

Senna gave him an uneasy stare. "I'll go discuss this with the pilot and sort out the launch positions." She rose, heading for the cockpit.

"Why are you such a jerk?" Marie said to David.

"What did I do now?" The insinuation affronted him.

"Just then, 'Of course.' As if it was the dumbest question anyone could ever ask."

"Wasn't it obvious it was where I wanted them to land?" David retreated into silence, as if wondering what was wrong with everyone.

Half an hour later, Senna returned. "OK. We have the release points worked out. Let's prepare the gear."

They headed for the storage compartment to fit out the probes, get them online, and make them ready to slot into the drop tube. The tube had a double-hatch lock so that the outer hatch could not open when the inner hatch was ajar and vice versa. It meant that they did not need to don spacesuits to complete their tasks. David directed Marie to secure the microbiology instruments in a chamber of the probes. Senna and Jade helped move the equipment into position and loaded one into the tube, ready for launch.

Senna notified the pilot to let him know they were ready. "He will announce when we're over a launch zone on the comm."

Jade waited by the controls.

"Bombs away!" the pilot said, jauntily. Jade pressed the release button, and the probe jetted out of the lander. The outer hatch closed again.

"Next drop in thirty minutes," the pilot said.

They loaded the next probe into the chamber and waited.

They launched it at the right time, and then the others progressively. Overall, it took four hours before they had completed the task. David connected the radio links in the meantime and checked that he was collecting data as expected. The first probes had landed, nestling in the self-produced craters they had made when they crashed into the ground.

"That's a problem," David said as he studied the results on the screen.

"What is?" Jade asked.

"The atmosphere has only fifteen percent oxygen in it. That's lower than we need to survive unassisted."

"Oh. We still have to chart the planet and collect information about it. Who knows? We might terraform the atmosphere."

"Yeah. They could live under domes or in underground chambers until they can boost the oxygen to the needed concentration," Marie said.

"I wouldn't want to live that way," David said.

"I wouldn't either, but everyone isn't like us, and it depends on the incentive to do it."

"Everyone has their price, hey!"

"Something like that."

"So, what are you getting?" David asked Marie.

"Nothing yet. The units are just exiting the probes. They should come online soon. I didn't tell you, but one instrument is a camera, so we can view the ground."

"That'll be interesting," Jade said with a hint of excitement.

Senna's cameras had collected the images she needed, so she packed them away, commenting that she had a lifetime of data.

Jade stayed near Marie, eager to gain a view of the terrain. The view from the first camera flickering into life didn't disappoint her. "Wow! Look at that!" Jade pointed at the image on the tablet screen. "That's incredible. Can you get it on the cabin screen?"

"I'll try," Marie said. She transferred the video after a few minutes, adjusting settings on her tablet.

A very alien landscape appeared on the display in front of them. Giant green things one could only describe as blobs confronted them. Giant tumors of greenery that presented no uniform shape or form. Various sizes from just ten centimeters to over five meters covered the viewing area. Scattered nodules had a rainbow of colors on them, others dappled or striped. They looked spongy in texture and composition.

"That's amazing!" Senna exclaimed.

"It sure is," Jade agreed.

"Fascinating," David said.

"I wonder what they're made of?" Marie queried with professional curiosity. "They look like a fungus, but could they be colony structures, like sea coral on Earth?"

"We could throw you down to find out," David suggested.

"You'd like that," Marie riposted.

"Any other sites transmitting?" Jade asked to change the topic and the deteriorating atmosphere.

Marie looked back at her tablet. "Yes. Here is another one —

more or less the same." She diverted the image to the cabin screen for the others to see but kept a frame of the original image in one corner. They saw very similar structures but different. The earlier ones looked like they grew in a tropical region, but the ones they now viewed were more compact and ragged, as if struggling in a hostile, colder and tempestuous clime. The blemishes on them were darker and more sinister looking. "I haven't seen animated movement anywhere."

"Maybe they're hiding," Jade suggested.

"Insects and other bugs are rarely shy. I'm sure Zane will have a field day with these images. He'll be itching to gain samples to dissect."

"Are the transmitters on the probes strong enough to send data to the ship at its current location?" Jade asked.

"Yes," David replied. "We don't need to stay here forever collecting data. The probes will store what they can't send. We can upload again when they return to the ship's view."

"What about you, Marie?"

"My data goes through the probe, so the probe will store it along with David's."

"There's no need to stay then. Let's go back to the ship — unless anyone objects?"

The rest agreed to return. Jade informed the pilot, and they were on their way.

25

CHARICLO

E than organized a meeting the following day to discuss progress and their next moves. The images of the biological matter filled Zane with excitement. He wanted an immediate return to the planet to gather samples. But Ethan doused any thought of descending to the surface without further analysis of the information David and Marie had collected. The discussion continued until they decided they should fly to Chariclo and replicate their survey there. Zane volunteered to join the crew to gaze upon the vista first-hand. No one had any objection to that.

The lander, loaded with Senna, David, Marie, Zane, and Jade, streaked toward the inner of the two planets, Chariclo. Being further away from them than Chiron, it would take much longer to reach its orbital destination, making their trip at least two days, possibly three. So, they took extra provisions.

Fourteen hours later, the planet started increasing in size as they approached. The telltale color of oxygen tinged the hazy edge of the orb, where the atmosphere gave way to the void of space. The familiar signs of water, vegetation, and a magnetosphere were distinct, too. Those in the cabin became agitated as they braced for their arrival, eager to discover what lay below them. As they positioned in orbit, Senna conducted her scans and produced a map of the world.

"A more complex geology here," Senna said. "More landmass. Here, David, you can mark the drop locations on the map." She gave her tablet to him. "The surface gravity is good too: one point one to two g."

"What was it on Chiron?" Jade asked.

"Less than Earth's: point eight-three g."

"Still suitable. If only the oxygen level were higher. Let's measure this planet's atmosphere."

David determined the intended drop locations and marked the sites on the tablet, which Senna took to the pilot to confirm the launch positions. He had nominated six. Once set, they dropped the probes. David started receiving data from the first probe as it entered the upper atmosphere. He tensed as the probe plummeted lower, beaming a smile when it broke into the lower atmosphere.

"What is it, David?" Zane asked.

David looked away from his display. "The oxygen level is twenty-one-point six percent, higher than Earth's, but should be perfect for us to breathe. That means this planet is potentially habitable."

Zane came over to view the screen, excited over the biological possibilities. "When can we see the ground?"

"Keep your pants on," David said. "The probe has to land first."

Zane's body language immediately registered withdrawal, and, for once, David realized the effect of his words. He usually thought the person could take it or lump it, whatever manner he portrayed. "I'm sorry," he said, repenting. "It came out wrong. I didn't mean it like it might have sounded. I meant we won't get any visual until the probe lands and Marie's analyzer equipment unloads and starts operating."

"OK then. Well, I'll hang around if it won't be long," Zane said, slightly appeased.

"Another ten minutes. You don't have anywhere else to go."

"Good point." Zane sat and waited. The probe landed without incident, and Marie started up the buggy with the test gear on it, including the video feed. Zane stood and paced as he waited for a first glimpse of this new cornucopia of potential biology. Marie placed the visual feed up on the cabin screen for everyone to see.

"What's wrong? Why is there only static?" Zane asked, as a snow-flecked display appeared.

"I haven't turned it on yet." Marie glanced at him with a mischievous smirk.

"Oh. Sorry. Maybe I'm too eager."

"It's fine. Everyone wants to get started," Jade said.

Moments later, Marie pressed a few buttons, and the first sight of Chariclo ever seen by humans appeared on the screen. The cabin went quiet as the team soaked in the vista the ground camera transmitted to them. The probe had landed in the middle of a typical earth jungle environment, but it could be anything on Chariclo since they were ignorant of the planet's ecosystem.

"What on earth is that?" Jade asked.

"Extraordinary." Zane's eyes drilled into the display to interpret the sight. Vegetation greeted them but like none they had ever seen. There were tall tree structures with purple-colored trunks and green foliage, but instead of smooth straight components, they comprised ovoid shapes. These elliptical structures were glued together end to end to form long trunks, and branches and twigs, one bifurcating into two independent new offshoots at random locations, continued the ovoid progression. "The evolutionary development here has used the egg shape as a basic building block — the vegetation form of life, at least. See, it's plain in the trees and the smaller varieties that resemble grass. Look." Zane pointed to one spot on the screen. "That resembles a flower, but it's composed of the oval architecture. I wonder how they grow. We have to go there."

"Whoa, hold on a minute!" Jade cautioned. "I know we're excited and intent on exploring, but we aren't going anywhere today. Not until we have a full understanding of the planet's meteorology, geology, and especially microbiology. So be patient. View from a distance for now."

"But we must collect samples and analyze this."

"And we will. But in due time and with attention to proper procedure."

Zane pouted his lips in disappointment. "You're the boss."

Jade laughed. "And don't you forget it." The others chuckled at Zane's expense.

After three hours, the rest of the probes landed, with the sampling and testing systems feeding information to the lander.

Zane jumped with excitement. "Look! Look!" He pointed to the screen. "An animal, insect, whatever."

The group turned to see the source of Zane's agitation. A creature moved in one corner, three centimeters long. It was red and had the same oval segmented architecture as the plant matter. One part, identified as the body, had rotund components; the parts that allowed locomotion were more elongated, with one ovoid serving as one limb section, three per limb, and six limbs altogether acting as legs. They must have had structural integrity to support the torso as it moved. The pseudo-ant, as that was what it looked like without the feelers and nippers, noticed the alien device filming it and started moving toward it. Two small ovals, spheres resembling eyes, protruded from the front. It seemed to sense that the camera had a special significance because it headed straight for it, becoming gigantic as it neared the lens before it disappeared underneath it. Moments later, a monster mounted the screen; the ant had climbed the vehicle and was now investigating the mysterious glass to determine its composition. The camera struggled to stay in focus with the object so near it. It mesmerized Zane. He had his tablet out, making copious notes on the experience. The ant, suddenly losing interest, left the lens for other climes. They didn't see it again.

They spotted no other animated life, but Zane overflowed with enthusiasm, confident of discovering more.

Zane giggled.

"What's so amusing?" David asked.

"I devised a designation for the plant and animal group of species on the planet, but it's a bit vain."

"Well ...?"

"Zaniology," he murmured and blushed.

"You're darn right — it's too vain."

"I don't know. It has a certain ring to it," Senna said.

"OK. My systems are functioning," Marie interrupted.

"Are we ready to go back?" Jade asked the team.

"Why can't we descend for a peek?" David asked.

Jade folded her arms in defiance. "Because it's not on the schedule, for starters."

"But we didn't know what we'd find when we put that together."

"Yeah, and a sample of plant matter would be valuable to dissect," Zane pleaded.

Jade looked around the cabin. She started wavering, even though she knew she mustn't. Marie saved her.

"We know nothing about the planet yet. We don't know what microorganisms exist there and how they might affect us. I want to explore like the rest of you. But I won't risk our wellbeing for it, so you shouldn't ask Jade to do it, either."

The others grumbled under their breath.

Jade's shoulders slumped as the tension escaped her. "Thanks, Marie. At least someone knows not to scamper off like a toddler."

The remark brought a grin to their faces as they reflected on their behavior.

"OK. You win," Zane said, imitating a childish voice. "You never let us play. It's not fair."

The comment made everyone smirk as Jade informed the pilot to return to the ship.

26

RELOCATION

The atmosphere on board *Destiny* sparked with electricity as the news of breathable air and animal life on Chariclo circulated. Ethan called a meeting the morning after the lander crew returned to the ship. They sat in the conference room waiting for the proceedings to start, everybody discussing the implications of the discovery. Zane threw his arms every which way as he described what the biology of the planet might mean, almost hitting people next to him when he became very excited.

Ethan finished his personal discussion with Hu. "OK, everyone. Let's quieten and get the meeting started."

The others pulled their attention away from each other and refocused on Ethan. Zane was the last.

"Hmm ... hmm, Zane, please."

Zane turned. "Sorry, boss. I'm listening," he said as he folded his hands in front of him to stop them from flapping.

"Fine. So, we have several topics to discuss. First. Safety. Everyone has heard of Max's unfortunate accident by now. It highlights that we need to keep our wits about us. His mishap happened while constructing the portal, but our activities in the coming weeks will include associated risks. Hugo and I thought we had covered the potential hazards, but we hadn't."

"Hu should have used more care," David said.

Hu felt rage build in her at the insensitive and arrogant comment — and one that she feared was true.

Ethan shot daggers at David with his eyes. "Enough, David! When you shoulder as much responsibility as Hugo has and show a better safety record than her, you can offer constructive advice. In the meantime, I suggest you keep your comments to yourself."

David was visibly shocked at the rebuke. "Sorry. It just came out. It won't happen again."

"No. It won't. As I was saying," Ethan continued in a calmer and more business-like tone, "we need to keep our wits about us. We will enter a phase soon where we meet unknown dangers and may be tempted to improvise. I urge you to avoid that. Stop and assess the condition first at every opportunity. It's far better to lose a few minutes identifying the risks and taking measures against them than plunging into uncharted waters."

The group nodded at the wisdom of the advice. Hu, her composure recovered, smiled at Ethan in appreciation of his support.

"So, as I understand it, we have two planets, Chiron and Chariclo, that have had a preliminary exploration from orbit, and we're still receiving data from the dispatched probes, both meteorological and biological. We also have preliminary geological information on the general tectonic and mineral distribution of the worlds. Correct?"

David, Marie, and Senna nodded in affirmation.

"Senna, please give your report first."

Senna gathered her thoughts. "Chiron has simple geology as if it has existed longer than Chariclo and has settled itself into a rhythm. There is evidence of tectonic movement with interesting mountainous regions. No current volcanic life is visible. The planet is eighty-seven percent covered with water, so it has less land to explore and catalog. Given that, it still has an extensive surface to investigate. The gravity is point eight-three g, a comfortable force for exercise. That's it for Chiron.

"Chariclo is very different. There is much more tectonic action and significant volcanic eruptions along presumed fault lines between plates at present. The planet is sixty percent covered with water and has interesting mineral formations that call for further exploration. The gravity is one point one-two g, again a comfortable weight to endure. That's it for now."

"Any questions?" Ethan asked.

"Have you seen any potential deposits for steel-making materials?" Hu asked.

"It's too early to know what minerals exist, but several spots suggest high iron and other alloying ores on Chariclo. Chiron is more problematic at present and needs more study."

"Any reason for the question?" Ethan asked Hu.

"I may need to make parts for the repair. I've brought a printer with me, so I could produce them if we collect the raw materials."

"OK. Anyone else? David, you want to go next?"

"Sure," he said, preening himself for his moment in the spotlight. "First Chiron. It has fifteen percent oxygen, so it's not breathable without a supplementary supply or artificial oxygen boosting. No other poisonous elements in the atmosphere that I have detected. The planetary climate is placid. There are ice-covered regions at both poles, but none anywhere else except at very high altitudes. Temperatures range from ten below freezing up to forty Celsius in the areas the probes fell, and although tropical zones exist, most of the planet is temperate. Wind speeds are moderate. There has been no cyclonic weather. It is a boring world, meteorologically.

"Chariclo is different. It has twenty-one-point six percent oxygen, just right for us. Again, with no poisonous components. The climate is diverse. Ice fields at the poles and major glaciation in various other regions in elevated areas. There is an obvious tropical band around the equator, progressing through temperate climates to polar zones. Deserts exist. Temperatures range from minus sixty to plus fifty. There is evidence of extensive cyclonic weather in the tropics during the summer season. In summary, not too dissimilar to Earth."

"Thanks, David. Questions?"

Silence persisted before Zane asked, "This may be more in Celeste's field. What tidal movement exists? Are there any moons?"

David looked annoyed but remained civil. "You're right. That is more Celeste's specialty. I can't tell from the data I'm collecting."

Celeste responded. "I briefed the lander pilot on the moons for astrogation, but I didn't inform any of you yet. Sorry. Chiron has three small moons that circle the planet in close and rapid orbit. They project little tidal effect unless they line up, which only occurs every twenty days.

"Chariclo has two moons. One is half the size of Earth's moon, and the other is two-thirds the size. Again, they fight each other, but they produce decent tides when in alignment and opposition. That may be part of the explanation for the diverse ecosystem we see, but I am stealing Marie's thunder. I assume that was why you asked, Zane."

"Yes, it was, and thanks."

"Anyone else ...? Marie, you're next."

"OK. Let's see. I've detected no pathogens on either world yet. That doesn't mean they don't exist, just that I've identified none. The biological matter of Chiron is simple and undeveloped. Wouldn't you agree, Zane?" Zane nodded. "Sort of contradicts Senna's comments about the planet being old and stable. Maybe the primeval environment was too hostile for organic development. Amorphous tumor-like material exists that grows to various sizes, although they display different patterning. That could show distinct species. I have little else to say about Chiron.

"Chariclo is much more biologically interesting. I've detected no pathogens either, though. Zane should summarize the rest for us. He is the biologist."

Zane was paying scant attention but perked up when he heard his name. "Oh ... um ... OK. Chariclo has a diverse ecology. The weird observation is that everything comprises ovoid units of various eccentricities, depending on the role performed. We have detected flora and fauna, very exciting. I can't wait to go there and explore the physiology further. The plant matter has only slight eccentricity. The animal species viewed so far show low eccentricity for what appear to be body parts and high eccentricity for limbs. One can only conjecture how they connect, but we could imagine a loose cartilage and tendon arrangement–"

"Let's not delve into detail, Zane," Ethan interrupted, redirecting him back on topic. "Anything else you can tell us?"

"Oh ... Well ... no."

"OK. Questions for Zane or Marie?"

"Marie, is there any sign of the biology's organic architecture? Do proteins, enzymes, etcetera exist like ours, or can't you say yet?" Jade asked.

"The equipment I am using doesn't analyze in that detail. But it's an important question to answer. It'll tell us how we will live in that ecosystem unprotected or, more important, if we can safely live there. It will also clarify whether we can use the plants and animals as a food source."

"Thanks, Marie," Jade said.

No one else had a question.

"OK then. Let's see if I can summarize our position," Ethan said. "Chiron is tame but unlivable without supplementary oxygen. Chariclo is geologically dynamic and has a breathable atmosphere and a diverse ecosystem. How is that?"

"Sounds good in a nutshell," Jade said.

"So, where do we go from here?"

Zane raised his hand. Ethan gestured for him to speak. "We need to explore Chariclo in more detail, including descending to the planet's surface to continue our work. But we are too distant from Chariclo at present to do an efficient job. We should move closer."

The others, except Ethan, Jade, and Hu, nodded.

"That sounds great. But the portal is here," Ethan highlighted.

Hu sat in contemplation before saying, "The portal is solid. It incurred damage, but that isn't structural. We could use magnetic clamps to secure it to *Destiny*, like you did Loki's ship, and drag it with us to Chariclo, if that's what the expedition needs."

Ethan considered the proposal. The portal was larger than *Destiny* in the cross-section. But they'd exert minor acceleration stress, as the trip was short, and he needn't hurry. Excited, pleading faces gazed at him. "Are you sure, Hugo?"

"Yes, it'll be helpful for me. Senna can locate the ore deposits I need to produce the damaged parts I can't replace. They would be quicker and easier to locate on Chariclo than Chiron."

"OK. That's a plan." An instant murmur of excitement circulated the table. "But we won't be descending to the planet at once." The murmurs turned to disappointment. "David, Senna, Zane, and Marie need to complete their assessments and modeling before we do, and when we do, it will be in full environmental suits until Marie confirms our safety without them."

The team grumbled their reluctant agreement.

"Is there anything else ...? I just have one more thing on my agenda. Hugo, when can you power up the portal again?"

"It depends on how long it takes to locate the materials for the parts. But if we can find them quickly, a week, no longer."

"Good. I'd prefer an open emergency path back to Earth before we progress too far — in case we need it."

"So, you needed me along," Hu joked.

"I'll admit it was on my mind when you requested it," Ethan said with a grin. "Anything else?" There was silence. "I'll get started on relocating the ship. Hugo can help clamp the portal, and we will be on our way. Let's get to it."

They vacated the conference room and went their ways.

Ethan and Hu needed a day to clamp the portal onto the ship. Ethan then started the EM drive and sped up at point five g, moving to a similar orbital position around Chariclo, Hu having relented on the separation distance. She suggested one hundred and fifty-thousand kilometers instead of the prior two hundred and fifty thousand. The trip took another day to complete.

27

DOWN TO THE SURFACE

Another week elapsed before the remote studies on the planet were completed to Ethan's satisfaction. More disgruntled mumblings of disappointment echoed through the ship when Ethan insisted on further work before he would consent to a trip to the surface.

Ethan finally signed off on a preliminary expedition once the study team provided him with their clearance. He nominated himself to lead it. Marie, Zane, David, and Senna would go with him.

"I don't want you to go," Jade protested when they were alone.

"I'll be fine. Why do you think I've delayed it this long? I wanted to be sure it was safe with full environmental suits," Ethan said, trying to placate her concern.

"What if the suit tears?"

"You know that's unlikely."

"I suppose," Jade said, still determined to coddle him. "I just dread something happening to you."

Ethan pulled Jade close and hugged her, rocking from side to side as he did so. He kissed her on the forehead. "And I want you safe, but we need to do our jobs. If I didn't go, I'd have to send you, and I'm not doing that."

"Humph! It's fine for me to worry, but not you!"

"Sort of like that."

Jade stayed grumpy for a while, but then surrendered to Ethan's warmth as he hugged her. She snuggled up to him. "OK then. But I insist you make up for it."

Ethan laughed.

"What's so funny?"

"We're acting like a married couple ..." Jade pulled away and looked at Ethan. Ethan reddened but continued, "Oh hell! I love you, Jade, and you know that."

Jade blushed with joy and hugged him hard. "Yes, I do, and I love you too."

They pulled apart and joined lips in a passionate kiss.

"I'd better go," Ethan said, gasping for breath.

Jade stepped away and pretended to adjust her clothing. "I suppose you should."

They stared at each other and started laughing.

"We make a great couple," Ethan said.

"We do. Now move and good luck and stay safe. I will have something waiting for you when you return," Jade said and pulled back as Ethan tried to advance. "I said when you return."

Ethan pouted in disappointment. "OK then. Keep the ship in one piece," he said, still trying to move closer to her again.

"Oi! Get going before I change my mind."

"I'm going ... I'm going," Ethan said as he started walking out of Jade's quarters. Jade watched him, concerned love in her eyes, as he disappeared.

Ethan walked to the lander bay, where the others were waiting impatiently for him at the vessel they were to use.

"About time," David said with a knowing smirk.

"Patience." Ethan gestured the others to board. "Let's get this show moving."

They entered the cabin, Ethan going up front with the pilot. The rest found seats and strapped themselves into them.

"We're set, Jim?" Ethan asked.

"Yeah. Ready to go when you are."

"Let's do it then. You can fly it. I'll watch and let you know where to land."

"Roger." Jim busied himself at the controls. The cabin door closed, and green lights blinked on as the cabin sealed, signaling they were ready for departure. Moments later, the lander emerged from *Destiny*'s belly on a gentle descent to the surface. Ethan pointed out the landing site the team had decided on, and the pilot aimed for it as they came closer to ground level. They landed on the planet thirty-five minutes after they left *Destiny*, the first humans to land on a planet outside the solar system. They settled in a clearing large enough for the ship's footprint. The spot abutted a watercourse, and they could investigate the territory without having to negotiate difficult terrain or vegetation.

Ethan unbuckled and joined the rest, who were busy putting on their environmental suits. They lined up at the airlock hatch after they suited up and checked their seals. The airlock stood separate from the normal hatch, allowing a quarantined entry and exit from the lander to prevent contamination. Only two could use its chamber simultaneously. Ethan used seniority to be one of the first. He chose Marie to go with him, as she could spot any danger once the outer hatch door opened. They carried various tools and instruments on them, as did the others, for their exploration.

"Ready?" Ethan asked Marie.

"You bet!"

"Let's go then."

They entered the airlock and closed the inner door. The chamber isolated itself from the inner cabin and equalized pressure with the outer atmosphere. Ethan pressed the button to open the outer door. The door slid aside to a vista of unearthly green, as a vast field of short grass met their gaze. Ethan glanced at Marie. Her eyes were wide with amazement. The scenery impressed him too. She froze into a statue with the incomprehension of their achievement.

"Impressive, heh?" Ethan said, to break the spell.

"Incredible."

"Can you two step aside?" Ethan and Marie heard from their earpieces.

They both laughed. "Be patient. It's not going away," Ethan said as he started walking out. He lowered a short staircase to the ground and descended it, stepping onto Chariclo, the first human to step on a planet circling a star other than the sun. "I should say something momentous now, but words fail me."

Marie followed, closing the outer hatch as she did so. She kneeled when she stood on the ground to study the plants they trampled. They had the same ovoid arrangement observed from the probe cameras. She gazed at them, fascinated. When she heard the outer hatch opening, she turned and saw Zane emerge, stepping to the stairs before the hatch slid back. She smiled through her visor at him. "This is incredible."

Ethan turned. Senna was with Zane. *I wonder why David is last.* He had expected someone so cocky to be jostling for first position. Ethan moved further away from the lander and toward the water-course nearby. He reached a red sandy beach extending off the concave side of a sweeping bend. There were a few pebbles scattered in the sand. When he arrived at the water's edge, he bent to peer into the stream. It was crystal clear where he stood and reflected the distant scenery. He sighed in peace, contented as he watched the flowing water.

Movement out of the corner of his eye, one meter away to his right in the water, caught his attention. It was purplish-red and had the same ovoid architecture. Four extensions of the body, used as legs, provided locomotion to the lifeform, whatever it was. It had a streamlined body, making it adapted to rapid motion in water. It was eight centimeters long and four wide. Eyes at its front watched as it crept toward him, drawn with an inquisitive interest in the unfamiliar creature it saw. When it was fifty centimeters from Ethan, it stopped. Ethan wasn't sure whether the animal was aquatic or amphibian. He couldn't tell from its shape or behavior. It possessed nothing that looked like gills, either. It seemed to search for danger elsewhere for a moment. Once it reaffirmed its safety, it advanced on

Ethan again. Its back broke the water's surface, eyes still searching furiously. Ethan extended his hand to touch it, but the creature retreated to a safe distance. It didn't hide, though. It just waited, taking stock.

Marie came over and stopped beside Ethan. "What are you doing?" she asked.

"Look." Ethan pointed to the creature. "It approached me when I stood still but scampered away the moment I moved."

"That's interesting."

"Look. It's coming again."

They both watched as the creature crept closer. Ethan didn't reach out to it, and it emerged from the water and stopped. It observed them, swapping its attention from Ethan to Marie and back again, seemingly wondering what these unworldly creatures were that had encroached on its territory.

"Well, I suppose I should do something else," Ethan said. The creature darted back into the water when he spoke.

"It's sensitive to noise," Marie pointed out.

"Yes."

They both returned to the ship. The others were pulling equipment from external access lockers on the lander.

"There's a marine creature in the water by the bend. Fascinating to watch," Ethan told them.

"Where?" Zane asked, his ears pricking up at the discovery.

"Over there," Marie said as she pointed out the direction to him.

Zane finished setting up a table and rushed to investigate it himself.

"Like a kid in a toy shop," David commented drily. The comment had derogatory overtones, and Ethan felt it reflected David's envy at Zane's uninhibited enthusiasm.

A forest dominated the landscape away from the stream fifty meters from the ship. Ethan wandered over to the verge to peer into the gloom of its depths as it became dense within ten meters of the edge. He walked along the border of the woods for one hundred meters. The trees were the same species, constructed from the same ovoid building blocks. He heard rustling noises somewhere further in but didn't go to explore on his own. He returned to the lander.

After returning from the stream, he found Zane had set up his instruments, one being a microscope. He had cut samples of grass and other nearby plants to study their details. Marie was helping him and setting up her own sampling machines. She collected water from the stream to investigate any microbiological life in it. David was establishing a meteorological station. Senna looked lost for something to do. Ethan supposed the geology of the immediate vicinity lacked any excitement for her. He headed to the lander and opened a security-coded compartment, pulling two pulse pistols from it. "Senna," he called out.

"Yeah?"

"Come over here."

Senna walked over, a curious expression on her face. She stopped in front of Ethan and looked at the pistols. She raised her brow. "What's with them?"

"Protection. Remember how to use it from training?"

"Yeah."

Ethan handed her one with a holster, and they placed them around their waists.

"Want to go hiking? Find something more interesting for you?"

Senna's eye lit up with interest. "Sure."

Ethan called out to the others. "Senna and I are going walking. We'll stay within communication distance. Anything you want us to check out?"

Zane looked up from viewing his microscope. "Wait." He strode to the equipment he had unloaded and rummaged through it, picking out a shoulder bag, and brought it over to them. "Here, take this. It has sample containers in it. Put anything that looks interesting into them and bring them back."

Ethan took the bag, pulling the strap around his neck.

Marie approached them, too. "Take these. They're swab sheets. You just wipe the sheet over goo and put it in one of Zane's bottles." She returned the swabs to the bag.

"OK. Anything else?" Ethan asked.

They shook their heads, as did David.

"See you in an hour."

They started walking toward the stream, following it to its source. The forest approached the stream as they ventured away from the lander until the path pushed them onto the water's edge. They wove in amongst the trees as they walked after that. Ethan noted the landscape rise to a ridgeline before they left, so he and Senna headed that way. "How are you enjoying the expedition?"

Senna stared at Ethan, surprised by the question. "Could've done without the lengthy trip, but this experience is exhilarating. I'm seeing things no one else has seen and gazing at the geology of a planet in an alien star system. How will it compare with Earth? Will it be similar or different? How do the tectonic plates move? Do different minerals exist here than those on Earth?"

"Too many questions," Ethan broke into her soliloquy.

Senna laughed, which made Ethan laugh too.

"Well, don't you get that sense of wonder and awe, too?"

"That's another question. But yes, I do. My realm is gadgets and drives and ships, but I can appreciate your enthusiasm for exploring the unknown. That's why I wanted to lead this expedition. I've always dreamed of reaching for the stars one day, and here I am. Talking of minerals, don't forget to keep an eye out for what Hu needs."

"I am, but we won't see much here. We need to visit a more geologically active location."

"OK."

"What happens after this?"

"What do you mean?"

"Once we have explored this star and returned to Earth."

"I don't know. I suspect we'll schedule more trips back here. We can't learn everything in the time that we intend being here. People might build a colony here if it proves practical. Apart from that, no one's told me. I doubt they've given it much thought. Explore other stars."

"I want to do that." Senna's eyes glistened.

"What about drilling into fault lines?"

"Boring — forgive the pun."

They both laughed.

"Yeah, I can't imagine going back to the work I was doing either," Ethan conceded.

They reached the top of the ridge. They didn't realize it while they were talking, but the stream had veered into a ravine while they were climbing the cliff next to it. They could see the lander below when they turned toward it, having walked three kilometers. As they gazed back over the apex, they viewed densely forested undulating hills extending far away before higher-reaching mountains towered in the distance.

"The vegetation here's not much different than where we landed," Ethan remarked.

"No. Let's enter the forest and search for specimens of interest growing in the underbrush. Seen nothing that looks like animals."

"No, we haven't," Ethan agreed, and they walked into the forest nearby. It became harder to negotiate a path as they ventured deeper.

"Wait," Senna said. "Look!" She pointed to a mushroom-fashioned plant comprising the same ovoid-shaped components. Several of them grew there, so Ethan got a sample bottle from the bag and pulled one from the ground. He looked at the root ball before he put it in the container. The roots comprised the same elliptic shapes but had elongated and bifurcated connections at the junctures. He placed some of the soil it was growing in into the bottle, too, for Marie to study.

They walked another ten meters and halted. A trail bisected their current direction. It was a meter wide and wound into the distance in both directions. Ethan got his pistol out and ready, just in case. He kneeled and studied the track for footprints. A multitude of elliptical prints in a trident shape covered it; each oval was broad at one end, narrowing to a point like a flower petal at the other. The narrow ends joined into a circular focal segment. They were fifteen centimeters long and ten wide. Ethan filmed video footage to take back to Zane. "I wonder what makes those?" Ethan asked no one in particular.

"I don't know," Senna replied. "By the looks of the path, it's in regular use." She looked both ways again to check they were alone. "Shh, I hear something coming."

They both stepped back into the tree line to camouflage themselves from whatever it was that was approaching. After twenty seconds, Ethan could hear the rumble too. It was getting closer and sounded heavy as they heard a thud, thud, thud of movement. They stood as still as statues while the sound grew louder. It was thunderous when they saw the beast. It plodded along the path, eight legs carrying its three-meter-long girth. The body distorted where the legs joined it, as if muscles rocked the limbs to produce the locomotion. Ethan estimated it must have weighed over three hundred kilograms. It had a head of the same ovoid shape as everything else on the planet, with several appendages, elliptical of various eccentricities.

The creature stopped right where they stood, as if it sensed a strange presence. It was just two meters from them. Ethan's hand tightened on the grip of his pistol. The creature moved its massive head toward them, looked directly at them, and shook its head as though trying to decipher what it saw. Once it perceived no danger, it turned its head straight again and started its thundering plod, growing smaller as the distance from them lengthened.

Ethan turned to Senna in time for him to see her gulp in relief. He relaxed his grip and put the pistol away. "I'd follow it, but we need to return," he said.

"Look," Senna said as she pointed to where the creature had stood. A gooey mess remained from it. "It left a present."

"We might be glad we're wearing our suits. I'm not sure I want to smell it. We had better collect a sample. It'll be invaluable for both Zane and Marie." Ethan retrieved a container and used a swab sheet to scoop up an excrement fragment, carefully placing it in the bottle. He replaced the lid and bagged the sample.

They returned to the cliff and retraced their steps to the lander. The others glanced up when they approached.

"How did you go?" Marie asked.

"We saw an enormous monster," Senna said, eyes bulging in the excited delight of a storyteller. "It was at least three meters long, and it looked at us."

"And you're still here?" David asked.

"It wasn't interested in us," Ethan said. "And we got an excrement sample from it for Zane to examine."

"Where?" Zane asked, eager to study it.

Ethan took the bag from around his neck and removed the specimen bottles they had filled. "This one," he said as he stretched his hand to give the container to Zane.

Zane grabbed the specimen and looked at it. "Amazing. You might find bugs in it too, Marie. Get an insight into its digestive process."

"Maybe," Marie said as she studied the sample. She selected the other containers one at a time, scanning what Ethan and Senna had collected.

"What's been happening here?" Ethan asked.

"We've been studying the organic makeup to decide whether the proteins and amino acids are like that of Earth. So far, the proteins are different. That's good as we can't assimilate them, nor they us. Although it also means we can't use them as a food source without processing. We haven't investigated their cellular structure yet, and we still need to produce a genome map, assuming they have the same DNA sequencing we have, which they may not have."

They kept working the rest of the day and returned to the lander as dusk advanced. Once they decontaminated in the airlock, they removed their suits, gaining access to the interior cabin at last, which allowed them normal movement again. The lander flew back to *Destiny*.

Various parties continued commuting to the surface for a week.

28

MINING RIGHTS

S enna spent most of her time during the week studying the planet surface for potential mineral deposits. She located two promising sites with a high probability of finding the minerals Hu wanted. She discussed the possibilities with Hu and Ethan, and they organized a separate expedition to investigate. David tagged along, as he needed to collect more data on the climate in other locations on the globe for his modeling.

They descended to the planet using a second lander. Senna gazed out of the window as they approached the ground. They headed for a rocky outcrop in a mountainous region on a different continent to their exploration location. It extended across the landmass, gently ascending to a ridgeline before ending as an escarpment. Anticipating new discoveries always exhilarated her — especially now, knowing no one had set eyes on these geological structures before her. The lander settled on a flat spot on one edge of the site. They suited up and exited.

Senna removed her sampling equipment and analysis instruments from the external locker of the lander and started walking over the landscape. She noted David had left to do his own thing, which was fine with her. He had his own objectives. "Keep within communication distance," she called to him.

"I sure will," he called back. Senna thought he was scanning his surroundings rather nervously for someone usually so sure of himself.

Hu followed Senna. "What are we looking for here?"

"The information I collected and analyzed suggests iron ore deposits. That was one item on your shopping list. There should be outcrops on the surface." Senna searched the ground for signs as she walked across the crumbly rock. They both had to watch their step as they went. Rocks and pebbles dislodged from the pressure of their feet. They cleared a slight ridge to give them a view of the other side. "There. That's what we want." Senna pointed to a rocky outbreak, a dark brown to black color. Fault lines ran through it like planks of lumber stacked on top of each other. "Hematite, I hope."

They walked over to it. The boulder was one enormous mass, so Senna used a small pick to hammer a sample of stone from the bulk of the material. She placed the lump in the analyzer and pressed the test button. "If my suspicions are correct, you'll have the iron you need," she said as they waited for the results.

"Good."

"How will you refine the ore?"

"I have machinery to extract the metals and other elements and combine them into the parts I want in a 3-D printer."

"Oh. I've seen nothing like that. I'd be interested in watching when you do it."

Hu nodded. "My pleasure."

The analyzer sounded, and Senna looked at the screen for the results. "Sixty-seven percent iron. Perfect. You have your iron source. By the looks of it, there's a large deposit here. We should lay claim to it," she joked.

"Find me gold, and I'll claim that."

"I won't tell you it's gold until it's too late."

They laughed.

"Help!" Senna and Hu heard over their comms, as David called out to them in obvious distress.

His panic alerted them to full awareness of their surroundings. They scanned for him but couldn't spot him anywhere. "Where are you?" Hu asked as they both dashed to the lander, slipping on the loose terrain.

"I'm north of the ship. Hurry."

"What's wrong?"

"I'm trapped."

Hu and Senna returned to the ship in five minutes and then headed north. They reached a ridge and gazed below to see David pinned by an animated lifeform, its foot on his chest and two extensile eyes examining him curiously. The animal itself must have weighed two hundred kilograms. They stopped short on seeing the creature and smirked as they took in the scene's visual comedy, even though David's predicament wasn't funny, given they didn't know the creature's intentions.

David looked up at them in obvious distress. "Why are you waiting? Get this thing off me!"

Senna and Hu drew their pistols from their holsters — a stipulation for crew to carry when remote from the landers — and crept forward and downhill to where David was. He seemed too panicked to have considered using his own. The creature sensed their presence, whether by vibration, noise, or sight, Senna couldn't tell, and it removed its foot as it moved to study the new intruders. The terrain's color camouflaged it. It glanced back at David and toward Senna and Hu before moving away, sensing they outnumbered it, and the wise strategy was to retreat.

David stood up when he felt safe as the creature lumbered off, and he started walking toward Senna. "You can get those smiles off your faces now," he said, sulking.

"Yes, it's not funny. I would have panicked too if I were in your position," Hu said.

"How on earth did it sneak up on you?" Senna asked.

"It didn't sneak up on me. You saw how it camouflages itself. It was standing here staring at me. When I came close enough, it bowled me over and stood on me. That's when I called for help. I don't know what it was doing. It was curious about me but not interested in eating me. Thank God."

"Did you get any video?" Hu asked.

David looked at her in disbelief. "You're joking! The thing was going to crush me."

Hu gave a mocking smile. "Didn't look like it wanted to hurt you."

David brushed himself off indignantly. "You could be more supportive and concerned."

"We came to your aid."

"Humph. Where did it go?"

"I don't know. It's too camouflaged."

"I hope I don't bump into another one. That was freaky. It was just eyeing me. I couldn't see any mouth or nose, so it's a mystery how it eats or breathes. Spheres protruded from its head. They could be ears."

"Yeah, well. No harm done. Can we leave you alone?"

David became angry. "Of course you can. Stop belittling me."

Hu snickered, enjoying David's embarrassment too much. "If you say so."

Senna knew Hu still didn't much like David, not after the bar incident when she first boarded *Destiny*, and despite his subsequent apology, but it was the first time Senna had seen Hu's nasty streak. She conveyed it in jest. Still ...

"Let's finish what we were doing," Senna said.

Senna and Hu walked back to the ore body.

"You weren't being fair to David," Senna ventured.

"You think? Maybe I wasn't. I can turn on people I dislike, and I'm sorry if it offended you. I might apologize to David ... later."

They arrived at the ore body and collected more samples to analyze. Hu placed one lump into a portable smelting machine she had carried with her and processed it. They produced a quantity of iron when the smelting was complete. It satisfied Hu. "Can we place a beacon here?"

"Yes, I brought several with us."

"Is this the only mineral here?"

"Yes, unfortunately. We'll locate your other elements someplace else."

"It's a good start. There's plenty here for steel production. What should we call the place?"

"What do you mean?"

"This spot. We have to name it. Senna Peak or something."

Senna laughed at the implied honor. "I don't think so. Hematite Hill might be more apt."

"Hematite Hill then. By the way," she added, "I respect a person who sees something that goes against their values and calls it out. It shows character."

Senna blushed. "Thank you. I had to keep two boisterous brothers in check. What about you then? You have to keep anyone in check — brothers, a husband, boyfriend?"

"No ... I don't want to talk about it."

Seeing her lighthearted comment had touched a nerve, Senna tried to repair any damage she may have caused. "I'm sorry."

"You needn't be. It's just a sensitive issue with me."

Silence fell between them as they started packing up to return to the lander. They carried their equipment back and packed it, ready for departure. David was busy packing his belongings away.

As they prepared to board the ship, Senna spotted movement fifty meters away, at the edge of a thicket of trees. "What's that?" she asked, pointing in the spectacle's direction.

"Don't know," Hu replied. "Let's go find out."

The three of them walked over to where Senna had seen the disturbance, stopping abruptly ten meters from it. A creature — perhaps the same one that had pinned David — was now overpowering and devouring a smaller, equally camouflaged animal. They stood with mouths agape in astonishment. Senna turned her video on to capture the event. What amazed them was they didn't see how the consumption occurred since the predator didn't have a visible mouth to ingest food.

After a time, Hu said, "Look. It's engulfing the other creature through an opening in its thorax." The others watched what Hu had pointed out. The smaller creature was being assimilated into the larger creature's body. Half an hour elapsed before the meal disappeared. The animal shook itself afterward and stared their way when it realized it was being scrutinized. It bounded away, disappearing into the surroundings.

"That was incredible," Senna said.

"Sure was. It reminded me of one amoeba engulfing another single-celled organism," David said. "Marie and Zane will have a field day studying that. Thank goodness they don't find us desirable." David gave an involuntary shiver as he realized what could have happened to him. "That's not a death I ever want to face."

"No," Hu agreed, and this time her tone was more sympathetic to him.

"Let's return to the ship," Senna said, shivering from what they had watched.

After decontaminating, they flew back to *Destiny* to relate their discoveries to the others.

29

SUITS OFF

It took another week of painstaking research by Zane and Marie before Ethan felt they could explore the planet without environmental suits for protection. Ethan called a meeting to discuss the issue before making a final decision. His team, plus Hu, was at the conference table, except Max, who was still recovering from his injuries.

"OK now," Ethan said to silence everyone so he could get the conversation started. "Let's focus on the meeting. The agenda notice has the safe discarding of the environmental suits and decontamination procedures when visiting Chariclo as the sole topic of discussion."

"It'd make life easier," David said.

"I'd love to smell the place," Jade said.

"Yes, our lives would be simpler, but we need confirmation that it's prudent. Zane and Marie have worked at a Herculean pace to analyze the planet's biology from the samples we've collected. Whether it's possible depends on what they recommend about the danger the native lifeforms present to us. It'd be untenable to colonize the planet if we couldn't work outside an isolated environment. Marie, Zane, can you lead us through the discussion?"

"I don't get it," David said. "Why don't you just decide after talking to them? Why are we needed?"

Ethan looked at David, frustrated by his cavalier manner. "David. First, I want everyone to review Marie's and Zane's data because you might highlight something we've missed. Second, this decision needs team agreement and individual acceptance since it affects our lives. Is that reason enough for you?"

"Just asking. You don't have to bite my head off."

"Well, that's the reason. Zane, Marie."

Zane glanced at Marie and said, "I'll leave it to Marie to lead the discussion as the microbiological interactions between organisms are more her field than mine. I will elaborate as required."

Marie looked at Zane and nodded. She turned to Ethan and the others. "First, thanks to everyone who collected samples and took videos for us. We wouldn't be here without that. Second, Chariclo is one weird planet, biologically. It still has carbon-centric biology as its basis, but it has an unusual evolution.

"I take it most of you are familiar with the double helix DNA architecture. Life on Chariclo has a DNA arrangement, too, but based on a triple helix, and it uses a couple more amino bases than we use. That is fortunate, as it means this planet's life is incompatible with us — nothing there is interested in eating us. It is unfortunate, too, since it means we can't digest native products.

"The interactions of a mixed culture of our organisms and ones from here have resulted in complete separation. They have a phobia toward each other."

"So, what happens if we breathe in these organisms?" Hu asked, leaning forward.

"From my analysis, nothing. Our body would eject it like it does other foreign bodies now."

"And if we ate it?" Celeste asked.

Marie sat back, gesturing for Zane to answer.

"As Marie said, the biology here is carbon-based. And our stomachs, being acidic, should tend to breakdown the material. But our metabolism uses a bacterial breakdown of food. It is this bacterial digestion that we believe would fail. The stuff would just pass through with little nutritional value."

"It is the same the other way. That's why David's beast had no interest in him as a meal. It sensed he was incompatible."

"Wise choice," someone sniggered under their breath, but Ethan couldn't work out who. David heard it, too, and indignantly scanned the room for the culprit.

Zane had the trace of a smile. "In saying that, our biology has a persistent talent for adaptation, and I suspect this biology does, too. A time may eventuate when organisms on both sides develop a means to assimilate each other's organic material. The implications are uncertain, but it should be controllable."

"And touching things?" Senna asked.

"As Marie saw with her tests, we both have a phobia. There'd be no effect. No rash or irritation."

"What if someone cut themselves, and something got into their bloodstream?" Jade asked.

"That is trickier. Marie?"

"I raised a few cultures to study that. As before, they stay separated, so in many respects it's like a foreign body in our blood stream on Earth. But, since it has organic origins, Zane and I believe the kidneys would filter it from the blood and expel it with your urine. Would you agree with that, Angelo?"

"Yes, I would," Angelo said with an air of the medical practitioner's authority in his manner.

There was general silence, having exhausted the barrage of questions.

Marie glanced at Zane. "That's everything we have to say, except it's safe to remove our suits." Zane nodded in agreement. "And anyone who knows me, and my work, understands that I only state that after serious consideration, having worked with the most dangerous organisms on Earth," Marie continued, her stern professionalism on display.

Ethan surveyed the others for signs of disagreement or consternation, but they looked happy with the recommendation.

"So, is there anyone who disagrees with Zane's and Marie's conclusions?"

No one showed any dissent with the findings.

"OK then. We can remove our suits. If anyone's uncomfortable with that, they have a right to continue using them."

A buzz of excitement circled the table as people started discussing the experience of walking unimpeded on the planet.

Ethan raised his voice. "Silence for one more moment, please ..." He waited for the chatter to die. "Does anyone wish to discuss any other issues while we're together?"

A drone of 'No's' echoed across the table to Ethan. "OK. You are free to go."

The buzz of conversation started again as people vacated the conference room.

"Can you stay back, Hugo?" Ethan asked.

Hu, who had stood, sat down again, eyebrows raised.

"How are you going with locating the materials for your repair work?"

"Good. Senna has found ore deposits for them. Once I collect enough to produce the parts, the manufacture time will be short. It'll speed up now without the suits."

"How long before you restart the portal?"

"Four or five days."

"I want it working as soon as possible. I know we have no guarantee that ships can pass through it over this distance but having it one stage closer to achieving it will help me sleep at night."

"What worries you? You don't normally worry."

"We've never been so far from help before, either. I prefer a backup — in case we need to return in a hurry."

"Pioneers in the past didn't have that luxury. The maritime explorers were away months, years, without home support, but they survived."

"Many didn't. They kept sending them regardless, I suppose. I want to improve my odds of returning."

Hu chuckled. "And so do I, Ethan. I understand your sense of responsibility for the crew's safety. I'll get the repairs completed as fast as I can."

"Speaking of which, did you find the technician?"

"Yes. He said he thought it didn't matter. He's not working on it anymore."

"Good. We don't want another mishap"

"Is that it, then?"

"Yes."

Hu rose and left.

Ethan sat alone, considering the state of the expedition's progress. Overall, everything was going to plan. They had discovered a compatible planet for human colonization. The need to grow their own food was a minor matter, he thought, although reconditioning the soil to accept terrestrial plants and organisms without destroying the local ecology might be problematic. The climate and air quality were suitable. No hostile forces had given them cause for concern so far. Maybe Hugo was right. His worry might be unfounded. One thing was sure: he wanted to be the first to breathe Charicloean air. He booted up his tablet and looked at the lander schedule. A lander was leaving first thing tomorrow morning. He booked a seat on it and nodded to himself in satisfaction. Things were looking good. He stood and headed off to find Jade.

THE NEXT DAY, Ethan, Zane, Senna, and Hu descended to the planet. They brought Angelo with them, suited when they opened the hatch for the first time and prepared for action in case they had an adverse reaction to the local environment, despite Marie's and Zane's assurances. Senna and Hu planned on using the lander to flit between the sites of the mineral deposits to collect what Hu needed for producing parts, replacing the ones damaged by the explosion on the portal. They intended to leave Ethan, Zane, and Angelo and then return, ready to fly back to the mother ship. They flew to a familiar site for Zane. It had a menagerie of fauna to examine.

The lander settled on the surface without incident. Angelo put on the environmental suit and gave the thumbs-up when sealed and ready.

"Here goes then." Ethan opened the hatch.

A gentle breeze washed across the faces of the unsuited occupants of the shuttle, and delicate exotic scents met their nostrils as they inhaled, like landing in a foreign country for the first time. Ethan took a deep breath and stepped to the ground. The air felt pleasant and invigorating. It made him want to run to enjoy the freedom of being outside the constraints of the ship and the suit. He saw Angelo monitoring the vital sign readouts he had for them to detect any change in their condition in the alien environment.

"How does it look, Angelo?"

"Nothing apart from excitement at the moment."

"Good. With luck, you can remove that suit too before long."

"That'd be great." Angelo surveyed the site with interest, being his first experience of the planet.

"Come over here, Angelo," Zane called out.

Angelo and Ethan walked over to investigate what he was pointing out.

"Look at that." Zane pointed to an ovoid creature resembling the ant they had seen when David and Marie had dropped the probes.

"Fascinating," Angelo said as he squatted to have a closer inspection. He stretched out his hand to see its reaction to placing his finger across its path. The ant neared it and stopped, undecided, until it sidestepped and rounded the digit at a leisurely pace. Angelo tried to touch it, but it scurried off when it felt the pressure of a foreign substance.

Having stayed for half an hour, Hu and Senna took the lander and left to complete their own duties.

Ethan, Zane, and Angelo reveled in the alien life's mysterious presence for the rest of the day. It was prevalent where they were.

30

FIRING UP THE PORTAL

Hu finally had the portal ready for testing again after repairing the damaged parts with materials from Chariclo. Ethan sat with her as he was eager for her to succeed. "Let's do it, Hugo," he said, smiling at her, "and good luck."

"I hope I don't need luck." She smiled back, thankful for the moral support. Hu typed in the start-sequence command, as before, and green lights sprang to life as each segment started. She had a circle of light showing full portal integrity. They both gazed through the porthole nearby and saw the portal's green halo. Hu released a sigh. "So far, so good." She ramped up the power and passed thirty percent without incident. The power level increased to sixty percent. The portal still operated as expected. Hu sat bolt upright in her chair, tense with concentration. Her heart rate rose as her hope for success peaked. The power rose to sixty-five percent, and the portal interior shimmered and collapsed as spacetime warped and funneled to an unknown destination. A smile appeared on Hu's face. Ethan held the top of her backrest, knuckles white with tension.

Hu transferred to a different display. She punched in a command and read the data displayed, delighted with what she saw. She was in the center of the moon's portal, so she sent a message through, knowing that the project monitored the portal twenty-four hours a day, waiting for such a transfer. The transmission informed them of the portal powering up again in two hours' time at fifteen hundred hours GMT. She kept the portal open to check its stability and the status of the various systems. Ten minutes later, she received a message back acknowledging the transmission. Once she completed her checks, she shut the portal off, turned to Ethan, and said with a beaming grin, "Stage one complete."

Ethan slapped her on the shoulder. "Congratulations! What happens now?"

"We wait till fifteen hundred, and I restart the portal. The team on the moon will power up theirs, and we'll produce a full-sized wormhole. I have requested they send an unmanned craft through with various spares, a larger smelting machine, and an organic refining unit."

"OK. I'll go do systems checks in Engineering and return in two hours. I don't want to miss this."

Hu grinned. "Yes, it'll be another momentous achievement to add to the expedition log."

Ethan smiled back. "Yes, it will."

Hu watched Ethan leave the command center, and she returned to her tablet screen, running diagnostic tests on the portal systems to fill in the time.

The designated time approached, and Ethan returned from his duties, his eyes shining with eagerness. "I haven't missed the start?"

"No, you haven't. I'm powering up the portal again," Hu replied with a grin, appreciative of Ethan's enthusiasm. *His boyish vitality radiates from him and warms those around him.*

Moments later, another person hobbled into the command center. Max had healed from his injuries enough for Angelo to allow him to walk. He had heard of the imminent test. "Can I look on?" he said as he approached.

Hu and Ethan turned to the voice. She smiled. "Of course. It's the least I can do for you."

"Nothing'll fly out at me, will it?" Max said, seating himself at the station next to her.

Hu paled, feeling a stab of guilt at being reminded of the accident.

"Oh. Sorry. I didn't mean to embarrass you. It's just my sick humor," Max said, trying to reassure her he had no ill-feelings.

"That's OK. I have thick skin, and the reminder doesn't hurt to keep my wits sharp for the potential dangers of what we intend to do here."

"I have a personal stake in its success now."

They both grinned and relaxed while they waited.

When the clock reached fifteen hundred hours, Hu started powering the portal. She was about to ramp up the power when she pointed to it. "Look. See that pinpoint of light?"

Ethan stared. "Yes. What is it?"

"That is light from the sun. They've powered up their end and are waiting for me."

Hu escalated the power to her portal and passed thirty percent with no change in the spot's image of space in the portal. She kept increasing until the power reached forty-three percent. At that point, the zone inside the portal shimmered as before but instead of the spacetime funnel ending in a pinpoint, the small light they had seen expanded until it filled the whole portal enclosure. They saw the moon in the lower right quadrant of the orifice. A transmission came through it.

<Congratulations. Test wormhole establishment completed. Proceeding to send through supplies in five minutes. Message sent fifteen-o-eight and ten-seconds.>

Hu checked her chronometer to compare with the time stamped on the delivery. It was showing fifteen-o-eight and sixteen-seconds. That meant a six-second travel time through the portal at light speed, which translated to a distance of one-point-eight-million kilometers through the wormhole hyperspace environment. She studied a calculation she had brought up on her tablet. "Perfect." She looked at Ethan. "As the theory predicted."

"That's great," Ethan said.

Jade walked into the command center at that moment. "There you are," she said as she strode over to Ethan and Hu. "What's keeping you so enthralled that you don't hear your comm?"

Ethan blushed. Hu had noted that it had sounded several times but had been too busy to mention it.

"I've been helping Hu commissioning her wormhole," he said. "I must've been concentrating too much to notice."

"Humph ... How is it going?"

"I've established a wormhole, and my package will arrive in ..." she glanced at the clock, "... nine minutes."

"Oh. That's exciting. Mind if I watch?"

"My pleasure."

Neither Hu nor Ethan had noticed, but most of the others working in the command center had dropped what they were doing to witness the historic event unfold. Hu peered around, delighted when she spotted everyone watching. "Come and have a closer look." Several crew members looked guilty over neglecting their duties, but they were too eager to view the outcome to deny their inquisitiveness. Nine minutes elapsed, after which a projectile shot from the portal space and decelerated at a lethal rate until it came to rest. Cheers erupted from the audience, which Hu acknowledged. She pulled up another screen on her tablet to give her control of the capsule. She fired it up and directed it to the ship's lander bay to unload.

It took fifteen minutes to maneuver the craft to the ship and settle it in the bay. Hu sent a message back to the team at the moon, notifying them of successful delivery of the package. After informing them when she intended operating the portal the next day to conduct the test, she turned off the portal. The moon base did likewise, the point of light disappearing soon afterward.

"What now?" Ethan asked.

"Now I see if my parcel came through in one piece and, if so, tomorrow we'll consider transporting a person."

"I can't wait for that. I'll sleep at night, knowing we can transport people through the portal."

Hu rose from her seat and left the command center, heading for the lander bay and the consignment that had just landed. She exited the elevator and walked over to the craft.

Keying in the unlock code, she pressed the button to open the hatch, which slid inside the shell cavity with a swish. She noticed movement on the floor when the door opened and gave a yelp of fright — a rat had darted from the cargo compartment into the bay. Those in the bay turned toward her cry of distress, and two maintenance workers, spotting the rat, gave instant chase. Nobody wanted a rat living on the spaceship. Two would be worse, especially if they were male and female. They'd never get them off unless they drained the ship's atmosphere. *At least I know mammals can safely traverse a wormhole*, Hu thought. *It must be one tough rodent to survive the deceleration forces the ship underwent.*

After calming herself, she checked through the shipped manifest. The cargo had stayed secure for the journey and survived the transit. She emerged from the hatch again and organized two crew to unload the vessel onto the floor space allocated for the Chinese equipment.

Moments later, the two who had gone hunting the rat returned, one of them carrying the now corpse by the tail, a proud smile on his face. "We caught it," he said to Hu.

Hu laughed at the comedy of their achievement. Anyone would have thought they had hunted a tiger. "Good for you. Don't eat it all at once." The one holding the rat gave her an odd expression, as if she had gone insane. It only made her laugh more. She left the lander bay and returned to the command center to prepare the portal for its next performance. She then switched off her tablet and headed to her accommodation to rest and prepare for dinner.

Hu activated the portal again at three the next day and waited. Max was with her. He displayed an interest in the quantum physics side of the portal generator, so Hu was glad to educate him. She felt relieved he wasn't showing any resentment toward her for his current condition, although Angelo had said he'd make a full recovery, given time. A shuttle came through ten minutes after the message of its imminent arrival. The ship decelerated at a lower rate than the earlier one, even with the gravity field matrix, for the crew's safety.

"Hello, *Destiny*. Is anyone there?" A familiar voice came over the ship's comm in the command center. Hu recognized Chang Jian Zha, the Chinese project leader.

She gestured to the communications officer that she would reply. He nodded and transferred to her. "Hello, Jian. Nice of you to drop in on us. Did you draw the short straw?"

"Ha! You kidding me? I get to do an exciting thing for a change instead of paperwork."

"It's good to hear your voice. I'm sure you will delight the crew when you meet them."

There was a moment of silence. "Pilot informs me we land in thirty minutes."

"Fine. I'll arrange a welcoming party."

"Then we have a proper party. I bring supplies."

"Ha-ha. You would. See you soon."

The comm disconnected. Hu closed the portal and left with Max for the lander bay after informing Ethan and Jade of Jian's arrival. They were both on board instead of one on the planet, contrary to the usual arrangement.

They assembled in the lander bay near the shuttle's landing position and waited. The shuttle entered. The hatch opened, and Jian emerged, waving his hand above his head in greeting as if he were a distinguished head of state. Hu and the others moved forward to meet him, and Jian descended the steps to the bay floor. Jian straightened his uniform.

Hu approached him and shook his hand. "Welcome."

"Good to see you."

"I will introduce you to the crew."

Ethan came forward, and Hu did the introductions. "This is Ethan Richards, the leader of the expedition to Centauri."

"Welcome aboard *Destiny*. I hope your stay here is pleasant," Ethan said, shaking Jian's hand.

"Pleased to meet you. Hu has spoken grand things about you. She holds you in large respect. I too hope pleasant stay. I have gifts to make sure pleasant."

Ethan looked at Hu with suspicion. "She has told many lies."

They laughed.

"I will get to the truth then when we have serious talk over refreshments."

"You are welcome."

Jade stepped forward next. "Hello, Jian. Good to see you again."

"Ah! Jade. The gem that shines and keeps this one in order." Jian gestured to Ethan as he talked. "It is magnificent to meet you again too."

Jade laughed. "I'm not sure about keeping him in check, but he has his good points."

"Yes, he does." Jian studied Ethan again. "We thank you much for allowing Jade to leave you to spend time with us. It was most valuable and contributed to my presence now."

Ethan blushed. "You're welcome. She spoke well of you and your team."

Max hobbled forward.

"This is Max Roberts, the team's fusion specialist. He had an unfortunate accident while helping me assemble the portal. I am humbled and embarrassed that I placed him in such danger," Hu said to Jian.

Jian looked at Hu with concern. "We shall have to discuss later." He turned to Max and shook his hand. "It is a pleasure to meet you. I hope you do not have unpleasant feelings for the Chinese republic because of this issue."

"Good to meet you too, and I have no bad feelings. Hu helped to rush me to medical attention."

"Ah, I am pleased." Jian surveyed the bay. "And what do you intend for me?" He looked at Ethan. "I need your help in unloading provisions for celebrations later."

"I will organize personnel to unload them, but I wish to escort you to a cabin to freshen up and then give you a tour of the ship if that pleases you."

"This is good, very good."

"After that, we'll take part in discussions with Hu and Jade and investigate this celebration you have brought with you afterward."

Jian nodded in agreement. "Yes, most proper."

"If you will follow me, then." Ethan turned to Jade. "Can you organize someone to unload the cargo, please?"

"Sure," Jade said.

Everybody entered the elevator except Jade, who supervised finding labor for the unloading.

As Ethan had said, he gave Jian a tour of the ship, which fascinated Jian. The warp bubble drive the Americans had developed piqued his curiosity, and he was eager to learn more about it. They had update and information discussions after that, with Hu and Jade present, and Jian was Ethan's guest at dinner that night. They retired to the bar afterward, the rest of the team joining them.

"Now I show you special delivery from China for everybody to share," Jian said. "Bartender, could you please open what I delivered to you this afternoon and give everyone a glass?"

The bartender obliged.

"Oh, no!" Hu gasped with amused anticipation when she spotted Jian's surprise.

Jian filled everyone's glass with a serving of the liquid from the bottle. When finished, he lifted his glass and said, "I present baijiu, one of China's finest drinks. I offer to you in honor of our countries many cooperations and for the successful completion of this expedition."

"Thank you, Jian, and may you have continued good health and achievement with you project, too," Ethan replied. "Cheers!"

Everyone repeated the toast and took a sip. The taste and potency of the elixir surprised them, several gasping for breath.

Jian and Hu sniggered.

Ethan said, "I take it you don't drink too much at once."

"You are correct," Jian confirmed.

The celebration continued until late, everybody wandering off to sleep in jovial state. Hu was last to leave. As she surveyed the bar, the evening's success and the warmth of relations established between Ethan and Jian pleased her. She said goodnight to the bartender and left for her quarters and bed.

31

FURTHER DISCOVERIES

The team filled the following days with extensive surveys in other areas of the world below them. Some members stayed on the surface for several days at a time before returning to the ship to report their findings about the exotic differences from terrestrial life on Earth. Jade, Senna, Marie, Zane, Ethan, and the technicians from the spaceship conducted the latest expedition in a tropical equatorial region of the planet. They camped in an open field by a stream that percolated past them with a variety of species eking out their existence in backwaters that the current's turbulence bypassed. The towering mountains near the camp were the destination for Ethan and Senna to explore. They planned to use the all-terrain vehicle they had brought with them for such an excursion. With equipment and supplies packed, they headed out.

The general terrain was simpler to negotiate along the stream, so they followed a route toward its source initially. The vehicle rocked as it traversed the steep and rocky terrain but still made steady progress. Travel alongside the stream became more difficult, so they left the it behind and continued to climb as the landscape increased in elevation to a vast plateau before scaling toward the towering peaks. The vegetation was easier to penetrate than Ethan's first impressions. It spread out into a savannah that filtered across the broad plain. Senna pointed to a spot she wanted to investigate on the plateau's far edge, where the mountains rose sharply up an escarpment. They arrived at the site at the base of the cliff twenty minutes later.

"What's special about this place, Senna?" Ethan asked.

"This cliff shows massive plate movement beneath that goes on for kilometers in both directions away from here. That is why the mountains are towering above us. One plate is pushing against another. This plane is descending into the planet's core and is pressing on the top plate. I want to study this cliff's formations to understand its geological history."

"Sounds like rock collecting to me."

Senna laughed at the simple analogy Ethan had made. "Yeah. Rock collecting."

"I might go for a walk and investigate anything else of interest."

"No problem," Senna said. Her mind was elsewhere as she concentrated on her own work.

Ethan strolled along the base of the escarpment, studying it himself. It was one hundred meters tall. The talus was narrow, and he could climb it if he had the urge. He rustled the alien grass as he wandered, his feet leaving an impression after him as his weight broke the delicate blades. After half an hour, he stopped at a spot that seemed different from the main cliff. He stepped back, trying to put his finger on why. He walked further away still until he was three hundred meters distant, giving a panoramic view of the cliff face. Senna worked to his left. He cast his gaze across the cliff face, scanning for the irregularity that his senses had detected and worked out its origin. A small section of the surface, five meters high by three wide, differed from the surrounding rock mass. It started at the top of the loose rubble gradient and appeared to extend into the ground, following the solid rock. He took a photo to show Senna and returned to the cliff, to where he had noticed the anomaly, and scaled the scree.

Once he reached the escarpment, he could just discern the discontinuity between the native cliff and the irregularity. He touched the wall and passed his fingers over the juncture but detected no variance; yet it was there. He pulled out marking paint and sprayed an X next to the peculiarity so that he could find it later. Afterward, he kept walking for another half an hour before he retraced his steps, finding nothing else to interest him.

Senna was busy taking seismic soundings when he returned. She glanced up at the sound of footsteps. "You're back," she said as she tucked away a stray lock of hair.

"Yes. I have something to show you."

Senna stood up straight, stretching as she did so. "What is it?" she asked, walking closer to Ethan.

Ethan took his comm from his pocket, brought up the image he had taken, and showed her. "I snapped this half an hour away. Any idea what it might be?"

Senna took Ethan's comm and studied the picture, staring at it with puzzled concentration. "No. I've seen nothing like it. I need to study it myself. Tomorrow."

"I marked the place, so it's easy to find. Are we returning?"

"Yes, I am leaving monitoring equipment here overnight to take measurements. We need to return tomorrow to collect it."

"OK then. It's time we started getting back if you're almost ready."

"Yeah. A couple more instruments to set up, and we can leave." Senna left and continued with what she had been doing.

She finished her tasks ten minutes later, and they packed up and drove off, returning to camp just before sunset. The others were busy preparing for the night when they returned. They made a campfire from dead timber collected nearby. It burned well, and they heated food in ashes from the fire. Their faces reflected the flickering firelight as they relaxed and talked, and the shadows grew.

Ethan sat next to Jade, content with her being near him. The others started to tease them over their carefulness in acting professionally in front of them. They didn't need to be so puritanical — they weren't fooling anyone. Ethan and Jade blushed, agreeing that, since no one minded, they would lower their guard amongst friends. It couldn't extend to bedding arrangements that night, much to

Ethan's disappointment, because of the sleeping gear they had, but they slept next to each other.

The sun greeted them with a spectacular sunrise, the air still warm and humid as the climate in the region dictated.

Ethan opened his eyes to the sight of Jade looking at him in return.

"Good morning, sleepy head," Jade said.

"Good morning," he replied with a contented smile, the wonder of Jade's sparkling green eyes warming his soul as he woke. He sat up and stretched his arms out with an enormous yawn. "You look like you just stirred, too."

Jade chuckled. "I was watching you."

"Like what you saw?"

"I did."

"We'd better rise and prepare for the day before we embarrass ourselves," Ethan said, winking.

Jade gave a seductive pout. "Yes, boss."

"Stop it," Ethan said with feigned annoyance and a smile as he rose from his bedding. He went outside their tent and noticed the others stirring, too. He re-entered the tent. "Want to go for a jog?"

"OK."

They both changed into exercise clothing. The others had the same idea. When he saw them, Ethan called them over to run together as a group. They started off and invaded the sparse bush nearby. They had a homing beacon program on their comms that located their camp so they couldn't become lost. A few hundred meters into the woods, they encountered a track, which they jogged on for ease of negotiating the terrain.

Ethan was leading the pack of runners when he heard a thump and groan behind him. He glanced around to see Chris lying on the ground two meters beside the path, holding his thigh and arm, blood pouring from a deep cut on his leg. "What happened?" he asked, shocked.

Senna, who had been straight behind Chris, answered in a trembling voice, "... We ... were running and this ... this *thing* crashed through the brush and rammed Chris. It threw him over there. It was built like a tank."

Chris moaned in agony from his injuries.

Ethan bowed for a closer inspection. "That's a nasty gash. It must have had sharp protrusions on it, whatever it was." They had no medical kit with them. He was unsure what they should do. He looked at Jade for help.

"Can you walk, Chris?" she asked. "Are there any bones broken?"

"I don't think so," Chris managed to get out through the pain.

"That's a serious gouge," Ethan said. "You're losing blood."

"We must bandage it," Jade said, staring at Ethan's jogging shirt.

Ethan noted where she was looking. "Use your own."

"Really?"

"Oh ... OK," Ethan said in defeat as he pulled off his shirt. "I suppose I'll do the gallant thing, then." The others smiled in amusement. He tore it into wide strips to wrap around Chris's thigh. Jade and he wrapped the leg and used narrow ribbons to tie the makeshift bandage into place. It soon stopped the flow of blood. "How does that feel?"

"Better."

"Your upper arm looks like it took a whack, too."

"Yeah. Nothing's broken, though."

"You want to try standing?"

Chris nodded and raised himself. Senna and Troy helped him by holding each side. He stood, trying not to place pressure on his injured leg. He winced in pain but coped.

Ethan checked that the bandage was still staunching the blood flow. "You want to take a few steps?"

Chris started walking but with a pronounced limp. "I'll be OK once I get going."

"I'm still worried about that injury," Ethan said. "Jade, can you and Troy return to camp and bring the first aid kit? We need to improve the bandaging. We'll follow you as fast as Chris can walk."

"OK," Jade said.

"Don't run into anything else if you can help it."

"That thing's disguise was good," Chris said. "I didn't know what hit me."

"Let's hope that's the last of them. I wonder if something frightened it, or was it trying to chase us away?"

Jade and Troy started jogging back to camp, looking around for creatures as they disappeared into the distance. Ethan, Senna, and Chris walked slowly as Chris hobbled along, wincing in pain every so often. Ethan didn't mind their slowness, preferring Chris not to exacerbate his injuries.

Half an hour later, they heard a noise approaching them, crashing through the bush. Ethan realized it was their all-terrain vehicle and wondered who had thought of bringing it. He kicked himself for not thinking of it. Moments later, it appeared in front of them and stopped several meters away. Jade and Troy emerged, Troy with a medical kit.

"Good idea using that," Ethan said.

"I thought we won't get any thanks from Chris's leg if we make him walk back, even with the extra first aid," Jade said.

"Yeah."

Ethan and Jade worked on improving the bandage. They then helped Chris into the vehicle, and Jade and Troy took him back to the camp. Ethan and Senna jogged back, not meeting any other hazards on the way.

Chris sat in a chair, uncomfortable and morose.

"I contacted Angelo," Jade told Ethan once he had regained his breath. "He wants Chris on the ship so he can tend to him. He says there could be complications if he doesn't get prompt treatment."

"OK then. The pilot can fly him back and return. We have enough supplies." Ethan went to talk to the pilot, who was conducting checks on the shuttle. He returned after a brief discussion and told Chris to board it. Troy and Zane collected his things and placed them on the shuttle with him before it rose and sped off to the ship.

"Do you know what hit him?" Marie asked once they had regrouped.

"Not exactly," Senna said. "I was right behind him, but I saw nothing until it struck. That is how camouflaged it was."

"Didn't you have your cams?"

"Didn't think of that. I'll get it and replay it."

Senna got her camera, which she wore when out of the camp. She set hers up to display on a screen to view the image. She forwarded the recording to just before the beast injured Chris and pressed play. They still couldn't detect what had hit him. It happened too fast. She rewound it and played it again in slow motion. The recording played to the incident, and they saw a creature the size of a sheep colliding with Chris and rolling its horn-encrusted head into Chris's thigh. Camouflaged in the general vegetation and soil, it was difficult to discern.

"Amazing," Zane breathed. He asked Senna to rewind and stop it mid-frame when the creature appeared. "It's hard to tell whether it's angry or afraid. We wouldn't know what to check. Look at its head. There are three curved horns protruding, the ends are sharp as spikes. No wonder Chris got such a nasty gash."

"Whether it was charging us in anger or fear, how do we protect ourselves against them if we can't see them?" Marie asked.

"Good question," Ethan said. "We have motion sensors in our kits. We might need to use them. They are solid objects, as Chris found out."

"We should," Jade agreed.

"So, what do we do now?" Ethan asked.

"I'd like to return to yesterday's site and inspect your find in more detail — if it's not too late to start," Senna said.

Ethan looked at his chronometer. It was already late morning. "It's too late to get started today. Let's plan to set out at first light tomorrow. The shuttle should be back by then. I'd be more comfortable knowing it's available if we need it."

"OK then," Senna said.

They attended to other duties that day. The shuttle returned late that afternoon just before sunset.

32

SKELETONS IN THE CLOSET

Senna, Troy, and Ethan returned to the cliff face the next day, following the same route. They found the cross Ethan had painted and headed for it, reaching the spot with no drama.

Once they disembarked from the vehicle, they gazed at the wall to examine Ethan's discovery.

"Looks like the rest of the cliff to me," Troy said.

"Looks can deceive you. Walk out a hundred meters or two, and it's different from the main cliff. It looks like a sealed entrance," Ethan said.

Both Senna and Troy followed Ethan's instructions and returned.

"You're right," Senna said. "It's like a blocked-up tunnel. But I see no evidence of sentience or technology here. What could have done this?"

"I don't know," Ethan replied. "We're only just discovering many things. Who knows what's out there somewhere? Aliens may have visited the planet in the distant past and tunneled into the cliff face."

Troy smirked. "Let's hope it's not a super-sized wasp nest."

Senna and Ethan stared at Troy, unimpressed by his imaginings. "Doubtful," Ethan said. "We don't know what we'll discover here, or anywhere else in the galaxy."

Troy sobered, thinking of the possibilities.

"What do you want to do?" Ethan said.

"I'll get my equipment out and profile the region first. Check if the material in this spot differs from the surrounding rock." Senna got to work with Troy's help.

Ethan sat in the vehicle, reviewing his backlog of reports. He contacted the ship to update himself on Chris's condition and smiled when Angelo confirmed he was mending, with no permanent consequences. An hour and a half later, Senna came up to him. He glanced up with a questioning expression on his face.

"It's hollow. A thirty-centimeter crust covers a significant space."

"That's interesting. How would that have developed?"

"No idea. The symmetry of the shape suggests that it's artificial."

"That's even more intriguing. Jokes aside, Troy's suggestion could explain it, couldn't it?"

"Maybe. But we'd see several if animals created this for breeding."

Ethan considered the implications. "OK then. What do you want to do?"

"I'd like to drill into it and pass through an endoscope to view the interior."

Ethan paused in thought. "Sounds reasonable. Let's do it." He hopped from the vehicle and followed Senna to the cliff to watch as she drilled the hole.

Senna readied the machine and other equipment and started drilling. The rock was hard. The drill took an hour to penetrate the wall.

"At last," Senna said as the bit plunged into resistance-less space. A puff of air from the inside blasted her face with dust. She wiped the dust from her goggles.

Removing the drill, she switched the endoscope on and threaded it through the hole. Ethan and Senna studied the display. She rotated the camera through various angles. "Looks empty," she said, looking at Ethan. "You can see the walls, floor, and roof, but it just extends into darkness. There's no debris. That surprises me. Rock should have fallen from the roof and walls after such a long period. Then again, the floor's our level, as if the wall was just raised. The walls and roof are smooth, artificial. Strange."

"What do you suggest?" Ethan asked.

"I don't know. Is it safe to knock down this wall for a better inspection?"

Ethan wasn't sure. He contemplated the risks. The cave seemed stable, so the roof collapsing wasn't likely. They could verify that before they entered. Why was this façade there? What was it hiding from the world? How long had it been sealed? He froze in indecision. The only prospect he feared was harmful microbiologic organisms, even though Marie had cleared the rest of the planet. He should check first. He hoped it wasn't too late and they hadn't already released something they shouldn't have. "Plug up the hole. I want Marie here to test for microorganisms before we go further. Can we figure out this wall's age?"

"I can figure out what it's made of, I suppose. If it has organic matter, I can check for carbon fourteen. Or I can analyze for radioactive elements and review the decay ratios."

"Do that."

Senna collected samples to take back to the camp, where she had specialized equipment available to conduct the tests she needed to do. She sealed up the hole with a cement compound she had with her. It was early afternoon, so they had lunch. They returned to the vehicle and moved out two hundred meters from the escarpment, where they could get an unobstructed view of potential anomalies. They traveled along the cliff before returning to the campsite for the night.

When settled, they reviewed the day's events with the others, and Ethan outlined what he wanted to do. The rest agreed with the plan, so they broke up and continued with their own activities before supper and sleep.

~

THE NEXT DAY, they piled back into the vehicle, this time taking Marie, Jade, and Zane with them, and trekked back to the cliff. Only the shuttle pilot and another technician remained at the camp. Senna drilled out the cement she used to seal the hole, and Marie collected a sample of air from the cave. She held an analyzer to test for organisms and tested the specimen. The results came back negative for organic matter.

"So, it's safe to remove the wall, then?" Ethan asked, wanting the others to confirm his conclusion.

"Nothing organic lives inside," Marie said.

The others nodded.

"Did you get any dating information, Senna?"

"I conducted a uranium–lead dating analysis. The wall is two million years old. That confuses me because the cave hasn't moved compared to the surrounding rock plate."

"Too young, isn't it?"

"No. It should have moved."

"OK then. Let's look inside the cave."

Senna retrieved a laser torch from the vehicle and started working on the rock wall, cutting an entry into the cavern. It took over two hours to cut a suitable opening, others taking a turn with the cutter to give Senna a break. They cleared the rubble away and used torches to illuminate the interior.

"Let's go check it." Ethan led the way.

The others followed, with Senna next to Ethan. Beams of light bounced off the surfaces they illuminated.

"The walls are smooth," Senna said as she touched one, her voice echoing in the confined space.

"Could it be from erosion?" Jade asked.

"I don't think so. It's too flat for erosion. You get smooth faces but not perfectly flat, and the cave's dry. The atmosphere isn't musty from dampness."

"Strange," Ethan said.

They moved further into the cave, having traveled two hundred meters from the mouth. Ethan saw a barrier up ahead. "Looks like we've reached the end," he said as his flashlight reflected from the wall.

"There's an opening on the side," Senna advised.

"You're right."

They approached the corridor and turned into it, freezing where they stood. Bones lay in front of them. They looked uncannily humanoid.

33

CONTAMINATED

"What the ...?" Ethan whispered, looking at the pile of bones before them. Hundreds of bodies lay lined up on the cave floor, as far as their torches shined.

Zane moved forward to inspect the find. He examined the skulls, in particular, at least ten of them. "This is unusual," he said, staring back at Ethan. "The crania are split open but not from injury or a weapon. They're separated along the coronal suture as if the skull popped from too much internal pressure. No other part of the body looks affected."

"I've got a bad feeling about this," Marie said, lines of worry creasing her brow.

"What do you mean?" Ethan asked, concerned over Marie's reservations.

"The bodies are in top condition except for the cranium displaying the same defect, according to Zane. One explanation is a plague."

"But you tested for microorganisms."

"I checked at the mouth, not here. There've been no bipedal creatures on the planet except here. Did whatever kill these creatures wipe out the entire population? That's a virulent organism if it did, the deadliest I've ever seen."

The others started expressing their conjectures of doomsday outcomes following Marie's comment.

"Stay calm," Ethan said, trying to regain control. "Let's look at this rationally, shall we? Marie hasn't found one microorganism on the planet that can affect us. It's a good presumption that whatever killed these still exists outside — if an organism killed them. Is that a fair presumption, Marie?"

"Yes, it's reasonable that it should still be present in the environment. But it might be dormant, especially if these bones are two million years old. It may have had nothing on which to feed."

"But you and Zane determined that this planet's biology is incompatible with ours and Earth's. So, even if it's there, it can't affect us."

"I have a question," Jade said. "Who lay these bodies here and closed the entrance? And where did those that sealed the cave go?" Jade moved closer to Ethan, wanting the comfort of being near him.

"I don't know. Something we must find out." Ethan pondered their predicament. "OK, Zane, Marie, how do we study this and get scientific answers?"

Both Marie and Zane stared at each other before speaking. Zane started, "I can investigate the skeletons to figure out how humanoid they are. Can you analyze the bone composition, Senna?"

"Yes. The equipment's at the camp," Senna said.

"And age? Carbon dating?"

"I can do that too."

"I can check for residual organics. See if we can answer that part of the puzzle," Marie said. "It still concerns me, though. We've disturbed something we should have left alone."

"Well, it's too late now," Ethan said. "Let me consider the consequences, and you start testing so we know more about what we're dealing with."

"What should the rest of us do?" Jade looked scared.

"Troy and Senna can help Marie and Zane. You and I need to talk."

Ethan and Jade walked back into the open air. The others started their work analyzing what they had found, emerging from the cave occasionally to collect equipment or other supplies for their investigation. Ethan led Jade to a quiet place where they could speak in reasonable privacy.

"What's on your mind?" Jade asked.

"I don't like this. I'm catching Marie's awful feeling. If they find something, I'll have to quarantine us on the planet until we understand what we're dealing with and whether it's safe."

"As you mentioned inside, let's do the analysis first. We shouldn't jump to conclusions before we get evidence. It's easy to panic after such a shocking discovery. We mustn't let our imaginations get the better of us."

"You're right. It's just so creepy, those skeletons, and they look so human. Where did they originate? I can't believe they came from here. The morphology is different, even after evolving for two million years. It would suggest things went backward, not forward. My bet is the skeletons have the same DNA as us. Then what?"

Jade paced in thought. She stopped in front of Ethan again. "If they are the same as us, it would raise many questions. 'How did they get here?', for starters. We'd prove we're not alone. Someone moved them here. And if they brought them here, where did we originate? Did we evolve on Earth, or were we brought to Earth as well?"

"Isn't the evolutionary history conclusive that we evolved on Earth?"

"I don't know. Somebody might've taken a population from Earth and planted it here as a bizarre scientific study, but it had disastrous consequences."

"Maybe." It was Ethan's turn to pace while he thought. Jade watched him. He came back. "You're right. Let's see what they find."

They returned to the others and waited for them to get results. Zane collected a sample for Senna to date. He then compared the bones to normal human dimensions based on the information he had stored on his tablet.

Meanwhile, Marie scraped material from the bones and inside the skulls that she could analyze.

As he waited, Ethan walked up to the row of skeletons, laid to rest in perfect order. He noticed that only adults populated the crypt — there were no children. That seemed odd to him. As if only adults were affected. Usually, children and the elderly take the brunt of an attack. The line of bodies ended at the tunnel end wall. He searched the surface. It was flat like the other walls except for a slight depression that he couldn't see from standing height because it was low, so he sat on the floor and shone his flashlight into it. It was a smooth and circular hole, as if drilled, five centimeters deep and two centimeters in diameter, so he stuck his little finger into it. He felt a sudden prick, so he extracted it. *That's strange*, he thought. He had seen no sharp projection at the end. A bead of blood congealed where the injury was, but the wound healed, and he forgot about it. He studied the end wall, but couldn't detect any other detail, so he strode back to the others and the worried looks of Marie and Zane.

"What is it?" Ethan asked.

"I've found an organism, a virus, and it could be a threat. It reacts to terrestrial stimuli. And we've had exposure to it."

Ethan frowned and looked at Jade as his fears were being realized. "How do we decide what risk it poses?"

"I need to conduct a DNA analysis on it, but the equipment for it is on the ship."

"OK. Senna, do you have results yet?"

"Yes. The bones are two million years old."

"Zane?"

"The skeletons are like Homo sapiens, but I don't have enough detail to figure out if they are or not."

"That's not good," Ethan said. "Is it?"

"No, it's not. If this virus killed these beings, it's our worst-case scenario." Marie grimaced in anguish.

Ethan paced his worry into the floor, thinking through his options, before talking again. He faced the group staring at him, fear on their faces, expecting leadership from him. "We must quarantine here until we understand the problem's extent. I can't allow a superbug on the ship or Earth. We'd have to destroy the spaceship if that happened."

Senna, Troy, and Zane complained, but Jade and Marie didn't. Marie spoke. "Ethan is making the right decision. We don't know what we're dealing with yet."

"We can't do anything more here. Let's return to camp," Zane suggested.

"What about the pilot and the technician?" Troy asked.

"Good point," Ethan said. He considered their position before replying. "Senna breached the seal to the cave yesterday, so we've infected the camp already if we brought it back with us. I know Marie didn't find any in her sampling this morning. But they may have dissipated from the hole."

"The cave was under pressure when I drilled, I remember, and I got a whiff of it when I pierced the wall," Senna said, depressed at the implications.

"They and the shuttle must stay on the planet," Ethan decided. "Let's get back to camp. I have calls to make."

They packed up their belongings and traveled back.

Just before arriving at the camp, Senna rubbed her temple.

"Something wrong?" Marie asked.

"I've got a headache."

Ethan turned his head, and Marie glanced at him, worried. He faced the front before anyone saw his expression.

34

OUTBREAK

After returning to camp and settling necessary housekeeping matters, Ethan contacted *Destiny*.

"Celeste, please assemble David, Angelo, Hugo and yourself in the conference room at six."

"I can do that. Why? Is everything alright there?"

"I'll enlighten you when you're together."

"OK. Well, it's just after five-thirty now. I'll get everyone ready for six."

"Good. See you then."

Ethan cut the connection. His dread of possibilities was mounting by the minute, and he couldn't hide it. This was a potential disaster, even a deadly catastrophe, and it was his fault. He had let his natural caution slip. He started thinking about the people he had failed in the past, such as his siblings and Jake, his best friend. He recognized he was spiraling into a depression, a depression that was self-fulfilling. He took several deep breaths to calm himself. The others were looking to him for leadership. Being a leader was a lonely occupation.

Jade entered the main assembly tent, where he sat with those tortured thoughts. "Are you alright?"

"No. I'm scared, and I can't afford to be."

Jade came over and perched next to him. She gave him a tender peck on the lips and hugged him. "It's OK to be afraid. This is serious. You aren't a huge superhero who defeats everything in his path, but you're my superhero."

Ethan was almost overcome with the emotion Jade instilled in him. But he kept himself under control as he gazed into her eyes with a love that connected their souls, like two metal plates fusing into one. He acknowledged the love reflected to him from Jade. It gave him strength, resolve, and purpose. He rested his forehead against hers for support. "Thank you."

"You're welcome," Jade replied, her voice husky with emotion.

"I love you."

"I love you, too."

They sat in that position for several moments before Ethan came back to the meeting he had organized. "Can you get Marie, Zane, and Senna in here at six? I've arranged a conference call with the team on *Destiny*."

"Sure. I can do that."

Jade left Ethan to consider what he would say. He needed to learn if this virus could infect humans and its mortality potential. He must prepare for his exploration team developing symptoms and must devise treatment. A twinge of concern pinched him as he recalled Senna and her headache. He had to instigate a total quarantine until he could guarantee their safety. He felt too much responsibility again.

His concentration broke when the others came into the tent for the meeting. Their somber mood entered with them as by now they all realized the seriousness of their predicament and its consequences. However, Ethan also saw a professional determination in their disposition. That professionalism would make his job easier. They sat around the table positioned to face the screen for the call to the ship.

Six came, and Ethan placed the call. The display showed Celeste and the others sitting in *Destiny*'s conference room. "Hello, everyone," Ethan said. Concern and questions lined their faces as they awaited the reason for the meeting.

When he glanced at Hu, he could tell she knew this wasn't just a project catch-up meeting from his expression. She stayed calm and said, "Hello," as did the others.

"You're probably wondering why I've called you together. I won't hide anything from you. The point is, I'm quarantining us on the planet until further notice ..." A chorus of consternation reverberated from people on both sides of the communication link. Hu continued watching Ethan. Ethan waited for the commotion to subside before continuing. "... We have discovered an organism here that might infect humans, and the virus could have already infected us."

"Are you sure, Marie?" Angelo asked.

Ethan allowed Marie to continue the conversation.

"I'm sure it's an organism with DNA compatible with ours. I'm not sure if it can infect humans yet," Marie replied.

"What do you need to verify this?"

"I need to run culture tests and generate the organism's full genome map."

"For which you need the apparatus on *Destiny*?"

"Correct."

"Can you give us a sample to test?"

"I'm not allowing anything from here on *Destiny* for now," Ethan interjected. "I don't want the entire ship infected."

"Hmm. We'll transport the sequencing equipment there then," Angelo said.

"You must use full sterilizing procedures," Ethan said.

"Will do. Is anyone feeling ill?"

"Not that I am aware, although Senna has a headache. Not sure how she feels now. Senna?"

"I'm OK. I took a painkiller for it before, and it's going away."

"We found rows and rows of humanoid skeletons sealed in a cave in a cliff face," Ethan explained. "That's where we detected the preserved organism. I was careless. I should have used more caution."

"You didn't know," Senna said.

"Maybe. It's too late now."

"The strangeness is they displayed the same cranial bone condition. Each one had a split along the coronal suture," Zane said.

"That *is* odd," Angelo said.

"Where do those humanoids originate?" David asked.

"Good question. We don't know. We've taken samples for analysis, but we need to concentrate on identifying this organism first," Marie replied.

"What do you want us to do?" Celeste asked.

"You'll just have to stay put, I'm afraid."

"That's OK. I have plenty to do with the astronomical observations. Not sure what everyone else is doing."

"Since I'm stuck here on the planet, I'm putting you in charge up there, Celeste."

Celeste jumped in surprise. The others gaped, too, and David looked irritated.

"Isn't she too inexperienced?" David asked.

Ethan sighed, having his reservations realized with David. "David, you're great at what you do and the decisions you make in your field. But Celeste understands the big picture and the implications of her choices, and she can fly the ship. Hugo can help her, too."

"Whatever you say," David replied, sarcasm dripping from his voice and his expression peevish.

Celeste braced herself for the responsibility Ethan had given her. "I'll do my best. What else do you need from us?"

Ethan glanced at the others to check if they had any requests, which they didn't. "Doesn't look like it. That's it from me. You could pray I am being over cautious."

Celeste smiled. "Will do. So, we will get a lander prepared to bring the sequencer to you. I'll inform you when we are ready."

"That's it for now," Ethan said. "Celeste, Hugo, and Jade, please stay for a moment."

The others said their goodbyes and left the conference on both sides.

"What's on your mind?" Celeste asked when they were alone.

"You can do this, Celeste. I've seen how you work when you pilot the ship, and you have the skills."

Celeste lowered her gaze, embarrassed by the show of confidence. "I won't disappoint you."

"Don't take any insubordination from David. Discipline him hard if he gets out of line. Hugo will help you if you need it. You've observed how she handles delicate matters," Ethan said with an attempt at a cheeky grin.

"I can be subtler than that," Hu said, chuckling.

"Anything else?" Celeste asked.

"No. I just wanted to offer encouragement."

"We'll be off then."

"Can I have a private word with you, Ethan?" Hu asked.

"Sure."

Celeste and Jade left, leaving Ethan and Hu sitting alone in their respective locations. Jade turned and gave an inquiring glance at Ethan before she disappeared. He shrugged his shoulders and frowned at the unspoken question.

"What's on your mind?" Ethan asked Hu.

"Are you OK?"

Ethan turned away to hide his fear. He reverted to the camera again, staring into Hu's eyes. "I knew I didn't fool you with my calm façade when the meeting started. I'm terrified."

Hu chuckled without humor. "I've seen that expression before. That's why I recognized it. I'm scared for you too. I wish I could do more for you from here. Just remember, you're not alone, especially since we can use the wormhole to reach the solar system and Earth's best facilities. That and our Chinese resources are at your disposal if you need them."

"Do you have that much clout?"

"Nothing will stop me from getting my way when your and Jade's safety is at stake."

Ethan glanced away again, overcome by emotion. He turned back. "Thanks. You're a great friend."

"You're welcome."

"Anything else?"

"No. That was it, and I'll keep a maternal eye on Celeste."

"You have a maternal instinct?" Ethan asked, laughing in amusement.

"I still have dreams. I am not that old yet."

"Yeah. OK. I hope to see you in the flesh soon."

"Goodbye."

The screen blanked. Ethan sat where he was for a few minutes, contemplating how fortunate he was to have friends like Hu. He remembered how she had nursed him back from his depression when he had injured himself in the explosion while researching warp bubbles years ago. She was an exceptional friend. He recovered from his reverie and headed for the outside air. Jade was standing, waiting.

"Everything OK?"

Ethan looked at her and smiled. "Yeah, it's good to have friends." He placed his arms around her and gave her a hug. "Let's go have something to eat."

ETHAN BROUGHT himself to full wakefulness at the sound of Marie's voice loudly calling him. It was just after eleven. He had hoped to let Jade sleep, but the noise and his movement roused her.

"What's happened?"

"It's Senna. Her headache is worse. I think it's becoming a problem and fear the virus is responsible."

Panic gripped Ethan, but he then calmed himself. "OK. Let's see her." He pulled on his boots. "Going to check on Senna," he told Jade as he left. He walked with Marie across their compound and entered the tent Marie and Senna shared. He headed to Senna's bed. She was in pain and perspiring.

"Hi, Senna."

Senna opened her eyes. Fear streamed out of them. "Hi."

"Marie says your headache is worse."

"A sledgehammer is bashing at my skull."

"Have you taken any more medication?"

"It's not working. I can't take any more."

"Do you have a fever? Has Marie taken your temperature?"

"Yeah. It's elevated, but not serious."

Ethan looked at Marie. "Can you prescribe something else so she can sleep?"

"We have supplies in the medical kit, but I should consult Angelo first."

"Get him on the comm."

Ethan turned to Senna again. "Try to rest. We'll discuss this with Angelo and see what else we can do."

Senna nodded.

Ethan left the tent with Marie. "Can you conduct tests? Check if it's this organism or something else?"

"I can sample her blood and analyze that. We should talk to Angelo first. He can give more advice than I can."

"Let's go wake him."

Ethan and Marie headed to the tent they had turned into a conference room and contacted *Destiny*. Angelo came on the comm twenty minutes later. "What's wrong?"

"Senna's headache is worse. She's in significant pain. We were wondering what we could give her to relieve it so she can rest," Ethan said.

"Hmm. Any other symptoms?"

"An elevated temperature."

"How elevated?"

"Do you know, Marie?"

"Thirty-seven point six."

"Hmm ... I need to come down there."

"You're not going anywhere. I don't want to infect the doctor," Ethan said, his voice firm.

"You think I want that? I'll wear an environmental suit. If it's a symptom of your discovery, you need me there with more advanced medical supplies, so I can be useful. I won't be of much value up here, having information relayed back to me and me providing remote diagnoses. I can override you if I need to, but I don't wish to circumvent your authority. You can see the logic, can't you?"

Ethan considered Angelo's argument and realized he was right. They needed his presence on the spot if more fell ill. The thought of Jade being infected was enough to panic him. He'd want Angelo there to give her the best medical treatment. "Yeah. You're right. OK. Get packed and bring whatever you think you need with you when you deliver the sequencer."

"Is anyone else showing symptoms?"

"No — not yet," Ethan replied grimly

"Shall I collect blood samples?" Marie asked.

"Yes, please. Run them through your scanning equipment to check if the organism is in her blood before I arrive. That should save time."

"I'll do that."

"What can we give Senna in the meantime?"

"You should have zopiclone in your kit. Give her a dose of that. It should be enough for now."

"Will do," Marie said.

"OK. We'll see you soon then."

"Yeah," Ethan replied. The comm disconnected.

"What do you think?" Ethan asked.

"I think we have a problem, but we already knew that. If this organism's causing Senna's illness, let's hope there's a simple cure."

"You had better give that stuff to Senna. Not much I can do, I suppose."

Zane exited the tent he shared with Troy, rubbing sleep from his eyes. "Thought you should know. Troy says he has a headache."

Ethan and Marie stared at each other. Fear gripped his stomach as Ethan absorbed the implications of Zane's revelation.

"Angelo's coming to check Senna," Ethan said to Zane. "He can examine Troy, too."

"It doesn't look great for the rest of us. First, Senna has a headache. And now Troy. We'll all be paranoid about headaches," Zane said, staring at Ethan, wanting reassurance from him.

"Stay calm, and we'll review our status as things unfold. That's all we can do."

"That's not good enough, Ethan. We need to solve this and fast."

Ethan, feeling the pressure of leadership, didn't have an answer, but knew Zane was making a reasonable demand. "I need Angelo's assessment first. We'll work out a plan then. OK?"

"I suppose that is the best course of action," he said, but he sounded disappointed.

"Go sleep. Tell me if Troy's condition worsens. Angelo can't get here soon enough." Ethan headed for his tent. Marie left to get the recommended medication for Senna, and Zane shuffled back inside his tent.

35

YOU'RE IN CHARGE

Celeste woke to the shrill noise of her comm chime. It was six in the morning, nearly her wake-up time anyhow, but she couldn't fathom what was important enough to disturb her at that hour. She rose from her bed and headed for the comm, pressing the audio button, "Celeste here."

"Celeste, it's Angelo. Can you come to the command center, please? We need to talk."

"OK. Let me dress, and I'll be there."

Fifteen minutes later, she walked into the command center to find Angelo and David at loggerheads. Their expressions were angry, daggers jabbing from one set of eyes to the other. She halted in mid-stride as she took in the scene. "... What's the problem?"

"I need to use a lander to go help Ethan with his medical issues. David won't allow it. You're in charge. Put David in his place."

Celeste raised a brow. "Really? Why is that, David?" She had a hunch what the issue was and tensed for the impending clashing of swords between her and David so early in her new position of authority. She resisted calling Hu as that would undermine the authority Ethan had given her.

"If we send the only uncontaminated lander we have to the

planet, we risk bringing whatever they have discovered up here and infecting the entire ship. That's too great a danger."

"Let's step back a moment, shall we? What has Ethan asked?"

"He needs me to look at Senna. She's very ill, and I can't do that from here. And, as you know, Marie wants the DNA sequencer so she can better understand this organism."

"Well, that sounds sensible, but how do we make sure we stay uncontaminated?"

"We have standard decontamination procedures. I'll wear a full environmental suit when I am outside the lander's sterile environment and undertake sterilization when going in and out."

Celeste nodded. It sounded reasonable. They had very stringent decontamination procedures for both the landers and themselves. "So, what's the issue, David?"

"It's too risky. One slip-up and we get whatever they have."

"True. So, we should leave Ethan and the others stranded?"

"I didn't say that. We should try to help, but we shouldn't risk our lives."

Celeste stared at David in disbelief. That David looked after number one was obvious, but such cowardice manner was beyond her understanding. "You'd want us to make the same decision if it were you?"

David hesitated at the dilemma Celeste had given him. "Well ... of course I'd want your help. But ... there must be another way."

Celeste folded her arms as she thought. She decided. "This is what I'll do. I'll contact Ethan and Marie to discuss any further precautions we can take to prevent contaminating the ship. I'll make my final decision after that. In the meantime, you load what you need onto the lander and prepare to leave, Angelo. One thing's for sure: I am not leaving those people helpless, thinking we won't support them because we're scared. We understood the risks when we signed up for this expedition and I, for one, stand by my team."

"This is ridiculous," David muttered. "I knew it was a mistake putting a greenhorn like Celeste in charge."

"David," Celeste said, raising her voice, forcefulness projected in the word, the tendons in her neck protruding. She quieted again. "Ethan placed me in charge because he knew I'd put the expedition and the entire team before my own personal interests. Grow up and don't just consider yourself. Now go do something more useful."

David gritted his teeth in anger. "Yes, *sir*," he said sarcastically as he stormed out.

Celeste sighed to let the tension out. "You had better get started, too. I'll tell you if we decide on any further precautions you need to take."

"OK. And thanks. The people below will thank you too." Angelo made to leave but stopped and faced Celeste. "By the way, you handled that well."

Celeste blushed at the compliment. "Thanks."

Angelo continued walking out after that.

Celeste noticed that there were others in the command center busy doing their assigned tasks, pretending that they hadn't seen the tense exchange. She became self-conscious and blushed again as she headed for the conference room to contact Ethan. She passed the threshold to a beaming smile of approval on Hu's face and halted.

"Sorry," Hu said. "I almost came out to help twice, but that would've made matters worse. You did a marvelous job of that. I see why Ethan wanted you in charge."

Celeste's blush became full-blown red as she accepted the compliment. "Thanks. It's getting hot in here."

"I didn't want to embarrass you," Hu said with a friendly smile.

Celeste giggled, "It's OK. I'm not used to compliments."

"Get used to them."

Celeste grew serious again. "What should I do with David? I don't think he's given up on stopping that lander going."

"Do nothing for the moment. Let him make the next move. He'll get over it."

"I had better call Ethan."

"I'll stay if you don't mind. This is important, and my support will help in backing up whatever decision you make."

"I'd appreciate that." Celeste put the call through to Ethan. She waited for Ethan to answer it, although she guessed he might be still sleeping. She would be.

But Ethan came over the audio straight away. "Hi, Celeste, what's happening?"

"Sorry to disturb you. I have Hugo with me here. David and I had a conflict of opinion. Nothing I can't handle, but I promised to make sure we'd confirm we had every measure in place to prevent the possibility of the virus getting up here."

Ethan switched to visual. He had a beaming face, which surprised Celeste. "I knew you could do it," he said.

"Do what?"

"Take charge."

"Oh ... well ... thanks. It wasn't easy."

"But you did it. Hi, Hugo."

"Hi, and she didn't need me either. I feel like a stowaway," Hu said.

Ethan chuckled. "So, what do you want to discuss?"

"I'd prefer Marie with you," Celeste said.

"Hmm. OK. Let me round her up, and we'll call you back."

"See you soon." Celeste disconnected. She stayed seated, pondering her options. "Have you seen our sterilization procedures?" she asked Hu.

"Yes. I had to study them before we started assembling the wormhole portal and again before I descended to the planet with Senna."

"Can you suggest any improvements we can make to them?"

Hu sat in contemplation. "No. They look very thorough to me. I'd say you're over conservative. I suspect Marie contributed to developing them since that is part of her field of expertise."

The comm buzzed, and Celeste answered on visual. "Hi."

"Hi — Ethan again. Marie is with me. We had a quick discussion about what you told me before I called back. We can only suggest two minor modifications to increase the confidence level. I'll let Marie explain."

"Hi," Marie said. "As Ethan suggested, we have two improvements to the procedure to be doubly sure nothing contaminates the ship.

One is that the occupants of the lander disembark when the lander goes to its sterilization bay before its sequence starts. This will allow a triple dose of UV radiation to be washed onto and inside the lander and set it for double the time. No organic life will survive that. And the occupants should undergo a secondary sterilization."

"OK. We'll do that. Thanks. How are things? Sounds like they are getting worse."

"They could be better. I hope I can find what we are dealing with when Angelo arrives with the equipment."

"I won't keep you. See you."

Celeste broke contact. "What do you think?" she asked Hu.

Hu pondered, staring at Celeste. "What do *you* think?"

Celeste sighed but then braced herself. "I'm happy to let Angelo go with the changed procedure in place."

"Good. I will back you up if you need me."

"That's it then," Celeste said, concluding the conversation. "I'll tell Angelo and David and make the changes."

They both rose and left the room.

36

FIRST CASUALTY

Ethan entered his tent after his discussion with Celeste and froze. Jade was rubbing her temples. She noticed him. "It's OK. I'm just getting the tension out of my head. That's all."

"Don't scare me like that." Ethan pulled off his boots and clothes and slid in under the blankets of their bed again. She lay next to him, allowing him to place his arms around her as they cuddled. Ethan felt comfort in her warmth but couldn't suppress the nagging worry of what lay ahead.

Jade, sensing his tension, pulled away from him to gaze at him and said, "It will be OK."

"Yes. It will," he mimicked, his voice sounding unconvincing to him. He turned off the light and reclined, trying to doze.

He rose from the bed soon after a sleepless night.

"Let's get breakfast."

Ethan and Jade dressed, and he looked at his comm. He saw he had a message from Angelo. He read it. "Angelo should be here mid-morning."

"Good. Maybe we will sort this out then."

They headed for the mess tent, where Zane and Marie sat with the pilot and two technicians. They got their meal and sat at the same table.

"How is Senna?" Ethan asked.

Marie met the question with dread bleeding from her eyes. "The sooner Angelo gets here, the better."

"He should be here mid-morning. That serious?"

"She has severe pain. She's delirious. I'm surprised you didn't hear her shouts of agony during the night. The zopiclone did little for her."

"Not good. And Troy?" Ethan asked as he turned to Zane.

"He's OK. Just complaining he still has a headache. And he has a fever now. I told him to stay in bed, and I'd fetch him breakfast."

"Similar symptoms," Marie commented.

"Let's hope Angelo can resolve it," Ethan said

They ate the rest of their meal in silence as Ethan pondered their predicament. He wondered what he should do if things deteriorated. At present, they didn't even know what they were fighting. It may have no connection with the organism Marie had detected. Ethan hoped not, but it was too coincidental. And the skeletons. From where did they originate? Why seal them in the cave? Why had their skulls split open? Who put them there? These were questions that baffled him. He spent the morning housekeeping to keep his mind busy instead of fretting about what might happen. Marie said she'd collect blood samples from both Senna and Troy, so she was ready when Angelo arrived.

The lander carrying Angelo and the medical and test equipment landed just after ten-thirty. Ethan waited by the hatch as Angelo put on his suit and completed the anti-contamination procedures. The airlock opened, and Angelo descended to the surface. "I made it," he said through the full sterilizing filter he wore.

"Welcome. I wish it were under better circumstances."

"Shit happens. I stored the sequencer in the forward compartment, and I placed other medical equipment and supplies in the side compartments. It might be easier if your people unload them."

Ethan immediately called two technicians over to carry out the tasks.

Marie came over when she noticed Angelo had emerged from the lander.

"I was just telling Ethan that the sequencer is in the forward compartment," he told her.

"Good. I've collected two samples and can start running them straight away."

"A couple?" Angelo asked, raising an eyebrow with concern.

"Yes — unfortunately. Troy is experiencing a headache and fever, too."

"I see," Angelo said, gazing at Ethan with the same concerned expression he had given Marie.

"Yes, it doesn't look good at present," Ethan agreed. "So, what do you want to do?"

"I want to examine the patients, and we'll take it from there. Although I suggest you erect another tent as a hospital ward so that I can keep a better watch on them and segregate them from you and the others who appear to be healthy so far." Angelo turned to Marie. "Can you get blood samples from everyone and analyze them? We may as well check if everyone's infected."

"OK. I'll set up the sequencer first," Marie said. She walked toward the lander to unload, calling Zane over to help her.

"Catch up with me once you've looked at Senna and Troy. Let me know your conclusions," Ethan said to Angelo.

"I will." Angelo strode to the tent Senna was in, leaving Ethan standing by the lander, considering their position.

Ethan left for a quick stroll to clear his head. After that, he headed for the office tent, made himself a coffee, and sat at his desk playing with a stylus. He was staring intently at the stylus as he flipped it in his fingers when Angelo entered. He didn't raise his eyes to meet him as Angelo closed the door behind him.

"Killing time?" Angelo asked as he found a chair, placed it by Ethan's desk and sat.

Ethan grunted acknowledgment and looked at Angelo with a

melancholy expression. He couldn't see Angelo's face hidden by the covering he wore. "It'll be tiring wearing that all day."

"I've only been here a few hours, but it's becoming a nuisance already."

"So, what's the verdict?"

"I don't really know. Senna's brain is swelling, causing her headaches. I'll scan her brain once we move her. I'll do the same with Troy."

"What makes brains swell?"

"Usually, trauma causes it, a knock on the head. But she's experienced none. A variety of viruses can cause it. Her symptoms don't mirror any I know. If her condition doesn't improve soon, I may have to give her a decompressive craniectomy."

"A decompressive what?"

"Remove a part of her skull to relieve the pressure."

"Oh. Doesn't sound like something you want to be done to you."

"No. I have her in a coma. She's stable, but I'm worried."

"And Troy?"

"He's OK for now. But he says his headache is worsening and, again, his brain is swelling."

"Hmm ... hope no one else gets it."

"So do I."

Marie entered and stared at them with a look of analyzing concentration. She sat in another chair as she mulled over the wording for her report. "Running Senna's sample through the sequencer now. What have you got, Angelo?"

"I was just telling Ethan that it would appear the brain is swelling. The symptoms aren't any I have encountered."

Marie pondered the revelation. "I've found nothing like that in my research, either. Everything I've seen produces many more physical symptoms first. It's obvious that the person has caught something. This is ... specific."

"Yes, specific," Angelo agreed. "We need to understand how this organism functions. I hope you get the results soon, as I'm uncertain how to treat Senna other than make her comfortable until the infection passes."

"I'll work on the analysis as fast as I can. Not sure what we can decide with our apparatus."

"What do you mean?" Ethan asked, his interest increased by the news of their limitations.

"Well, we only have the basic equipment for analysis, and we have nothing to develop a vaccine or treatment drug."

"We could change that."

"Let's check our results first. I can offer a better direction for our actions then."

"I won't keep you here then. We need quick answers," Ethan said, suggesting an end to the discussion.

The door opened, and Jade poked her head inside, dread and fear plastered on her face like a horror film costume.

"What is it?" Ethan asked.

"It's Senna. She's dead."

37

EPIDEMIC

Ethan, Angelo, and Marie jumped in astonishment at the news like someone had sneaked up on them from behind and shouted 'boo.'

This worst-possible news was too much for Ethan. "How could Senna have deteriorated so fast?"

"Good question," Angelo replied. "I thought she was stable. Whatever this thing is, it progresses rapidly." He walked out the door at a brisk pace.

"Marie, we need an answer yesterday, please."

"I'll get you something when I can," Marie said as she moved to leave, too. Ethan knew her task took time, and she understood how important it was, but the pressure of finding a solution to their dilemma mounted.

Ethan put his head in his hands and rocked back and forth as though to shake his worry away. Jade came over and rubbed his shoulder with tender concern. He lifted his head and sighed. "This wasn't my expectation when I signed up for this expedition," he said. "I wanted an adventure, history-making discoveries, not for people to die or to become embroiled in this nightmare."

"We *have* made history. Senna is the first person to die on an exoplanet. Ethan, someone had to perish sometime. We're the unfortunate ones who met alien organisms that are hostile to our lifeform. We'll be the first to solve this problem, too. Early explorers to the New World had similar problems to resolve, but they survived and triumphed."

"But at what cost?"

"Whatever it takes, I suppose."

"Yeah, whatever it takes." Dejected, he rose and hugged Jade. He sighed again. "I won't change things by just sitting here moping."

They both left, Jade heading for the makeshift hospital, and Ethan taking another walk to clear his head.

THE AFTERNOON WAS WELL underway when Ethan entered Marie's workroom, curious to view her setup. Marie spotted him. "May I help you?"

"No. Just sticking my nose into your hideout," Ethan said. He sighed. "To be honest, I'm trying to find something useful to do."

Marie grinned. "You can keep whipping us for results." She was only half joking. "Preserve our morale, too. It's difficult knowing we may never see Earth again if we don't get on top of this."

Ethan acknowledged her wisdom. "Anything to report yet?"

Marie smiled with a patient expression. "Things don't happen that fast. I can say that the organism is an unusual strain. My first analysis suggests it has a DNA sequence unlike any I have seen before, yet it seems familiar. I can't put my finger on it. I'm having trouble finding where it attacks our genetic makeup. What's even more disturbing is that it resembles an artificial organism. I've experienced nothing natural like it."

"Full of positive news," Ethan grumbled.

Marie sighed with mock indignation. "Kill the messenger."

They both uttered a sad laugh.

"What does that mean, then?" Ethan asked.

"If it's synthetic, who made it and how did it enter the cave, for starters? Anything manufactured should have a key to unravel it, to negate its effects. But it's too early for me to speculate much further."

"Well, keep at it," Ethan said, preparing to leave when Angelo entered.

Angelo was pleased to find them together. "Good. I have interesting and important information. I have conducted an autopsy on Senna's brain. It has grown thirty percent more than normal."

"Isn't that what you'd expect if it was swelling?" Ethan asked, in ignorance of the implication.

"You don't understand, Ethan. It didn't swell. The actual brain mass increased. That's what caused the extra pressure. The added mass had nowhere to go. The skull couldn't expand anymore because the plates had fused. The skull usually grows four-fold from birth, but that happens while the plates of the skull are still floating. This ... I've never seen. I can't explain how this could happen."

Marie took in the information. "That's a good bit of intelligence. It may help zero in on what this organism does. I was just telling Ethan that this strain is artificial. It has a DNA sequence that affects our genetic makeup. I was having trouble with where to concentrate my attention on the genome, but that knowledge helps. It's only one case, though. Does Troy have the same symptoms?"

"Yes, he does. His brain is swelling too."

"How's he doing?" Ethan asked.

"Not too good. He's not deteriorating as fast as Senna, but he's getting worse."

They stood in concentrated misery when Jade opened the door to Marie's makeshift laboratory. "There you are," she said, worry lines etching her brow. "I have more grim news. Fiona, Nigel, and Sullivan are experiencing headaches. I've told them to go to the medical tent for you to examine them, Angelo."

"That leaves us three and Zane," Ethan said, panicked.

"I'd better check them," Angelo said and hurried out of the room.

"I need to keep working too if we want a cure," Marie said, turning to her machinery and readouts.

"Leave you to it," Ethan said, dejected. He left the laboratory with Jade following him.

Angelo caught up with Ethan several hours later. Ethan sensed he had bad news. He was wearing worry like a mourning suit at a funeral.

"How are they?"

"Not good, disastrous in fact. Troy has lapsed into unconsciousness, and the swelling in the others is increasing. Their headaches are getting worse."

"Can't you do anything?" Ethan asked in frustration. "What about that craniectomy thing?"

Angelo watched Ethan, searching for signs he wasn't coping. "If I thought that'd help, I'd do it, but the growth is too massive. I'd be removing the top of the skull, and that's impractical."

Ethan realized he was being over-demanding and panicky. "Sorry. I'm just frustrated. I know you're doing what you can."

"That's OK. You're allowed to get frustrated."

Ethan stood in silence for a time, exploring his own thoughts and feelings. "Is there anything we can do?" He hoped Angelo would take the question constructively and not him lashing out in frustration.

Angelo rubbed his faceplate with his fingers as he thought. "There's little I can do until we understand how to treat whatever it is. I can ease those suffering with the condition. You've more resources available to you. You need to make sure you use them to the fullest."

Ethan considered Angelo's words. "At present, we're relying on Marie to guide us on how to attack this problem. There's a hell of a weight on her shoulders. How could we reduce that burden?"

"She's the only one here with the skills to analyze this organism and understand how it affects us."

"That's a major responsibility."

"It is."

"How could we shed that load?"

Angelo considered his response. "We need to contact Earth and give them the problem. Can we do that?"

Ethan brightened as he saw an exit instead of just treading water, but he realized the danger in it, too. "We can't send them a sample of this thing. It could infect the whole planet."

"That isn't what I meant. But if that's what's needed, I'm sure we can deliver a specimen while keeping Earth safe. From what I understand, Marie's dealt with similar things we've created."

"That is food for thought, Angelo. Thanks for this."

"You're welcome."

Marie walked up to them, looking distressed and tired.

Ethan stared at her. "What's wrong?"

Marie avoided Ethan's eyes. She glanced at Angelo instead. "Zane is complaining of headaches, and Jade doesn't look much better. She's said nothing, though."

Ethan froze.

38

JOHN, WE HAVE A PROBLEM

Ethan held Jade in his arms. "Are you sure you're feeling well? You look exhausted."

He had walked the perimeter of the camp after he heard Marie's news, not wanting to believe what she had said, refusing to accept that Jade, his Jade, could succumb to the present crisis.

"I'm fine. Just tired," Jade said. She glanced away.

She sounded fatigued and in pain to Ethan, but he decided not to press the issue. "OK then. Rest ... please ... for me."

"I will." She moved over to the bed and reclined.

"I'll see you soon. Try to rest."

Ethan walked from their tent and headed for the office, where he sat gazing at the ceiling in thought, frustration, and fear. Something had to be done. He couldn't let things get worse. He decided he needed to contact John and placed a comm call through to *Destiny*. When the command center answered, he asked them to get Celeste and Hu so he could talk with them. The officer acknowledged the call and broke the communication. Celeste buzzed him ten minutes later. Ethan accepted. "Hello, Celeste. Thanks for getting back to me so quickly."

"Not a problem. Hugo is with me." Celeste moved so he could see Hu on the screen.

"Hi. I'll get to the point. Our plight here is deteriorating. Senna is dead ..."

"Dead!" Celeste and Hu both exclaimed in unison, shocked.

Ethan sighed. "Yes, unfortunately. And three more have symptoms besides Troy, and I am worried about Jade. She says she is alright, but I'm not sure."

"What do you need?" Hu said, instant readiness for action reflected in her tone and the change in her stance as she leaned forward.

Celeste glanced at her with a hint of resentment.

Hu spotted the look. "Sorry. I didn't intend to go over your head. But these are my close friends."

Celeste regained her composure. "That's alright." She returned her attention to Ethan. "As Hugo said, what do you need?"

"I want Hu to open the wormhole so you, Celeste, can send a message to General John O'Conner with a secure comm link for the two of us. Celeste needs to do this, not you, Hugo. I hope you understand."

"Perfectly," Hu said. "Consider it done."

"What do I say to the general?" Celeste asked.

Ethan thought for a moment. "Just tell him I need to speak with him urgently, and he must talk to me to get further information. I don't want you, Hugo, or anyone else telling him about what's happening. He needs to hear it from me and only me. We can't have any unauthorized leaks to Earth while the wormhole is open, either. I think you understand why."

Celeste glanced at Hu and back to Ethan. "Yes, we do." She turned to Hu. "How long before you can activate the portal?"

"I can get it open within two hours." Hu replied.

"So, how do I reach this general?" Celeste asked Ethan.

"I'll send you his contact details. If anyone says he is unavailable, tell that person to relay an urgent message to him. The message is 'Centauri'. He'll talk to you at once."

Celeste reddened again, suddenly feeling boxed into a position beyond her ability. "This is very cloak and dagger. I'm not sure I can handle it with everything else that's happening."

Hu responded, "Celeste, Ethan chose you to command for a reason. He has observed you and seen your ability. What you are experiencing now is just your questioning of your competence to handle this. Everyone has these moments, don't we, Ethan?"

Ethan chuckled. "Yes, we do, even you."

"I wasn't talking about me. I'm invincible," Hu riposted in mock affront at the suggestion.

"You're right, as usual," Celeste said, regaining her composure. "Can Hugo be present when I talk to the general?"

"Yes, that's fine. He knows her."

"Why don't you get her to do it, then?"

"She isn't a member of our expedition. It wouldn't be right. She can support you, though. John will know why I'm doing things this way."

"OK then. If Hugo can open the portal in two hours and we reach the general, can it stay open, Hugo?"

"It will stay open for as long as I say it will," Hu said.

"I'll get back to you, Ethan, as soon as we've contacted the general."

"Good, I'll be waiting."

The connection broke, with Ethan staring at the blank screen in dumb fear.

GENERAL JOHN O'CONNER sat next to the conference room door in a joint military chiefs-of-staff meeting discussing defense budgets. He twirled his pen absentmindedly, displaying the boredom he felt. An aide opened the door and entered. He presumed the aide was about to impart a message to one of the higher-ranked officers, so it surprised him when he zeroed in on him. John eyed him as the aide lent over to whisper something to him.

"I have a message from the Chinese base on the moon. The message is 'Centauri'. They are waiting on the link for you," the aide said.

John became fully alert, as if someone had just announced an impending air strike. He nodded, and the aide left. John packed up his belongings, data pad, pen, and diary and quietly rose to leave. He leaned over to his commanding officer sitting next to him and explained his need to be excused. His commander nodded acknowledgment, and John left.

The aide stood by the doorway. "This way, sir. There's a secure link set up in an office if you will follow me."

"Thank you."

The aide led John to an office nearby.

"Is the office shielded?" John asked.

"Yes."

"Good." John entered and closed the door behind him.

The room contained a desk in the center with a large comm unit positioned on it. John circled the desk and sat, placing his belongings on the desktop. The display was blank, in hold status. He activated the link, and a Chinese person came online. "General John O'Conner here."

"General O'Conner, it's good of you to be prompt. I am Chang Jian Zha of the Chinese Wormhole Project. You can call me Jian."

"A pleasure to meet you, Jian, but I feel the call is not a social one."

"No, it's not. We received a transmission through our wormhole from our Comrade Hu, who, as you know, is in Centauri with your expedition. A Celeste Grüber wishes an urgent conversation with you. She said that you would understand what the message meant."

"Yes, I do, although I wasn't expecting it from her."

"This is everything I know. I'll connect you at once. But first, Hu has instructed me to extend our services should you need help from us. This is an unusual order from a subordinate, but Hu is no ordinary person."

John chuckled at the comment. "Yes, Hu is extraordinary, that's for sure. And I thank you for your offer and will take it up if necessary."

"Right. I will say goodbye then."

"Goodbye, Jian."

The display went snowy as they changed the connection. Celeste came on the screen a few seconds later. John saw she was worried about something. Audio activated, she fidgeted in her chair and then said, "Hello, General O'Conner. I'm glad you could speak to us straight away. I have Ching Hu with me."

"Hello, Celeste. You can call me John. Hello, Hu."

"Hello, John," Hu said in greeting.

"I wasn't expecting to talk with you, Celeste, although I wasn't foreseeing talking to anyone from the expedition before you returned. What's happened?"

"Ethan has placed me in command of ship operations until he returns from the planet where he has a major incident on his hands. I think it is best that I let him explain it to you as soon as we can connect him to the conversation."

John raised his brow in surprise that Celeste was in charge of the spaceship, but when he thought through what he knew of her, he recognized Ethan had made a wise choice. He realized too that, amongst other things, Hu was with her to give her moral support. Again, a sensible move. "Fair enough. I see the wormhole functions for communications, Hu."

"Yes, and we have transported a shuttle through it, too."

"Excellent. That'll be a tremendous help for future work."

"Yes, it will, and that prospect may be closer than you think."

"You alarm me now, Hu."

"Sorry, I do not wish to alarm you."

Celeste butted into the conversation after communicating with the ship's staff off screen while John and Hu were talking. "Ethan is joining us, John."

A dot on John's display faded, and an image of Ethan appeared, causing John concern. Something was wrong with Ethan. He looked tired and unkempt.

Ethan faced them. "Hi, John. Glad you could get to us straight away."

"You're welcome, but what is this incident?"

Ethan lowered his eyes, almost overcome with emotion, but he gathered his wits and stared at John. "We have a problem. We have encountered a living organism compatible with our DNA, and it has infected us."

"Oh. Tell me more."

"We are on a planet we have called Chariclo orbiting Alpha Centauri A. It has a breathable atmosphere and an interesting life-form inhabiting the world. Senna ... found a sealed-up cave, which we opened after testing the interior. Our exploration of the cavern uncovered something extraordinary, a mass interment of human-like skeletons and ... a surprise. Marie picked up a microorganism on her monitors. We evacuated the cave at once, but it had already infected us. Several have succumbed to the effects of the virus and ... Senna is dead."

John jolted in his chair. "That is serious." He was silent for a moment. "And the others?"

"Four of the eight of us have it in various stages of severity and ... one or two more concern me. Angelo is caring for them the best he can, and Marie is analyzing the virus for treatment solutions, but we need help before more die."

"I see. What are the symptoms?"

"The brain grows."

"Can't Angelo control the inflammation?"

"It's not inflamed, John. It physically grows in size."

John looked puzzled. "That's most unusual."

"Yes. It manipulates a part of the chromosomal DNA, but Marie can't pinpoint where yet."

John reclined in thought, fidgeting with his pen. A noise over the comm interrupted him. Ethan glanced to the side, alarm crossing his face a moment later.

"Troy?" Ethan asked whoever was off screen. He sighed and

turned back to John. "There are now two deaths. Troy, one of our technicians, just died."

John noticed the emotional stress on Ethan, like Atlas struggling to hold up the world. He needed to support him, to share the load as best he could from Earth. "OK, Ethan, what are our options?"

"We need a cure for this, and we need it fast. Marie needs help to solve it."

"Can you deliver a sample of this virus to us? I will get our biohazard strike team working on it at once."

"I'm worried about the virus escaping and contaminating Earth."

"We're more likely to crack this on Earth where we have everything than trying to send personnel or equipment to you in dribs and drabs as the need arises."

"I can give you complete access to the wormhole as a priority," Hu said.

"Jian said you can be persuasive," John said drily.

"What is the point in having clout if you can't use it when you need it?" Hu responded grimly.

Ethan rubbed his chin, thinking. "I know Marie brought biohazard containers with her. I suppose we can store the virus in those and then triple-sterilize the exterior."

"That sounds like the start of a plan," John said. "Keep Marie connected with our personnel on Earth to impart her knowledge through the wormhole. Is it hard to set up, Hu?"

"No. But the timing needs to be right. We could hold it open for an extended period of communication."

"Ethan, how fast can you deliver the samples to me?"

Ethan thought for a moment. "Three or four hours to get them to the ship. Marie might need containers sent here. I don't know if she has any with her. Then, passage through the wormhole is ten minutes, isn't it, Hu?"

"That's right. We'll then need to transport them from the moon to Earth. That takes twelve hours."

"I can send a lander to rendezvous with your shuttle at the moon when it gets there. I have one that can complete the trip in three." Hu raised an eyebrow at the lander's inferred acceleration rate. John chuckled. "Our little secret, Hu."

"Of course," Hu said, grinning.

"Let's do that then. I can't guarantee when we'll have a breakthrough, Ethan, but I promise I'll place Earth's best resources on it, from any nation."

"Thanks, John. Well, I'll get things rolling on this end. Thanks again for the quick response."

"That's fine. Celeste, Hu, stay on to coordinate our movements."

"Will do," Celeste said.

Ethan broke his connection.

"How's Ethan holding up, Hu?" John asked, concerned about the visible signs of strain on Ethan.

"He's holding up for now." Hu sighed. "I don't know how he'll cope if Jade succumbs to this virus, though."

"Well, watch him."

"I will."

"Celeste, I want you to take complete command of everything on *Destiny*."

Celeste sat in silence like someone shell-shocked.

John sensed she needed encouragement. "Ethan placed you in charge of the ship for a reason. I support that reason. Don't disappoint him."

She remained silent, but her posture altered from doubt and hesitation to determination to step up to the challenge. John liked the change. "I won't, sir."

"Good. How do we organize transfer our end then, Hu?"

"Discuss that with Jian. He is closer to the action there."

"I will. It's better to keep an open communication link if that's possible."

"I'll review it with our moon-based operators, but I don't see it as a problem unless it malfunctions, and we need a temporary shutdown."

"I have things to organize. Godspeed."

"Goodbye," Celeste and Hu said in unison.

John sat in the office, mulling over priorities. He remembered they had a self-contained biohazard laboratory in space set up for cases like this one. It would avoid the need to bring the virus to Earth. That was the best choice, in his opinion. He stood, left the room, and headed off to organize things at his end.

39

MUTINY

Ethan got busy after his conversation with John with getting the samples prepared for transport to Earth. He headed for Marie, as she would be instrumental in the task.

Marie glanced up from her work when he walked into her laboratory. "What's up?" she said.

"I've just finished talking with people on Earth–"

"How did you do that?" she interrupted, surprised that it was possible.

"We set up a comm link through the wormhole. Thanks to Hu and the Chinese team on the moon."

"Oh. So, what did you say?"

"Getting more resources working on a cure for whatever this virus is."

Marie jumped in surprise and, for a moment, looked offended. "Why — aren't I good enough?"

Ethan realized where this was headed unless he checked her reaction straight away. "You're doing an incredible job with what you have available, but you can only tell us how it behaves. You can't produce a cure. My gut says we need speed if we want to get off this planet alive."

Marie's indignation collapsed with the logic of what Ethan was saying. She sighed, drained from the long hours she had already worked. She brushed a tress of hair from her brow. "Sorry. I'm tired, I guess. What you are saying is perfectly sensible. I can't produce a cure with what I have here. I don't even know if I can give you a complete explanation for it or how it works. What do you need me to do?"

"We need to prepare samples to send to Earth so they can start analyzing it with more grunt."

"Are you sure that's wise? We don't want this infecting Earth."

"You tell me. Surely, you've transported lethal materials before in your line of work. How did you do that with confidence?"

"Of course. I'm not thinking straight." Marie walked to a chair by a desk and sat. She closed her eyes, placed her face in her hands, and rubbed it to remove her tiredness.

"Looks like you need to rest," Ethan commented.

"Maybe," Marie said as she raised her head again. "Yes, we use triple isolation containers. I have none on the planet, though. Lucky, I had the sense to bring them with us. There are five up on *Destiny*. Someone will have to get them."

"I'll get the lander Angelo arrived in to fetch them. We can prepare the samples in the meantime. How do the containers work?"

"We place each sample in the central canister and seal it. Then we irradiate that canister to remove any organics on the exterior. They make the bottle from a radiation-impervious material, keeping the specimen safe. It's then placed in a second container, which we clean and irradiate with a different disinfectant radiation source and the same with the third canister. We handle the whole procedure in a specific apparatus."

"That sounds secure enough. I presume they have similar precautions on the other end when they open the container."

"Yes, and I've been thinking. I am aware of a biohazard laboratory in orbit around Earth. If they have any sense, they'll use that to conduct their research. That way, it's still remote from Earth."

"I'm sure John has considered it. Can you prepare samples, and

I'll organize the lander to bring the containers? Is there anything else helpful to send?"

"Maybe my observations so far. That should give them a head start."

"OK. Get what's useful ready. The Chinese will keep the link open for comms, so you can talk with whoever is doing this research to compare notes."

"Oh. That would be helpful. Tell me who's in charge that end."

"I will." Ethan left, leaving Marie to concentrate on her sample preparation. He contacted the lander pilot and got him to power up and travel to *Destiny* to collect the containers. He then headed for his office to talk with Celeste. Once he organized everything, he made his way to the makeshift hospital to speak with Angelo.

Angelo looked around when he entered. His face held the fear of another patient being admitted. He sighed, relieved to see Ethan and that he seemed well.

"How are things here?" Ethan asked.

"Not much different. Conditions are stable at present. Nigel, Fiona, and Sullivan are under sedation, and Zane is just resting."

"I've arranged for support from Earth to find a cure for this. Marie and I are packaging samples to send through the wormhole so they can help us with our challenge."

"Good. We can use any help we can get. We're fortunate we have the wormhole."

"Yes. Very."

"What are your impressions of Marie and Jade?" Angelo inquired, probing for Ethan's assessment.

Ethan wondered why he asked. "They look tired, but they say they are healthy."

"I hope they aren't trying to hide their symptoms. What about you?"

"I'm fine. Exhausted but fine. I don't have a headache."

"Interesting."

"What do you mean?"

"You were among the first exposed to the virus, but you don't display any signs. Is there any reason for that?"

Ethan shrugged his shoulders. "Lucky, I guess."

"Luck doesn't come into it. May I suggest Marie take a sample of your blood and send it back with the rest of the specimens? You might have an anomaly that gives the researchers a clue about the cure."

"Sure. They can't have too much data. Do you want anything from the ship?"

"No. I have what I need. Just bring me something I can use to stop this."

"I second that."

Ethan left. Once the lander left for the ship, he headed for his cabin to catch up with Jade and wait for the lander to return. When he entered, he saw Jade was asleep. Standing there gazing at her, he took in her beauty as she slept, her peaceful face radiating perfection. He dreaded what he might do if something happened to her and feared waking her to check how she was in case he didn't like her response. He let her sleep and turned to leave.

"Where are you going?" Jade's dreamy voice asked.

Ethan moved to her. "You were sleeping, and I didn't want to wake you." He sat on the bed and bent over to kiss her on the lips.

Jade lifted her hand and placed it in his, rubbing the back of it with her thumb. "You can never disturb me."

Ethan stroked her forehead with his other hand. "How do you feel?"

Jade smiled. "I'm fine. Just tired. We haven't slept well of late."

"I suppose," Ethan said, keeping his concern to himself. "I'll leave so you can rest."

"OK." Jade offered another sleepy smile.

Ethan gave her a kiss as he rose to go. They parted, and he left the cabin, worry clenching his stomach as he entered the warm sunlit outside air.

The lander returned in two hours, and Marie packed the samples. Ethan mentioned what Angelo said about his blood, and Marie collected a sample and packaged it, too. The lander headed back to *Destiny* after another hour.

CELESTE WATCHED as the lander prepared to board the ship. She was in the command center monitoring the on-ship functions. A red light blinked for the lander bay door to open. She thought it was strange. It should already be open. "Why is the lander bay door closed?" she asked the logistics officer.

"I don't know. It should be open, but it's not. Let me check."

Celeste heard the lander pilot communicating a few moments later. "Lander 2 to *Destiny*, ready to dock. Repeat, ready to dock. Please open the door."

There was silence from the controller in the lander bay. That was odd. The controller should have responded. Celeste replied, "Lander 2 pilot, Celeste here. Please stay where you are. I'll investigate why the door isn't open."

"Roger. Will stay stationary till further notice."

Celeste rose from the command chair and headed for the lander bay.

As she stepped out of the elevator, she froze. Pandemonium filled the bay. The Bay Controller lay on the floor, unconscious or dead, and the panel that controlled the bay door was smashed with David and four others surrounding it, menacing everybody else with makeshift weapons of spanners, hammers, and other such objects. She strode up to David. "What the hell is going on, David?"

David looked at Celeste with restless eyes, ready for instant violence on anybody who came too close. "No one's getting through those doors and threatening us with that virus, and no one's contaminating Earth."

"Don't be ridiculous, David. They've contained the pathogen in sterilized containers. It won't contaminate anyone. Now give me that and let me open the door." She walked closer to him.

"Stay back, or you'll get the same treatment as him." David pointed to the controller lying on the floor.

Celeste stopped approaching when she realized David meant what he said. "So, you will let our friends on the planet die because you're afraid?"

"They knew the risk. No need for us to die because they were careless."

Celeste studied David. She understood at that moment what his true personality was. "You're a coward."

"I'm a survivor."

"You're a coward. You'd sacrifice this entire ship if it meant you were safe, wouldn't you?"

The others in David's posse shuffled, uncomfortable with the implied revelation, but stood firm to support him.

"I'm doing what's right. No one else can see the big picture, especially you. You are out of your depth. You shouldn't be in charge."

Celeste folded her arms, confronting David. "Really? And what gives you that idea? I'm not blinded by my cowardice? I consider the entire team and not just saving my butt? Really, David, you must do better than that. Now stop this ridiculous behavior before I have to resort to more drastic measures."

"You're the one that can't see the big picture. You're dazzled by your own sense of importance. Stay back."

Celeste shrugged and said, "Have it your way, then."

A smug expression of victory passed over David's face as she turned to go.

David doesn't know that Ethan told me of the weapon he keeps secure in his quarters and has given me the combination to retrieve it. She used the elevator to fetch the pulse pistol from Ethan's safe.

Celeste re-entered the lander bay ten minutes later, the pistol hidden in the small of her back. She walked up to David again. "Your last chance, David. Give this up or suffer the consequences."

"What are you going to do? Strike me with your charm?"

"No, stun you with this," Celeste said as she withdrew the gun from where she had hidden it. She altered the setting on the firearm to stun, aimed it at David's chest, and fired.

David's eyes widened in surprise and alarm and then deadened when his body felt the effect of the stunning and slumped to the floor, twitching with spasms.

"Any of you others want to stand in my way?" Celeste challenged the rest of the mutineers.

The group stared at each other, confused and directionless without David's leadership. One by one, they stepped aside from the panel to allow Celeste access to it.

Security had come with her. "Take these into custody for trial," Celeste said to the senior officer. David's accomplices were led away, and David's limp body was carried away with them.

Celeste looked at the board. It was a mess. She gazed at the controller and approached him, feeling for a pulse. He was still alive, thankfully, but that wouldn't open the door. "Someone, call for a medico." She went over to the panel. This was out of her depth. She needed help and turned to the crowd. "How do I open the door?"

One technician said, a nervous tremor in his voice, "I know there's a manual override."

"Where is it?"

"Over here," he said, leading Celeste to a separate station.

They arrived at their destination. "Well? Why are you waiting? Open the door."

The command flustered him. "Sorry. I ..."

"Stay calm. Just open the door."

The technician took a deep breath, glancing nervously at the pistol Celeste still held in her hand. Celeste noticed his discomfort and tucked the handgun out of sight. He turned to the panel with relief and folded away a part of it, revealing manual switches and levers. They had labeled one lever 'Lander Bay Door.' He pushed the lever to the open position, and the door whirred, pivoting on its hinges. Celeste headed to a comm when the door fully retracted and contacted the lander pilot. "Clear to land."

The lander entered the bay a few minutes later and landed with no further incident.

Celeste had the containers with the virus transferred to the Chinese shuttle at once. Hu came once Celeste notified her that the shuttle was ready to go.

"I hear you handled a commotion here before," Hu said to Celeste.

"You could say that. David created a small mutiny ... I had to use force to remove him. I feel guilty about it, but I could think of nothing else I could do. He wouldn't see reason."

"Don't be sorry. If people want to misbehave, that isn't your fault. You have a job to do. So, we can leave now?"

"Is the moon base ready?"

"Yes. They have dilated the wormhole. I just have to take it to wherever General O'Conner wants me to go."

"Hasn't he told you yet?"

"I think they know. They just haven't notified me. Anyway, hope to see you soon with an antidote for this thing."

"I hope so, too," Celeste said with a pensive look.

Hu boarded the shuttle and took off a few minutes later.

40

THE SEARCH

Hu arrived at the moon ten minutes after entering the wormhole. Two craft waited for her at the other end, one a Chinese shuttle, the other an American lander.

"Welcome back," came Jian's familiar voice over the comm as she shot from the wormhole portal orifice.

"Not a social visit, Jian," she replied. "Where do I take the samples?"

"General John O'Conner is on the American lander. He'll take charge from here. I will hand you to him."

"Hello, Hu," John greeted her. "Call me John. Glad to see you here so fast. We're going to our biohazard orbiting laboratory. I believe your people are ready to transfer the canisters to my ship."

"Hello, John. It hasn't been without its issues, but that's news we can discuss later. I'll get the containers ready for pickup."

The technicians outside came in, collected the samples, and sent them to John's lander.

"OK. I have transferred the specimens. I'll let you go," Hu said to John.

"Before you do, why don't you transfer to my lander? Your first-hand experience may prove useful. Jian suggested it, and I presume you would like to check our progress."

Hu raised an eyebrow in surprise. "Oh. I'll maneuver to docking distance and get a pilot to take over, then." Hu spent the next hour jostling her shuttle closer to the lander and extending the docking tunnel to connect the two ships so she could board. The tube connected, and Hu entered it a few minutes later, having given the shuttle controls over to the pilot. She approached the lander and opened the outer hatch, entering the airlock and the lander moments later. She opened the inner door once she had the green light.

"Welcome aboard," John said as he stood nearby.

"Good to be here. Thanks for inviting me."

"I'm glad to have you. Let's retract the docking tunnel and leave." John returned to the pilot's seat. Hu followed him and sat in the vacant copilot chair next to him. John had the shuttle pilot withdraw the tube and fired up his drives, heading for the biohazard laboratory. He increased power to generate the greatest acceleration, reducing the journey's time.

"How are things back there?" John asked once Hu had settled and he had completed the trajectory adjustments for the trip.

"Tense summarizes it. Ethan is worried sick and blaming himself for what has happened, especially since he is concerned Jade has symptoms. And to compound matters, an incident occurred on *Destiny* when the lander returned from Chariclo with the samples. David had smashed the lander day door control panel and was preventing anyone from gaining access to it, with the aid of a few others that he convinced to help him in his cause."

"Why? What was his problem?"

"The risk of the virus infecting the ship was too high for David."

"Hmm. Ethan and I discussed David at length before the expedition. We may have settled on the wrong choice after all. It's too late now. How was it resolved?"

"Ha! David may have been a wrong decision but placing Celeste in charge was the right one. I wasn't there but, from others' accounts, she tried reasoning with him and, when that failed, she used Ethan's pistol to stun him. I think she'd had enough of David's torment. Opposition evaporated after that."

John raised an eyebrow at the drastic measure Celeste had taken but then chuckled. "People amaze me every day. I didn't think Celeste had it in her. There's a powerful intellect and courage hiding inside that slight frame. Ethan must have seen that."

"I admit she's surprised me too, but she still lacks confidence. She'll grow. You may have to build another ship for her to command unless she takes over from Ethan permanently."

"Now that's food for thought."

"So, what happens when we arrive?"

"We'll dock. I have the team leader on standby for us, and he'll get his team working on the issue straight away."

"Oh. Marie sent research files with me. Might be useful to forward the data to them."

"Can you give them to me, and I'll send them? It's a classified laboratory, so I can't give you access to the systems even with the close relationship that we have on this."

"That's fine." Hu retrieved her data pad and transferred the information. He sent them.

"John, if there's anything you need that we can offer, please ask. I will make sure you get it."

"You have influence."

Hu smiled. "I am very persuasive sometimes."

"I bet you are."

They both sat back for the rest of the trip to the orbiting laboratory, making occasional small talk.

John contacted the lab as they approached it. "General John O'Conner wishes to speak to Dr. Kawoski of Bio-Lab Echo-Lima-Yankee-Zero-One."

"Bio-Lab Echo-Lima-Yankee-Zero-One acknowledges General John O'Conner. Dr. Kawoski here."

"Doctor, we are approaching the station now. Did you receive the package I sent you?"

"Yes, I did. Marie does excellent work. It will fast track what we need to do."

"Good. We'll contact you again once we have docked."

"Looking forward to meeting you and the parcel you are carrying."

The link broke, and John started maneuvering the shuttle to prepare for docking. They berthed at the laboratory twenty minutes later, and technicians unpacked the canisters, taking them away to begin their study of the enclosed virus. John and Hu boarded the lab to the welcome of Dr. Kawoski.

"Doctor Kawoski, Ching Hu of the Chinese Wormhole Project."

"Pleased to meet you, Ching Hu. I've heard of you, including your exquisite beauty. The words don't do justice to seeing you. I hope you don't mind me mentioning it."

Hu blushed but remained composed. "The pleasure is mine, doctor, and it's difficult walking around with your American definition of beauty. I don't mind you acknowledging it. I am used to the attention, but I'd prefer we concentrate on the issue at hand since very dear friends at Centauri need a successful outcome of your work."

Dr. Kawoski smiled. "Of course. My people are unpacking the containers and preparing the specimens for analysis, but we have a head start in finding what we lack, thanks to Marie's research."

"So, what is the procedure now?" John asked.

"We will continue the genome mapping Marie started and see where it aligns with the genes in the human body. Once we know that, we can design an antiviral treatment for the condition. This has me intrigued. This sequence looks familiar, but I just can't put my finger on it."

"We won't keep you then."

Hu and John stayed in a special cabin Dr. Kawoski arranged for them while they waited.

Hu kept fidgeting impatiently like she was waiting for the release of her final exam results. John saw her from time to time and tried to calm her. Her agitated state surprised him. He finally had to know what was bothering her.

"What is it?"

"Nothing. It's childish. I just want nothing to happen to Ethan and Jade. They are the best friends I have. I can't stand this waiting."

"We all wish them no harm," John said, sharing her anxiety. "The team's working as fast as they can."

"I know." She paused, in deep contemplation, as if choosing her words carefully. "I had a partner once," she said, somber and distant, remembering another universe of her existence. John listened without interruption. "We were so much in love. He was a fanatical adventurer, though, and always had his next venture to achieve. He'd return with tales of his quests in such excited detail ... and then one day he didn't. They found him days later at the end of a cascade of rapids. It ripped my heart apart. I felt lost for months. Ethan and Jade's relationship feels similar. I don't want ... that to happen to either Ethan or Jade."

John dared to reach over and take her hand in sympathy. "That is a tragic story. I am sorry."

Hu looked at him, a smile of gratitude on her face, absorbing the understanding he was giving her.

"Ethan and Jade are strong. They won't give up without a fight. They will come through this," John said. He and Hu searched each other's eyes out of curiosity to view each other's souls, just wishing to connect once to seal the conversation's meaning. But, at that moment, a spark jumped between them like a bolt of lightning. They both started in surprise and broke the connection, embarrassed to articulate what had happened. John withdrew his hand, and they both sat in silence.

They avoided each other after that, frightened they might have to confess something they wished to stay hidden.

41

DESPERATION

E than moped around the camp after the lander left. Jade worried him. It wasn't normal for her to be so tired. He couldn't think or concentrate, so he left to talk to Angelo.

"How is everything here?" Ethan asked when he entered the makeshift hospital, beds strewn where they were most convenient for Angelo to access the sick lying on them. Various apparatus stood monitoring the patients as he considered the prognoses of their illness.

"Not good," Angelo said as he looked up from viewing the latest sample taken from Zane, wrinkles of worry covering his brow. "Zane is comatose, and the others are deteriorating. I hope they can crack this thing soon."

"So do I."

Silence filled the air as Angelo waited for him to continue, but Ethan was reluctant to speak.

"Do you want something?" Angelo finally asked, breaking the deadlock.

Ethan pursed his lips. He couldn't face Angelo; his emotions would overcome him if he did. He looked at Zane instead. "It's Jade.

She's unusually tired. I know we're under stress and working long hours, but she–"

"You wish me to examine her," Angelo finished for him, saving Ethan the pain of saying it.

"Yes," Ethan said, gaining the courage to glance at him.

"Not a problem. I'll just finish here and then I'll pop over and check her. I'm sure she is fine."

"Thanks."

Ethan left, unconvinced by Angelo's show of optimism. Jade didn't appear OK to him. He headed for his office for solitude and sat at his desk, gazing out the window.

He remembered an occasion when he was a youth of fourteen. His ten-year-old sister became very ill with a virus she had picked up from somewhere. His father was away, leaving him to care for her and his brother. He didn't know what to do. She got worse, and nothing he tried gave her relief or remission from her condition. She lapsed into a stupor. Frantic, he dashed next door to ask the neighbor for help. The wife came over to check on his sister and rushed her to the hospital, chastising him for not seeking her support sooner. Ethan had sat with his sister until the nursing staff chased him away to rest, despite his insistence that he wanted to stay. His sister recovered, but he found out later that they had gotten her medical attention just in time …

He sighed as he realized he should do something instead of daydreaming or work himself up with worry. When he glanced at his data pad, he saw a message from Celeste to contact her, so he placed a call to her to see what she wanted. He waited for five minutes for her to answer. She came onto the comm screen.

"Hello, Ethan. Glad you could call me back," Celeste said.

"Hi. What's happening?"

"David caused a crisis here. I just thought you should know. He wouldn't let the lander enter the ship. He wrecked the lander bay's door controls and barred anyone from coming near them."

The news alarmed Ethan. He needed the samples sent to Earth. "You stopped him, didn't you? The specimens got on their way?"

"Yes, they did. I had to stun him with the pulse pistol, though. I have him in the brig. He and the others he convinced to help him."

Ethan sighed in relief. "Thank God for that." He lost his concentration for a moment before he came back to her. "You did the right thing."

"Are you alright, Ethan?" Celeste asked, frowning with concern.

Ethan groaned again. "Things are strained here. With everyone getting sick and everything."

Celeste spasmed with alarm. "Are you sick?"

"No, I'm fine. It's the others."

"Oh. And Jade?"

"I ... don't know," Ethan said, averting his eyes in distress. He looked back after recovering his composure. "Is that it, then?"

"Yes. I wanted you to know what occurred."

"Thanks for that. You should fill out a report for the record when we return to Earth."

"OK. I'll do that."

Ethan broke the connection. He reclined in his chair and closed his eyes to rest and think.

When he reopened them, it felt like seconds later, but it was over an hour. The door opened. Angelo entered, with a pensive stare behind the environmental suit. Ethan moved to an erect position in his seat. "Have you seen Jade?"

"Yes, I have, and I'm afraid she's infected with the virus, although it's affecting her slower than the others. That's good, I suppose, but I want her to move to the hospital tent so I can watch her, too."

The news devastated Ethan, even though it didn't surprise him. He braced forward and held his forehead in despair, shaking his head. He raised himself. "Is there anything you can do?"

"I'm already doing what I can. We need to pray they come good with a cure on Earth."

"Why can't you do more?" Ethan shouted.

The response took Angelo aback, but he said nothing. He recognized that Ethan needed to vent.

Ethan calmed. "Sorry. I didn't mean to shout at you. I just feel so helpless."

"Your reaction is understandable. I've watched it many times, and it's natural. Let's use it to help these people ... Jade ... have the best chance of recovery we can."

"Yeah, you're right. Thanks, Angelo. Have you seen Marie?"

"I popped in on her. She says she is fine, but I'm not sure. It's as if she believes she must solve this herself and won't stop."

"We can't let her pause if it helps fix this."

"I suppose not. I had better get back."

"OK. I'll move Jade to the hospital."

Angelo left. Ethan held his head again and started crying tears he couldn't stem. He needed someone but was isolated and alone. His lament ended. He decided he couldn't afford self-pity when others needed him to stay in control. It was so hard, though. He groaned to his feet as he made his way to Jade's tent, feeling tired and old, but he stretched to get the blood circulating again.

Jade still lay on the bed when Ethan entered the tent, asleep. Ethan sat on the edge and gazed at her with love and fear. She opened her eyes at the disturbance. "Hi," she said in a languid voice.

"Hi. I'm moving you to the hospital."

"Hmm, hm." Her demeanor changed. Alarm radiated from her, like lancing lasers piercing Ethan with needles of despair. "I'm frightened, Ethan."

Ethan kissed her. He wrapped his arms around her shoulders, raised her torso, and hugged her. "It'll be OK. We'll find a cure," Ethan said in as convincing a voice as he could muster. He was finding it difficult to believe his own words. He needed to keep his faith that John and Hu would return with a treatment. "Let's get you over to the hospital."

Jade rose, groggy, supported by Ethan. He had her put her arm around his shoulders and led her to the hospital tent. It was like a march of despair for Ethan, like helping the victim to the firing squad, waiting for the commander's order to fire. They arrived, and Angelo showed him a bed for Jade. Ethan eased her into it, and she collapsed once he let go of her, too exhausted from the walk. He made her comfortable.

Ethan gathered a nearby chair and planted it next to Jade's bed. He sat and placed her hand in his and stroked it with his thumb as he watched her breathing, shallow but regular. His eyes never left her face. He remained there for half an hour before he realized he should tend to other matters. Jade had fallen asleep, so there wasn't much point in staying. He laid her hand back on the bed and rose.

He trudged over to Angelo.

Angelo glanced at him and saw his worry. He gripped Ethan's shoulder. "I'll take care of her," he promised.

Ethan nodded his gratitude and left. He plodded over to Marie to get an update on her progress. When he opened the door, she turned to see who it was, and Ethan jumped in shock at the sight of her exhausted features and black-ringed eyes staring at him like an owl.

"Oh, hi," she droned with no enthusiasm.

"You could use a sleep."

"I'm too busy to rest. I need to solve this. How is everyone?"

"Similar. I took Jade to the hospital," he said, keeping his voice neutral, not daring to face her.

"I must keep going." Marie turned back to her work for a minute as Ethan watched. She paused as if an idea had occurred to her and faced him. "How are you?"

"I'm fine. Exhausted, but fine."

"Exactly. Why? You were with Senna and the rest of us. Why don't you have any symptoms?" A spark of excitement brought light to her face, hiding the mask of strain that had moved onto it. "Angelo was right ... there's something different about you."

"I don't know."

"Do you recall doing anything different in the cave?"

"Not that I remember. I handled the skeletons, too."

"Are you sure?"

"Of course."

"Hmm." The passion disappeared, exposing the underlying

anxiety again. She turned back to her work and the exhaustion it caused.

"Making any progress?"

"Not yet," Marie said, not diverting her attention.

Ethan stood watching her for another minute and left, walking in the open instead. He wandered from the camp, oblivious to any danger from the natural environment. The trees swayed in the breeze, rustling as the various fronds and leaves rasped each other. He stopped five hundred meters from the camp and listened. Apart from the trees, silence filled the air. The sun's rays broke through the tree canopy and warmed his face. He resented the serenity. It shouldn't be so splendid, he thought. It should be dull and gloomy, reflecting his mood. He started strolling again and pondering Marie's words. Had something else happened in the cave? Had he done something no one else had? He contemplated the question, but nothing occurred to him, despite an inkling that something had happened. He shrugged and returned to the camp, not wanting to lose his way. No one could search for him if he did. He trudged back and headed for the mess tent. He had dinner, since it was late, and came back to the hospital.

Seated in the chair next to Jade's bed, Ethan stared at her. He held her hand again, rubbing it with his thumb. He looked around and wondered whether the others were wishing they had someone by their side in this time of crisis for them, comforting them and giving them strength. *They'd envy Jade if they were conscious*, Ethan thought. It didn't diminish Jade's predicament or change the fear in Ethan's heart and his sense of helplessness, that same helplessness he had experienced when his sister neared death those many years ago. He reclined in the seat, still rubbing Jade's hand.

Ethan jumped with a start. He scanned the room. Everything was the same, except Angelo wasn't there. He glanced at the time and realized he had fallen asleep. It was early morning. He tensed and stared at Jade. She looked the same, her breathing still shallow and regular. He noticed Angelo had set up a drip for her during the night. Other tubes protruded. Wires extended from her, crazy radiating tentacles from a monitoring machine. He let go of Jade's hand and stood, stretching the kinks out of his bones.

Angelo came into the room. "You're awake. I could have moved you but didn't have the heart."

"Thanks. But my body's protesting."

Angelo gave a half-hearted smile.

"I have bad news, I'm afraid. Zane just died."

"Oh," Ethan said, not knowing what else to say. His posture flagged into defeat. He asked, "And the others?"

"Deteriorating. I've hooked Jade up to sustain her; she hasn't been eating or drinking. She's still stable."

Ethan sighed. His frustration reached a crescendo as he approached a solid section of the tent wall and punched it with all his strength several times. Fortunately, the material flexed, or he would have caused himself a serious injury. He stopped, and tears started oozing from his eyes, cascading down his face. "Are we going to lose everyone?" he asked Angelo behind him. "And why hasn't it got me?"

"I don't know the answer to either of those questions," Angelo said, walking to Ethan and patting his shoulder, "but breaking your hand won't help much."

Ethan chuckled. "I suppose not." He wiped his tears away and returned to Jade to continue his vigil.

"Why don't you grab a bite to eat? I'll keep a close watch on her."

"I'm not hungry, but you're right." Ethan left and went to the mess tent for breakfast. Surely, they've developed a cure by now, he thought as he sipped his coffee. He went to check on Marie and then contact John if he could.

He headed for the laboratory and entered. Marie sat slumped over in her chair. Ethan assumed she was asleep but wasn't sure. He shook her, but she only stirred, too weak to come to full consciousness. He looked at what she had been doing and read her notes. Her last entry was, 'Ethan is different. Must get another sample of b...'. His eyes gaped in surprise at the implications of her words.

He tried raising her again with the same result. He needed to move her to the hospital, so he left to tell Angelo. Both he and Angelo manhandled Marie to the hospital and a spare bed. *We won't need any more beds now*, Ethan thought.

A monitoring machine sounded an alarm. It was Sullivan's. Angelo glanced over and back at Ethan, sadness in his eyes. "Another one."

Ethan balled his hands into fists several times, hoping the exercise would leak the despair from him as he resisted the urge to hit the wall again. He stormed out, saying nothing to Angelo.

He headed for the office and contacted the ship to get John on the comm.

42

BREAKTHROUGH

John was looking through messages in an office the laboratory had set aside for Hu and him when his comm sounded. He noted it originated from the Chinese moon base and glanced at Hu. "You should join me on this."

She looked up from what she was doing, disorientated by the distraction. John's meaning registered. "Oh." She rose and came over, pulling up a chair to sit next to him. His closeness discomforted her. She noticed John move in his chair, too.

John opened the link to the Chinese. "General O'Conner here."

"Stand by to connect to *Destiny*," the speaker said.

John straightened at the revelation. "Confirmed."

Moments later, Ethan came on the screen. His image shocked Hu, and she saw John's eyes widen in the screen's reflection. Ethan looked like he hadn't slept for days, and he was even more unkempt than before. He looked angry and frustrated.

John gave a throat-clearing cough. "Hello, Ethan. Dare I ask how things are there?"

Ethan glared back at them. "What's taking so long?" he demanded, almost shouting.

Hu and John glanced at each other. She became frightened and concerned about Ethan's health and the conversation's direction. She gazed at the screen and answered. "This is significant work, Ethan. It takes time–"

"We don't have time," Ethan butted in.

Both John and Hu weren't sure how to answer.

Ethan's demeanor changed to fear, desperation, and despair. "Please, we have little time left. I'm the only one still free of this. Marie had started on something when she succumbed to the virus. I have four dead, two near death and two... well, you know, and one of them is ..." Ethan broke off and averted his eyes.

Compassion filled Hu like a torrent bursting into a ravine. Seeing Ethan break crushed her. She turned away from the display, stood, and walked out of view.

John glanced at her and back at the screen. "I don't pretend to understand what you're going through there. I can't promise anything. We don't have a cure yet. I am sorry. We're putting all our efforts into cracking this and developing a drug."

"I know I'm being unreasonable."

"No apology required. You mentioned Marie finding something?"

Angelo, who was with Ethan, broke in, speaking calmly and authoritatively. "The fact that Ethan is still showing no symptoms of the disease suggests to me that there is something different about Ethan. I asked Marie to take a blood sample. It should be among the samples we sent you. I suggest you take a look at it. Also, just before she collapsed, she implied in her notes that she had the same suspicions. She wanted to get another sample of Ethan's blood."

"Well, I'll pass that onto Dr. Kawoski straight away."

"Just hurry ... please," Ethan added.

"We will."

The screen blanked. John turned his comm off, and instantly contacted Dr. Kawoski to pass on Angelo's suggestion. He then stood and became aware of Hu in distress. "Are you OK?" he asked as he approached her.

"No," she got out before she placed her head on his shoulder and started crying.

John froze, unsure what to do. He finally wrapped his arms around her and let her exhaust her grief.

Hu's outburst of tears slowed and stopped. She pulled away and wiped the moisture from her face, averting her eyes from him. "You must think I'm overreacting."

"It would have surprised me if you didn't show any emotion, given how close a friend you are to Ethan."

She sat in a nearby chair. "That is the first time I've cried since my partner died," she confessed.

"It's a good thing ... crying, that is ... it releases the tension so you can refocus."

Hu stared at John, pondering the wisdom of his words. She looked at his damp shirt. "Sorry about the shoulder."

John peered, grinned, and said, "It will dry. I might keep it as a memento."

She gave him a quizzical look, not sure what to infer from that.

"What do you think Angelo and Marie meant?"

"You were listening?"

Hu beamed at him with mocking scorn. "Of course I was listening."

John chuckled. "I don't know, but it's in Dr. Kawoski's court now."

"Yes."

Twelve hours later, Dr. Kawoski came back to them. "We have it!" He wiped the tiredness from his eyes.

John and Hu brightened their outlook at once. "Really?" they both said at once.

"Really. The key was examining Ethan's blood, as Angelo and Marie suggested. And we made an amazing discovery."

"When can we leave?" Hu asked, eager to return to Ethan.

"Another hour to produce enough serum, and we can go."

"We?" John asked.

"Yes. With your permission, I'd like to travel with you. I need to confirm my theory back there. Something to do with what they discovered."

John looked at Hu. "Is that acceptable to you?"

"As long as it doesn't delay our flight, I'm fine with it."

"Good. Let's get cracking, then."

"I will see you in an hour with the serum." Dr. Kawoski left.

Hu and John busied themselves with packing. Hu headed for the lander to help prepare it for departure. Many emotions ran through her as she started running the checks for takeoff. She was eager to leave to deliver the cure to Ethan and Jade but feared they might be too late. Those passions were two titans fighting for supremacy in her heart and in amongst it was confusion about what was happening between her and John. She didn't understand why she was behaving the way she was with him. She sighed. *I am reading too much into it.*

She was just completing the pre-flight checks when John and Dr. Kawoski came on board.

"Let's get going," John said, placing his bags in a storage compartment. He directed the doctor to do likewise.

"Where is the serum?" Hu asked.

"I put it in one of the outer sealed compartments, but I have a surprise for you."

"What?"

"This," Dr. Kawoski said as he held up a syringe. "It is an inoculation against the virus."

"I don't like needles very much," Hu said, smiling nervously.

John laughed. "You're not as tough as you led us to believe."

"That's not fair. I never said I was tough," she said with a mocking challenge to John.

The doctor came over to her. She pulled up the sleeve on her left arm, and he injected the contents of the needle into her.

"Can we go then?" she asked, rubbing the site of the injection.

"By all means," John said as he parked in the pilot's chair. The doctor sat in a seat in the passenger cabin behind them.

John received departure clearance and disengaged from the laboratory, aiming the lander for the moon and the wormhole portal at its greatest speed.

They arrived at the portal and went through it in record time. When they emerged at Centauri, Hu had John headed straight for Chariclo, bypassing *Destiny* to save time. They could see the camp rush toward them as John burst into the atmosphere, braking as hard as the lander could tolerate.

43

SALVATION

Ethan returned to the hospital tent after his call to John. He couldn't see purpose in anything else. He sat in the chair he now called home and watched Jade as she slept in her coma and breathed in the same shallow, steady rate. Her face exposed an undercurrent of pain but looked peaceful otherwise.

Unprompted, he recalled the moment she had practically forced him to ask her on their first date. It was comical when he reflected on it. He was so shy, and she was so teasing. He didn't realize it then, but she told him much later that she had been nervous he wasn't interested in her. She said she was sure he was for her, but he was so ... antisocial, clumsy, naïve, it almost scared her away. She had almost given up. He smiled at the thought and sat dreaming of the wonderful times they would have in the future.

Angelo occasionally checked her condition but said little. Ethan presumed he didn't want to inflict more panic on him.

He ventured outside at one stage to watch the sun set below the horizon in the glory of its oranges, reds, and mauves. He got a bite to eat and returned to sit by Jade's bed.

Angelo came over to him. "Thought I should tell you. Nigel just died."

Ethan nodded, immune to the shock of the news after so many, his senses numb, emotions rubbed beyond raw and deadened to any more pain. He seemed in a realm between the living and the dead himself, experiencing existence but having no reaction to it. His sole focus was on Jade. His world would fall apart if she died. He'd lose his focus and purpose; it would be the last tragedy in his life because he would not be able to endure it.

The evening moved into night, and the lights dimmed. Ethan stayed by Jade's bed, sometimes speaking to her, other times just sitting and stroking her on the hand and face. He wiped her face now and then, moistening her skin from the dry air-conditioned ventilation. It was late when he felt himself drift off into sleep, his head resting on Jade's shoulder.

He woke with a start. It was early morning, and he didn't know what had woken him. He looked at Jade and the monitors. Her blood pressure had risen substantially higher, and her breathing was ragged. His heart missed a beat as he saw the unmistakable signs of the last stage of the disease. He started crying, tears moistening his cheeks. "Hang on just a little longer ... please," he whispered in despair. He heard a commotion outside but couldn't recognize its source, his mind numbed to everything but Jade.

The entry door opened, and Angelo walked in, accompanied by Hu, John, and someone else. The significance didn't register with him. Who are these strangers without environmental suits? One person held a box and rushed over to him and Jade, followed by Angelo. "What are you doing?" Ethan asked in a mechanical tone.

"Saving her life," the man said.

The world inverted from the surreal one he had existed in, and he recognized Hu and John. "You came."

Hu dashed to him and clasped Ethan's shoulder as she gazed at Jade. "I only hope we're in time."

The stranger removed a syringe from the container he held and injected the contents into Jade's arm. "We can only pray now." He moved on to inject Marie and Fiona, the other surviving patients.

"Why aren't you in suits? You'll catch the virus," Ethan asked, alarmed at the prospect.

"They have inoculated us," John said.

"Oh."

Now that they were together, Hu, John, and Ethan couldn't find words to speak. There was nothing to say until they knew whether Jade would recover. John left. Hu retrieved another chair and sat next to Ethan, holding his hand in support.

An hour elapsed before Jade's blood pressure stopped rising and stabilized. Hu and Ethan sat in silence by her side. There was no need to talk. Hu's presence was enough for him. Four hours later, Jade's blood pressure started falling. The room's atmosphere sighed in relief. Ethan glanced at Hu with a slight smile, not wishing to break the spell with optimism too early. An hour afterward, Jade's improvement was in no doubt. The others were recovering, too.

Hu gave Ethan a hug and rose to stretch her legs. "You want something to eat?"

"An energy bar."

"I will see what I can find." Hu walked out.

Another six hours passed, with Jade's vital signs progressively improving. She stirred. Ethan jumped at the sight and reached for her hand again, stroking it as tears returned to his eyes, tears of joy instead of despair. Jade's eyes opened ten minutes later.

"Hello, sleepy head. Welcome back," Ethan said with a massive smile plastering his face.

"Where have I been?" Jade asked, drowsy.

"To hell and back." Ethan leaned over, kissed her on the forehead, and then brushed her lips. "I love you."

A weak smile crossed her face. "Love you too."

"Rest."

"Hmm, hmm." She closed her eyes but remained conscious.

He rose to fetch Angelo and tell him the news. "Jade is awake."

"That is good news," Angelo said, smiling and patting Ethan's shoulder. "Let's examine her, then."

"I might stretch my legs. I'll be back soon."

"Take as long as you need. I'll make sure she doesn't go anywhere."

Ethan chuckled. "You do that."

He stepped out to a balmy evening air, walked several meters away from the tent and stretched both arms high. "Thank you," he shouted to the sky with every watt of the energy his lungs could offer.

Hu and John came running from somewhere behind one of the other tents. "What's wrong?" Hu asked, out of breath.

"Nothing's wrong. Jade's awake." Ethan beamed without embarrassment as he whirled a dance.

"Oh, Ethan," Hu said, excited, hugging him with joy as she joined him.

"That's great news," John said with a smile of relief.

Hu let go, and Ethan's normal mental processes restarted for the first time since this nightmare began. He stared at her, then John, and returned to her. "Why were you behind the tents?"

"Nothing, just talking," John said, giving a sheepish grin.

Hu blushed.

Ethan said nothing more on the issue but decided a covert eye on them would prove interesting. "We've got beer somewhere. Want one?"

"Sure," they both said as Ethan led them to the mess tent.

They had a beer together, and Ethan scrounged a supply of food, hungry for the first time in days. He then departed for the hospital and Jade again, leaving Hu and John to their own devices. He gave a quick glance round as he left. Two innocent-looking faces stared back at him. It didn't fool him, and the prospect filled him with delight if his suspicions were correct.

"How is she?" he asked Angelo.

"Good. Making an excellent recovery. The pressure on her brain is returning to normal. The others are improving, too."

"That's a relief," Ethan agreed as he walked to Jade's bedside again.

He sat in the chair and looked at her face. Her eyes were closed, but her face showed signs of the radiance and beauty he loved. He smiled, appreciating her features.

"What are you looking at?" Jade asked through sleepy and cracked eyelids.

"Your beautiful face," Ethan said, smiling.

"I must look a mess."

Ethan laughed. "You return from the dead, and the first thing you consider is your appearance."

"We always want to be our best for the one we love," Jade joked.

"You're perfect the way you are."

They stared at each other in silence.

"Guess what?" Ethan said, conspiracy in his tone.

"What?"

"Something's going on between Hugo and the general."

"General?"

"General O'Conner."

"How? He's on Earth and she is on *Destiny*."

"No. They are both here. They brought the antiviral serum from Earth that saved you."

Jade's eyes brightened. "Really? That is interesting."

"Don't let on, though. I think they think they are covering it up well."

Jades smiled. "OK. I won't."

"I'll let you rest."

"You look like you need it, too."

"Yeah. I suppose. See you in the morning." Ethan leaned over and kissed her on the lips, gently but savoring the feel and taste of her again.

The heartbeat-monitoring machine shot up and gave a soft beep of warning. They both looked at it and laughed as her pulse returned to normal.

"See you tomorrow," Jade whispered.

44

JOHN AND HUGO?

During the hour before Ethan blasted his outburst of gratitude to the universe, Hu and John had been sitting in a quiet setting, gazing at the gathering twilight and talking.

Hu had suspicions about her feelings for John. She didn't understand what had stirred them in her, but something had roused her at the laboratory. She sensed he thought things had changed, too, but she was reluctant to raise the topic for fear of embarrassing herself. She chastised herself for such teenage behavior. Maybe the period since anyone had affected her romantically had dulled her memory of its characteristics. She determined to seek John's attention and find a private spot to discuss it with him. She cornered him while busy working but convinced him to take a break and led him to the location they now were.

"This is ominous. Leading me behind the bike shed?" John quipped.

Hu laughed. "You could say that." They sat in a comfortable position, and she became serious. "I'm probably making a fool of myself, and be gentle if I am, but I can't help but speculate something unusual happened at the bio-lab, something ... personal ... a connection."

John stared at the landscape and the stars before responding. "I thought it was just me," he said, turning his face to gaze directly at her. "You see, I've had little opportunity for personal relationships, given the pressure of the work I do, so I'm not good at this ... but yes, I felt something too." He smiled and returned his eyes to the appearing stars.

Hu, grinning, did likewise. "The star field looks indistinguishable from here."

"In the scheme of things, we haven't moved location that far from Earth."

"I suppose not." They were subdued again. "Who is General John O'Connor?"

"Not much to know."

"Modesty will get you nowhere with me. Really. Who are you?"

John chuckled but stayed quiet until he said, "I grew up on a potato farm near Kalama, Washington state. I have three sisters and one brother. Mother and father are still alive and enjoying their senior years. Achieved above-average results at school and entered the military. Progressed through the ranks into my present job."

"Were you the oldest?"

"Yes, just. My sister is one year younger."

"Why did you join the military?"

"I don't know. Seemed like a good idea at the time. I ... was probably avoiding an event I was too immature to face ... I feel like running now."

"Oh ... well, you can try, but you won't get far here." She giggled.

"No, I suppose I can't. And from your reputation, I wouldn't escape, would I? You'd hunt me down quick smart," he replied, smiling.

"That I would," she said with a generous smile.

"What about you? What's your story apart from what you've already told me?"

"I grew up in a suburb of Beijing, an only child — a remnant of the one-child policy. My father was an engineer at a local manufacturing plant. I showed promise in engineering. They gave me a scholarship when they noticed my aptitude and sent me to the best education facilities in China, where I graduated in astrochemical engineering."

"No wonder you and Ethan understand each other so well. You're both from the same mold."

She laughed. "You could say that. Education is our only similarity."

John chuckled. "Yes, he is unique. You are, too."

They both sat in silence after that until John broke the impasse. "Hu ..."

"My friends call me Hugo."

"Hugo, when we finish here and return to Earth, would you have dinner with me sometime?"

Hu blushed with a delighted pleasure she hadn't experienced for ages, although John couldn't see it in the darkness. Her reaction surprised her. She tried to put off a reply with banter. "Why don't we dine here?"

"That'd be very romantic. A table for two in the mess tent seated under the soft glare of overhead lighting. I don't think so."

"Won't it cause an international incident?"

"I'm sure we'd iron out any diplomatic issues, but if you prefer not to, that's OK."

Hu sensed she risked taking her play too far and didn't want the opportunity slipping out of her hands. "In that case, how can I refuse? I'd love to, John."

"It's settled then. Not a word to the others, though."

"Ha! Do you think we'll fool Ethan and Jade for long?"

"It'll be fun trying."

They then heard Ethan's exclamation of gratitude to the universe.

45

THE FINAL PIECE OF THE PUZZLE

The next day, Dr. Kawoski asked if they could travel to the cave where they detected the virus. Jade was recovering well, and as Angelo had assured Ethan he'd look after her with extra attention, he agreed to take him. John and Hu came along, despite Ethan's reservations about their safety.

They started out from the camp mid-morning and arrived at the cliff and cave after lunchtime. Ethan kept an eagle eye on John and Hu as they traveled, looking for confirmation of his suspicions about them. It wasn't his business, but Hu deserved to find a warm relationship again, and he couldn't think of anyone better suited to her than John. Consequently, Ethan wore a contented, conspiratorial smile most of the way. Hu gave him a quizzical rise of the eyebrows a few times but said nothing.

They disembarked from the vehicle. "This is it," Ethan said, stating the obvious as he pointed to the gaping hole in the cliff.

"So, you found the cave sealed up, you say?" John asked.

"Yes, with thirty centimeters of ceramic material. It wasn't rock but something we hadn't experienced before. We could drill through it."

They advanced to the cave's entrance, lamps in hand. Ethan led them with curiosity mixed with trepidation. They followed the path he had tread before, stopping to inspect their surroundings with fascination as they progressed, finally reaching the niche where the skeletons lay. He shone his flashlight on them to show them how many bodies there were.

"Incredible," Dr. Kawoski said as he viewed the vista of bones laid out in a neat row in front of him.

They walked the line of fossils as though inspecting the troops until they reached the end wall Ethan had seen before.

"Of course," Ethan said, memory stirring.

"What is it?" Dr. Kawoski asked.

"People asked me if something happened to me here, and I couldn't remember. But there was something. See that small circular hole?" Ethan said as he pointed to it. "I put my little finger in it." The others stared at him in disbelief that he would stick his finger in anything without knowing what it was. "Yes, it probably was stupid. I recall getting pricked. I thought nothing of it at the time. Didn't mention it to anyone."

"Well," Dr. Kawoski said slowly, "that prick might have injected an antivirus into you, making you immune to the illness."

Dr. Kawoski walked over to the orifice Ethan had pointed at and inspected it with his flashlight. It was deep, but he spied a hypodermic protrusion in the center. "There's a needle in there. I'll extract a sample from it if I can." He opened his bag and extracted a rubber glove. He rummaged through his gadgets, looking for something, and pulled out gauze and stuffed it in the middle finger of the glove. After inserting his finger into the hole, he moved it forward until he felt the needle penetrating the skin of the glove. He pushed further and retracted it again, placing the glove in a specimen bag he had ready. "We'll see what we get from that," he said.

"But who placed it there and why since everyone was dead?" Hu asked.

"Maybe someone was alive. And it was a means of immunizing those that entered this space. Although there's no obvious survivors or signs to alert visitors of the danger," John said.

"Who were these beings? Was someone experimenting, and it went horribly wrong, so they covered it up before anyone asked questions?" The cave's puzzle perplexed Hu.

"We may never know."

Dr. Kawoski inspected the skeletons for over two hours before it satisfied him, and they packed up to return to camp. He was eager to use Marie's testing equipment to analyze the glove. The vehicle rocked them as they traveled the terrain familiar to Ethan now. They entered the camp just before sunset.

He saw Jade sitting in a chair, basking in the sun, just outside the hospital tent as he pulled the vehicle up at the site maintenance shed. *She's waiting for me to return*, he thought. They piled out, and Ethan conducted the standard checks on the vehicle before hustling over to Jade, eager to check on her recovery. "How are you feeling?"

"Much stronger. I'm enjoying the sun." She was relaxed and showed a better complexion. "Angelo let me escape out here after he checked me, so long as I rested and didn't wander off somewhere."

Ethan reached over and kissed her. He pointed inside the hospital with his eyes. "How are the others?"

"Recovering, as far as I know. They were both awake when I left a few hours ago."

"Do you want to go back?"

"Yes, thanks."

Ethan helped Jade from her chair and let her lean on him as she shuffled inside the hospital. Two smiling faces met them as they entered. Ethan smiled at Marie and Fiona as he helped Jade back to her bed. Once he settled her, he headed over to Marie first and then Fiona to ask about their recovery and answer any of their questions.

While with Marie, he thanked her for alerting everyone to why he, Ethan, had not gotten sick.

"It wasn't just me," she said, always a stickler for truth. "It was Angelo too. I only wish we had realized it earlier. It might have saved Senna and the others."

"Marie, think instead of how many you saved."

He walked over to Angelo to thank him too.

"They're recovering well," he said, looking at the patients.

"Yes, the antiviral serum works quickly. I conducted autopsies on two of the dead. The growth tissue in the brain differs from ordinary brain cells, so it's easy for the serum to attack just those cells, leaving the others intact."

"I see. That's good. A pity so many died. If only I had remembered earlier about sticking my finger in that hole ..." Ethan became melancholy.

Angelo patted Ethan on the back in consolation. "It's good that so few died."

"That's what I said to Marie."

Ethan walked away in thought. He headed for Jade, kissed her goodnight, and left for his own bed and sleep.

46

WHERE WE CAME FROM

Ethan awoke early the next day. He had a quick jog with Hu and John, who rose at dawn, too. They worked hard, bringing up a rapid sweat. Ethan hit the shower when they returned to camp and had breakfast with the others. Dr. Kawoski was there too.

"You look like you haven't slept," Ethan said to him.

"That's because I didn't. I've been trying to solve the mystery of this virus, and I believe I have."

"Well?"

"Not yet. I will meet you in the hospital at ten, where I'll tell you an amazing story."

"I'll be there."

Hu and John accepted the invitation too.

They gathered in the hospital tent with Angelo and his patients, now strong enough to move with shuffling steps. They sat on seats provided.

Dr. Kawoski took center stage in front of the others as he considered where to begin his monolog. "What I've determined is a story spanning two million years. But let's start with the virus itself. When I studied the genome of this pathogen, I felt it strange but familiar. I believe Marie had the same inkling."

Marie nodded in agreement.

"This puzzled me for a time until I analyzed Ethan's blood and found the antibody that stopped the virus from spreading. When I looked at the changed microorganism once the antibody attached itself to it, I realized where I had seen the sequence.

"This same sequence of DNA material, integrated into our own DNA chromosomal gene bundles, controls our brain size, and that is where the two-million-year-old story begins.

"Two million years ago, our brains were the mass of today's apes, and we behaved with similar characteristics from what we glean from fossil evidence. Something then triggered our brains to expand over many millennia, not rapidly like this virus's behavior. When you study the gene arrangement of this virus and the part of our similar DNA, one key distinction is obvious. Our biology caps the gene in our DNA once the brain has grown to a particular size, so the brain no longer grows. This is a mutated virus of that gene sequence but has no capping mechanism. So, it allows the brain to continue growing as the pathogen divides and multiplies rapidly, killing our people. The antivirus that we developed reverses the action and removes the tissue the virus added, providing the cure for you.

"Now, when we returned to the cave, Ethan remembered a hole where a needle pricked him. Why he merrily placed his finger in an orifice without looking, I don't know." Several snickered at Ethan's expense, which embarrassed him. "It was fortunate for him — and us —that he did. He became immune to the virus and showed us how to make others immune. I used a rubber glove to simulate a finger and placed it in the hole. The same needle that pricked Ethan pierced the glove, depositing a small dose of liquid into it. When I examined the material, I found it provided a cap for the pathogen, preventing it from multiplying, and that, my friends, brings us to the most incredible mystery I've ever encountered."

The group sat puzzled and stunned for a moment as they processed the information Dr. Kawoski had delivered.

"But why would the gene sequence appear on Earth, too?" Hu asked.

"It's not the same, but that is an excellent question. I believe the virus has mutated from Earth. Other questions are: why are those humanoid skeletons buried in the cave? And where did they originate? I can come to only one conclusion."

Dr. Kawoski paused for dramatic effect, making Ethan say, "Come on, out with it."

"Patience, my friend. Aliens migrated here and to Earth two million years ago and found lifeforms they postulated could develop into sentient beings. They attempted to speed up this development. Unfortunately, for the humanoids on this planet, the form of the virus administered to them made things happen too fast, exterminating them. The aliens placed the bodies in the cave and plugged it to stop the virus from spreading any further. More sealed caves may exist elsewhere. The intriguing question is, why place an antidote supply in the cave when it seemed no humanoids remained, and no signs alerted anyone of its presence? Of course, we might have missed reading them, or they deteriorated. Did the beings intend to return later?

"These creatures changed the gene sequence to retard the growth when they administered it to our ancestors on Earth. It took place over millennia and generations, not days, allowing the skull bones to expand and grow to compensate."

"Where's this virus exist on Earth now?" Ethan asked.

"I think it's become extinct. When it performed the intended task, the active sites became capped, and the pathogen died out."

"So where does that leave us in returning to Earth, John?" Ethan asked again.

John pondered the question. "We can sterilize everything that's been in contact with the virus, and we now have a cure if it accidentally spreads. They may quarantine us just to be safe. We should inject everyone on the ship with the antidote. If we do all of that, we shouldn't have a problem."

"That is an amazing story," Hu said. "But where did these beings originate, and how do we prove it? We've had no contact in recent history."

"I don't know," Dr. Kawoski replied. "They might have died out since, or they visit us from time to time if you believe in UFO sightings."

"Maybe."

A general buzz of discussion developed where everyone had their own thoughts and theories to put forward and debate.

47

HOMECOMING

The expedition party stayed on Chariclo for another week before packing up. *Destiny*'s crew welcomed them with enthusiastic cheer when they disembarked from the landers.

"Good to have you back," Celeste said to Ethan when they met. "I can hand over the reins and live a less stressful life."

"Ha! Not so fast. I'm still busy, so I'm leaving you in charge for now," Ethan replied. "You can't get out of it that easy. Anyway, from what I hear, you've been doing an excellent job of it."

Celeste swelled with pride at the praise but tried to sound humble. "We did little but sit here orbiting the planet."

"Don't be too eager to lose the position. It could grow on you."

"Let's have a drink to celebrate your return," Celeste said, veering from the topic.

"I'll say yes to that."

Ethan, Celeste, and the others strolled off to the ship's bar for a relaxing refreshment and to exchange stories about what had happened both on Chariclo and *Destiny*.

"DID you see signs of their blossoming relationship in the bar?" Jade asked Ethan as they prepared for bed in comfort again.

"No. If there's something, they're hiding it well," he said, recalling his observations. "But I'm sure something's brewing."

They both tucked in between the sheets, reveling in the renewed luxury, and cuddled each other, Jade's head on Ethan's shoulder, as his arm wrapped around her. He stroked her hair as he watched her tired face. She was recovering from her ordeal still and closed her eyes, ready to drift off to sleep. He refrained from any chatting and let her sleep. It was soothing and a relief to wrap her safely in his arms again. He sensed her descent into slumber as her regular soft breathing started. He gazed at the ceiling and reviewed the recent events that had happened over the month. They had made amazing discoveries but at the cost of losing five individuals: Senna, Nigel, Troy, Sullivan, and Zane. The deaths upset him, and it had been hard breaking the news to their families. He intended doing what he could to have Senna's and Zane's work recognized: *Senna Peak* for the mountain Senna had discovered and *zaniology* as the name for the new plant and animal group of species found on Chariclo.

But a whole fresh field of research had opened to understanding who the Chariclo people were, where the virus had originated, and how it connected Chariclo with Earth. If it was a bizarre experiment, what did it say of the experimenters' motives?

Ethan considered another puzzle to complement the human origin one. Why were the rest of Chariclo's lifeforms so different from Earth's and the discovered skeletons? He wondered if hominids still lived on Chariclo in a remote location or if they had become extinct.

Somebody else could work that out. Having Jade back was enough for now. He regarded his own emotions throughout the ordeal and realized how much he loved her and needed her in his life, how she completed him. As he sighed and turned off the light, he considered what their future held.

EVERYONE WAS busy the next day, preparing to return to Earth. They had intended to return through the wormhole until they realized the ship didn't fit through the orifice. Ethan was true to his word and kept Celeste in command, answerable only to him. Her increase in confidence pleased him. It vindicated his faith in her.

They started their homeward journey to Earth after lunch. Hu returned to *Destiny* instead of using the lander John placed at her disposal. Ethan wondered why she had made that decision and smiled to himself in conspiratorial glee. He couldn't wait to catch her if she and John slipped up in concealing a clandestine relationship.

Ethan was delaying the inevitable, but he needed to talk with David to understand what had possessed him to sabotage the lander bay door. He took John with him.

They met David in the improvised brig, the occupant grumpy and rebellious.

"What on earth were you thinking?" Ethan asked, throwing his arms up in a gesture of disbelief.

"Someone had to protect Earth. You were being foolhardy, and Celeste didn't know what she was doing."

"And you had the knowledge that we couldn't send the virus back without releasing it? We didn't have the proper safeguards?"

David shuffled in his seat. "Not sending it was the safest way of negating the risk."

"At the peril of our lives on the planet."

"Collateral damage. Are you going to arrest Celeste for shooting me? I thought you didn't allow weapons on board."

"She had no alternative from where I stand. You disobeyed a direct order. That's mutiny."

"I'm not in the military."

"You're still required to obey the ship's commander, and she was and is the commander."

"Even when you think she is making a mistake?"

"Even then."

"That's suicide."

"You haven't been on any merchant vessels, have you? They'd

throw you through the airlock and say you met with a nasty accident," John said.

David stared at him, thinking he was joking.

John raised an eyebrow and nodded that he was serious.

"Ultimately, you come under General O'Conner's authority and his commanders, so you must accept their decision when they try you."

"Whatever," David said, crossing his arms in defiance.

"Yes, whatever," Ethan agreed as he rose to leave.

John followed his lead. He turned as they were exiting and shot back at David, "I hope you have a talented lawyer."

THEY REACHED Earth after many tedious days. The ship was placed in an orbital position opposite to the moon and in quarantine, as Ethan expected would happen. The time gave him and Jade the opportunity to spy on Hu and John clandestinely to learn if a romantic relationship was indeed brewing. They thought no one noticed them, but they underestimated Hu's observational skills.

The four of them had formed a close-knit circle, only disturbed by the occasional addition of Max, Angelo, Celeste, or Marie.

As they ate dinner one evening, Hu said to Ethan and Jade. "As you two are so inquisitive about John and me with your covert snooping, we thought we might as well tell you that yes, we are considering whether we have personal interests to explore."

Ethan sat back, placing one hand on his chest in false innocence. "Hugo, you know I'd never–"

"I see through you, Ethan. You should understand that by now. Anyway, if we can accept that, we might return to normality instead of this cloak and dagger surveillance."

Ethan moved to protest again, but Hu raised her hand, gesturing for him to stay silent before he dug a deeper hole for himself.

"That's so great," Jade said.

John sat in silence, staring at them.

"You look stuck for words, general," Ethan said, holding back a smile.

"I ... am not used to this ... personal ..." He threw his arms up in annoyed embarrassment. "Give me an enemy to throw a missile at, and I'm your man, but this ... I'm confused."

They laughed at his admission of ineptitude.

"John has asked me to dinner when we get off this ship, and I'm holding him to it," Hu said.

John blushed for the first time Ethan could recall.

Jade felt sorry for him. "I hope you have a great time and disregard our teasing. We know how it feels."

They started eating again, but Ethan considered where his relationship with Jade had started and where it might lead. He confirmed a decision made during her recovery.

Quarantine requirements confined them to the ship for another week before being cleared to return to Earth and home.

48

WILL YOU MARRY ME?

I t felt marvelous to stand on planet Earth again. Ethan breathed in the fresh air, tasting the distinct aromas with his nasal senses. Yes, it felt great to be home. They had disembarked from *Destiny* and dispersed to their various homes for a well-deserved rest and reunion with families and friends, leaving a skeleton crew that rotated their duties with others on Earth. They undertook the usual debriefings, and life started to return to normal, whatever normal was. Ethan encouraged John to keep Celeste on and offer training for her, which he did.

Hu and John met for their dinner date, which foreshadowed their gravitation closer to each other. Ethan was happy for his friend, especially now that he knew more about her sad history. He knew little about John, but he was sure he would if they continued their relationship.

Ethan organized a dinner two weeks afterward for the four of them at Stars Seafood Selection, where he dined on special occasions. He considered that night special since Hu was returning to the moon soon to continue her work there. He had another reason, too, but kept that to himself.

Ethan and Jade arrived early and sat at a table in the restaurant's garden, the evening warm and fine. They ordered a drink and waited for Hu and John to arrive. The gentle breeze wafted past them with the salty taste of the sea blending with the perfumes of the blooming flowers.

"I love coming here," Jade said as she settled herself in to absorbing the view.

"It's a wonderful restaurant, and the scenery is great, even without you."

"Flattery will get you everywhere."

"Good."

They both laughed.

Ethan fidgeted, lost in thought and debate as he gazed at the ocean.

"What is it?" Jade asked, puzzled.

He took both of Jade's hands into his and changed his gaze and focus. He searched Jade's eyes and said simply, "Jade Eleanor Powers, I love you. Will you marry me?"

Jade sat dumbstruck. Her mouth half opened several times and closed again. Radiance burst from her face as tears trickled down her cheeks, including streaks of mascara. She finally found the words. "Yes. Yes, I will marry you. You've just ruined my makeup, but I don't care." She started laughing. It was contagious. Ethan laughed, too, with great joy.

He lifted his glass and held it in front of him. "To us and a wonderful life together."

Jade raised her drink as well and clinked it against Ethan's. "You've made me the happiest woman on earth."

They both took a sip, their attention so fixed on each other that they did not notice Hu and John arrive.

Hu stared at Jade, noticing the tears. "Is everything alright?" she said.

Jade glanced up, surprised. She wiped away her tears. "More than alright. Ethan just proposed to me, and I've accepted."

Hu whelped in glee and clapped her hands together. "I am so happy for you both."

Ethan and Jade both rose from their seats to accept congratulations from Hu and John, shaking hands or kissing cheeks as decorum dictated. Ethan had a beaming smile on his face that he couldn't remove.

"I suggest we order a bottle of champagne," John said. "My treat."

"That's good for me," Ethan said.

The champagne came and was poured, and they toasted the momentous occasion. Jade looked at her chronometer. "I hope you don't mind, but I just have to tell my parents." She rose from the table.

"That's fine," John said, and Hu agreed.

Jade left the restaurant's noise for five minutes. She returned, beaming with happiness.

"What did they say?" Ethan asked.

"Mum's over the moon, but Dad's not so happy," Jade said, laughter in her voice. "He says he hasn't even seen you yet, and you haven't asked him his permission, but he supposes it's OK."

They laughed.

"I'll have to share a beer with him then," Ethan said.

"Yes, you will," Jade agreed.

They enjoyed a hearty meal together, talking and drinking late into the night.

They left and went their separate ways. Ethan and Jade returned to Ethan's villa, where they drifted onto the rear patio to savor the warm night and their closeness as they stood arm in arm.

"What made you propose?" Jade asked.

"Do I need a reason?" Ethan riposted, grinning. He then changed his demeanor to seriousness. "When you were near death, I realized I couldn't live without you. I needed you in my life forever. And if you survived, I'd make sure that happened. You lived, and I proposed."

They fronted each other, linked arms, and kissed.

∾

THE END of Book 2 of the Reach for the Stars series

You can continue reading about Ethan's adventure in Ceti.
Type https://books2read.com/Ceti in your browser.

Thanks for reading this book. If you loved the book and have a moment to spare, I would appreciate a quick review on the site that you purchased the book from, as this helps new readers find my books.

Subscribe to my Newsletters and receive three free episodes of The Chronicles of Gatacus Todd.

Type http://subscribepage.io/g4r4f8 in your browser.

ALSO BY JOHN WEGENER

Books

Reach For The Stars Trilogy

FTL

Centauri

Ceti

Reach For The Stars Box Set (Books 1-3)

Loki's Fall

Zodiac Series

Scorpius

Libra

Halwende's Legacy Series

Halwende's Redemption

Halwende's Resurrection

Halwende's Reincarnation

Halwende's Legacy Box Set (Books 1-3)

Solar Dawn Series

Lunar Rift

Other Stories

The Dark Ages

SAGI

Short Stories

The Love Particle

ABOUT THE AUTHOR

John Wegener grew up in the Adelaide Hills of South Australia. He now expresses his imaginative dreams by engaging in writing after a 34-year career as a Chemical Engineer in the steel industry, which has taken him to many countries and allowed him to experience many cultures. John currently lives in Wollongong, Australia with his wife and children.

Click on johnwegener.com to find more of my books or read his blogs. Type subscribepage.io/g4r4f8 to subscribe to my emails for more stories and information.